W9-AHH-667

This first novel is dedicated to the muses, both human and ethereal, which enable emerging authors to gather their thoughts, apply them to paper, massage them into something worth reading, and then alert those new writers to the fact that they are finally done when that exciting moment arrives.

David —

Enjoy!

Pet

When executing advertising, it's best to think of yourself as an uninvited guest in the living room of a prospect who has the magical power to make you disappear instantly.
—John O'Toole, Chairman,
Foote, Cone & Belding Advertising

I am one who believes that one of the greatest dangers of advertising is not that of misleading people, but that of boring them to death.
—Leo Burnett, Chairman Leo Burnett Worldwide

APPRECIATION

As this is my first novel, I first want to thank the many folks who said "keep going" over the last eight years. Their energy and confidence are much appreciated.

Warm thanks to my wife, Carole Engler, my patient and savvy proofreader and "idea-reader." She kept me focused and sane.

My thanks go to my three sons, Rob, Scott and Jeremy, and two stepdaughters, Monika and Alexandria, who put up with way too many conversations about the novel while providing their own special support and love which was very useful in completing the book.

To Dean Pacalla at Bucknell University who overlooked my early academic transgressions and helped me to graduate, to the Marine drill instructors and Navy flight instructors at Pensacola, Florida, who trained me to be a Navy officer and to love to fly, and to the many people in the New York City and San Francisco advertising communities who allowed me to bask and flourish in the warmth and joy of their marketing and advertising brilliance, I say "Thanks."

Much appreciation to Arleta Quesada, my alert editor, Ruth Schwartz, my clever book production pro, Matt Hinrichs, our brilliant cover designer, and Judy Baker, my book marketing ace, as well as the many folks who critiqued parts or all of the novel along the long path to publication.

And to Sloan Wilson, the famous author of *The Man in the Gray Flannel Suit*, I say thanks for inspiring me at the age of twelve to write a novel about exciting people with my name on it. It looks great on my bookshelf.

CONTENTS

CHAPTER ONE

Ben Coleman, Advertising Man

June 22, 1992, 10:12 AM

"The client's never right!" roared Ben Coleman, Creative Director at Barry, Delgaldo & Fredericks Advertising, the tenth largest advertising agency in the world. Scowling at Dan Roth, his senior account executive who had just announced another client request, the slim, intense Coleman bellowed, "I suppose now they'll be sending some lousy research over here to support the ridiculous claims they want us to make in their ads." Once again, Ben felt a familiar anger well up in his stomach in response to clients meddling with his advertising copy.

"Why do I keep at this when they end up ripping the guts out of our ideas so they can stick in useless research statistics. People don't buy data. They buy products, not numbers, dammit!"

The two men, one forty-five and visibly angry, the other younger, leaned over Ben's immense glass worktable covered with advertising layouts for General Household Products, the agency's largest account.

"Ben, in this case, the client is right. Let's consider the basic strength and appeal of this new campaign concept for Super White Bleach before we worry about its accuracy. That can always come later," Dan responded calmly. "It's the way they do it at General Household Products and they pay our bills, including your bar bills at the Four Seasons."

The large corner office windows framed the darkly overcast New York skyline, reflecting Ben's gloomy mood. He had been awarded the palatial office eight years earlier when Charlie Fredericks, the canny and unpredictable head of Barry, Delgaldo & Fredericks Advertising had promoted him. Now in his late sixties but showing scant evidence of his age, Charlie was one of a handful of account executives Ben regarded with anything other than disdain. Most seemed to have just one purpose: keeping the client happy. But Ben thought there was more to advertising than happy clients. Happy customers were his focus. Well, at least during the day.

Ben's rise to Creative Director had been rapid relative to other creative stars. Charlie had made an uncharacteristic big splash by announcing the news to Ben in front of a group of his associates. Ben still refused to repair the chipped edge of his oval glass desk where he had dropped his highball upon hearing the news. It was a rare moment of loss of control, and Ben relished the recollection.

"Screw the bills," he said sharply. "If they keep this up they'll have to give the stuff away to get it off the shelves." Ben's outburst went on. "David Ogilvy wouldn't have stood for this crap and I won't either. People don't care that some bleach is 46% more effective at making clothes whiter. Get the client on the phone and let's convince them to let us do our job. And we'll tell 'em to forget about radio, too. It's television or nothing!"

As Dan sat down for what appeared to be another protracted meeting, Helen Mayfield, Ben's efficient secretary, poked her silver-haired head through the door of the office. Her eyes shone with unbridled excitement.

"The President's Chief of Staff is on the phone from Washington," she said in a breathless voice totally out of step with her generally serene demeanor.

Curious to see if the call was legitimate, Ben reached for his classic black rotary-dial phone, a gift from his second wife. He had hated telephones since his Navy duty in Vietnam when their shrill ring signaled the launch of his F4 Phantom jet on yet another Viet Cong target. These days calls generally heralded another impossible advertising deadline, but mostly Ben disliked phones because he preferred face-to-face conversations that let him track the other person's eyes and hands and watch their faces whiten with doubt or redden with conviction. His ability to deal effectively with the powerful successful corporate heads of the agency's client companies was based on his direct and frank manner in face-to-face meetings. Often his initial forthrightness seemed an affront to these willful men, but they quickly recognized Ben as a rare and extremely talented communicator. It was not unusual for a corporate chieftain to brag to his golf club buddies that he had "been through the wringer with Ben

Coleman again."

For a similar reason, Ben preferred making TV commercials, as compared to radio and print ads. They allowed words and pictures to work together to tell a more fully dimensional and powerful story about the service or product he was selling. "And selling it is," he always insisted to anyone in his presence. "Don't let anyone convince you otherwise." Ben was the undisputed "Big Dog" of television advertising, as proven with the dozens of CLIO Awards and other industry accolades that he kept in an old cupboard at his summer house on the Jersey Shore.

"Coleman," he rasped into the mouthpiece, his voice mirroring his earlier outbursts.

"Mr. Coleman, my name is Charlie Gaines, Chief of Staff to President Bradley Rogers," said a voice with a hint of a Southern drawl. "We met two years ago at a business leadership conference in Malibu. I don't remember what you look like, but I certainly recall the lady you were with," Gaines chuckled, with the condescending mirth of an overweight man sitting back in his chair savoring the memory of the lithe brunette standing with Ben in the reception room.

Somewhat put off by the man's recollection, Ben resisted an urge to make a rude retort, realizing that even though he had spoken to legions of powerful and famous people, a call from the President's office was a first.

"Yes, Mr. Gaines, had I realized CJ appealed to you, I would have traded ladies with you," Ben parried, warming to a volley of wits.

"Well, unlike yourself, I'm married to the lady I was with, and she doesn't let me share.

Anyway, I only have a few minutes to speak with you, if it's a convenient time for you to talk." Gaines now was clearly all business, but Ben could imagine the difficulty he had putting CJ's memory out of his mind. Many other men had experienced the same problem and, at one time, so had Ben.

"As you probably know," Gaines resumed. "President Rogers has had a most successful first term in office. He wants to stay with the job to complete several important initiatives and programs that have eluded us to date. We want his re-election to be the greatest landslide in history because, as our friend Chief Justice Blackstone has said, it's important to bring as many Republicans as possible into office on the President's coattails in order to guarantee a more supportive Congress. We want that majority and we want you to help us put the President over the top—way over."

"The Chief Justice?" Ben countered, taken by surprise at the involvement of a judge in a national election.

"Don't you worry your history book, Ben. The Chief Justice has been a long-time friend, attorney and advisor to President Rogers. They go way back, over fifteen years now. Blackstone helped him get his first election victory in Philadelphia, and two years ago the President put him on the Court to ensure some balance, which we sorely need. They keep it kosher, so no sweat," assured Gaines. "Now, obviously, the election will go our way; Rogers' ratings are strong. But, we want a really big win," Gaines added with a happy chortle, which caused Ben to clearly sense how much this Gaines fellow was relishing the political challenge that lay ahead. "That's why we're calling you. We hear you're the best. We need the best. And we'll pay you handsomely."

"How much is handsomely? I've always wondered about that." Ben smiled and noticed Dan was watching him with an expression of awe at such high-level horsing around.

"A million dollars, and more importantly, a lot of forgiveness concerning your last five or so income tax returns," Gaines chortled again, seeming to enjoy his skill at manipulating people on behalf of his boss and oldest friend, Brad Rogers.

"I think you've got the wrong man," Ben exploded, causing Dan to glance back up from his notes. "I can't believe you're threatening me with that IRS shit. I'm sorry this conversation isn't face-to-face or yours wouldn't look so great!"

"Hold on, Mr. Coleman," Gaines countered. "That was a goddamn joke; I thought you'd find it funny. Okay, I'll keep this totally straight. Brad Rogers is a good president. I imagine you probably voted for him. Why not put your talent to work for him? We need you. And it may even be fun. Hell, when's the last time you advertised a president?"

"Well, maybe you've got your man, because at least you're direct. I'm surrounded by way too much bullshit in my job," Ben admitted, wondering how much horse manure awaited him in Washington. "But in order to sell someone, I'd have to know a lot more about him."

"No problem, Ben. You're booked at the Mayflower Hotel here in DC, and you can spend the next few weeks living with the President and building his campaign. You'll know him pretty well by then, and I'm sure you're going to like him. He's pretty excited about this idea and wants to meet you. When can you join us? We need you here now."

"Well, as it turns out I need a change of pace," Ben said, glancing at Dan and thinking of their recent conversation. "I'll fly down tomorrow," he agreed, grinning at Dan, who was shaking his head with frustration at Ben's going AWOL from the agency. Dan began brusquely gathering up the ad layouts as Ben added, "Politics sounds a lot more exciting than bleach and toothpaste."

"Thanks Ben. The President will look forward to meeting you tomorrow night."

Ben hung up the phone with a fire in his belly he hadn't felt since signing up to fly Navy fighter jets, fresh out of college twenty-four years ago. He felt he'd actually get a shot once again at making a real difference, and that felt good, really good. Glancing pensively at the chipped edge of his glass desk, he enjoyed the sudden rush of a new challenge.

"Helen," he called through the door as Dan exited the office. "Come in here, please. I need a flight to Washington, D.C. tomorrow. And clear my calendar for at least three weeks; give Phil and Annie any new work. Mr. Coleman is going to Washington, for better or worse, and worse is not an option!"

CHAPTER TWO

The "Volga Boatmen"

June 22, 1992, 10:16 AM

The gates on the northernmost Champlain Canal lock, #12 near Whitehall, New York, groaned from many years of heavy labor as they released the sleek, 45-foot Hatteras yacht "Tempest" to continue its cruise into Lake Champlain. A hundred yards farther up the narrow canal, a rusting metal New York State historical marker described the ancient mill town as the birthplace of the American Navy under Benedict Arnold in 1775. Arnold's mission, urgently ordered by General George Washington, was to destroy the invading armed English flotillas on Lake Champlain. Although Arnold failed in his mission, his valiant efforts slowed the British advance, contributing to their decisive defeat on the broad fields of Saratoga weeks later.

In the cold early morning fog, four husky men on the deck of the yacht huddled over strong heavily sweetened coffee as the boat approached an old, decaying dock. Even if they had noticed the historical marker, they wouldn't have cared a wit about Benedict Arnold's mission. Their education hadn't included much American history. Even so, their secret mission on this chilly Monday morning in June, 1992, was designed to dramatically surpass Arnold's treachery.

Above them another man, larger than the others, turned into the spacious pilothouse. Picking up the short-wave radio microphone, he adjusted some dials and calmly uttered a few words. "In position, destination will be reached at 14:30 tomorrow. Out." He gazed out to the far shore where children were happily at play on a school playground.

"They will have to add an exciting new chapter to all your little history books, my children," the Captain said in a harsh voice, taking a deep pull on his cigarette before flicking it into the murky water. "And you will never know how close you were to the authors of that exciting chapter, kiddies." Then he hollered, "Prepare to dock!" at the others, who quickly jumped onto the deck to do his bidding.

Taking control of the helm again, the captain smiled broadly at a slighter, older man, Jared Jorgenson, who stood to the side, glancing first at the dock then back at the giant metal lock. Confused by the Captain's cryptic comment, Jorgenson turned his attention to his large logbook, which lay open on the chart table next to the helm, and made several rudimentary notes confirming the thirty-six hour period he had been aboard this yacht as a licensed New York state river pilot. According to maritime regulations, a licensed pilot had to be aboard any transiting yacht over forty feet that did not have a U.S. Coast Guardapproved captain on board.

This had been an easy trip, Jorgenson thought to himself. The large, brusque captain was a natural yachtsman, in spite of his size and his curt mannerisms. They could have done this without me, Jorgenson presumed, but the law's the law and this paycheck will take me through next month, unless my wife gets a hold of it.

Jorgenson never knew what hit him as the Captain turned briefly in his direction, grasped his neck in a visor grip, and neatly snapped his neck. Jorgenson dropped like a rock to the deck, his blue New York Yankee's ball cap falling to the floor beside him.

Returning to his position, the Captain spun the wheel in a relaxed manner and drew the gleaming blue-and-white hull close to the dock. One of the other men dragged the body down the interior staircase to the engine room while the other three leaped on the dock and gripped the thickly roped lines, fastening them to huge iron cleats. Once this was done, the Captain shut down the deep-throated twin engines.

"I never thought I'd be so glad to get off a boat!" exclaimed one of the men on the dock. "That Hudson River is as boring as an overweight hooker."

"Too bad about Jorgenson. I kind of liked the guy."

"Well, his fate was sealed the minute he stepped on board," said another. "Can't have anyone leaving this boat that might wonder about us later and blow the whistle. He's probably got a load in the bank, so his widow won't spill too many tears. I stuck him below out of sight. In twenty-four hours, this will be his grave," he said darkly, as a fifth man, who had been below getting dressed, appeared on deck.

As the men gazed at a restaurant sign that promised a hot breakfast at reasonable prices, the well-dressed man glanced up at the wheelhouse gesturing to the Captain.

"Tony, stay with the boat," the man ordered. "We'll bring you something back. They don't want any screw-ups, so I don't want to leave the boat alone. Neat work with the river pilot, clean and quick."

Tony glanced down at the crew and their leader. Squelching a sneer on his pockmarked face, he turned back to the wheelhouse without any objection. It had been quick and neat, as always. "Just be glad I've never been assigned to liquidate you, Mr. Dade, or whatever your fucking name is," he mumbled under his breath. "I may be big and slow, but I'm good at what I do. Especially the nasty stuff. And the little girl stuff."

Grinning at the thought, he shut down the electronic panel and glanced out the side window to the group below.

"Don't worry. We know what you like for breakfast," laughed the short man who was clearly in charge even though he was only half the size of any of the others. "And we'll look around for some young redheads for you, too. I still can't believe you didn't jump ship in Albany when we passed those schoolgirls touring the locks down there. Maybe you're finally getting some class. Nah, that'll never happen, right Tony?"

"Sure, Mr. Dade," Tony replied as he surveyed the surrounding shore. At least he would have time to enjoy the quiet of the sunlit canal from his perch fifteen feet over the water. Boy, if his friends could see him now, he mused. They wouldn't believe it. Tony felt like one of the "Volga Boatmen" but without the music and with a more unpleasant mission. Maybe some chicks will show up and want to come aboard, he imagined. But he knew he'd better not let that happen, or it would mean trouble for his large Russian ass.

Tony lowered his overweight frame into the pilot seat, looking down at the pilot's logbook that lay open and lifeless on the mahogany chart table. "Bad luck, my friend," Tony said out loud, thinking how easily the man's neck had snapped. "By the time your wife or whoever cares about you discovers you're overdue, we'll be done with this scow and long gone."

CHAPTER THREE

Washington Bound

June 23, 1992, 3:45 PM

Ben Coleman eased his athletic frame into the rich comfort of the leather Delta DC-9's first-class seat, accepted the first of what would be several well-chilled scotches from the youthful blond hostess, and reflected on his body's remarkable capacity to remain fit despite the professional torture he constantly put it through. As one of the country's top advertising copywriters and creative directors, Ben challenged himself with a non-stop schedule of work, travel and play. The only apparent physical effect seemed to be a hardening and leaning of his six-foot-three frame. While his intense, ultra-competitive personality concerned his physician, there was no physical evidence to cause his doctor to demand that Ben slow down. That was fine with Ben. He couldn't slow down anyway, even if he was strapped down, because the abundant energy of his powerful imagination was always driving him to create new ways of living, loving, firing the tennis ball into the far corner and creating advertising. If something wasn't "perfect" it wasn't satisfying to Ben. So in this very imperfect world, he always had a lot of work to do. I'm probably a classic ADD type, he mused. Mom always wondered how to settle me down in school. Staring out the window instead of reading books, or planning the baseball team's line-up rather than doing math problems always felt much more satisfying to him. He enjoyed stuff involving people, not scientific or mathematical things. Today they give kids pills, but in those days, after-school detention was the sole remedy, and it rarely worked, certainly not on him. What did work was writing for the school newspaper, creating ads for college friends starting businesses, and acting as the Public Affairs Agent for his Navy jet squadron, which was home-based in San Diego, California, or at sea on an aircraft carrier anchored off the coast of Vietnam.

As the Delta commuter jet carved its escape through the soggy, yellow air enveloping New York City, Ben wondered, as he often did on such flights, about the man at the controls of the giant aircraft. Although he hadn't been at the helm of an airplane since serving as a highly decorated Navy F4 Phantom pilot, Ben still fancied himself as an excellent aviator, one who had always flown with the distinctive measure of finesse that he felt was dismally lacking in many airline pilots today. When the plane approached its cruising altitude of twenty-eight thousand feet, his cynicism was confirmed as the jet abruptly lurched into a right-hand turn over Atlantic City before proceeding to Washington, D.C.'s National Airport.

"Air Farce" for sure, he murmured knowingly. You just can't get good talent anywhere these days, he thought. Maybe we need another war to bring back some talent in the cockpit. Talent, that's what's missing from everything in this world, from Congressmen on down to dry cleaners. "No one cares about excellence anymore," he grumbled softly, "and sooner or later everyone will be worse off for that failure."

Ben signaled the blonde flight attendant, or "air-nurse" as he liked to call them, and when she arrived he noticed her gold nameplate proudly proclaimed "Sunny" on her snug, full blouse. After asking for another double he eased his head back into the smooth headrest to contemplate the curious turn his life had taken in the last twenty-four hours. I've been waiting for something like this to happen, to break me out of the stalemate that has been my comfortable but boring life for too many years, he thought. The only time I've ever felt really alive was a thousand feet over downtown Hanoi releasing five-hundred-pound bombs on the bastards who had captured and at that very moment, were probably torturing my flight buddies. I've never wanted to do anything as much as drop those bombs right down the gullet of Ho Chi Minh, and get that crazy, useless war finished and our guys back home.

Well, it certainly seems like I'm back in the flack. This time it's political flack, something I know nothing about, but I'm willing to learn. If this guy Gaines is anything like the people I'm going to meet, Ben reasoned, this could be my best gig yet. I won't be dropping any bombs but who knows, my words may get more done than all those fucking bombs ever did.

Well, like we used to say at fifteen-thousand feet above North Vietnam as we pulled back the power, dropped our speed brakes and rolled inverted, "I'm going in." Ben chuckled, glancing out the window at the passing terrain thousands of feet below. Doesn't look any different from 'Nam, he mused.

Lost in thoughts of what might come of his new assignment, Ben was unaware of the impact his presence was having on Sunny and her equally attractive brunette flight associate, Amy. Whispering over the *New York Times* they were holding between them, they recognized Ben as the man pictured and profiled in the business section, the man referred to as an advertising legend, the best in the country. The man who also had weathered three wives, and raced through countless girlfriends, tennis matches, open-ocean sailing regattas and Black Label bottles. But in spite of all of this, he was a man who had worked at just one advertising agency since being handed an honorable discharge and $450 in travel allowance from the Navy.

The article also mentioned that Ben had just been hired by President Bradley Stewart Rogers to help elect him to a second presidential term. In an accompanying photo, standing next to the President was an older man identified as Chief Justice Robert Allan Blackstone. President Rogers was smiling pleasantly while Blackstone's appearance was one of studied confidence, a man accustomed to getting his way. The women sighed and looked longingly at the celebrity on their plane.

Unaware of being admired, Ben handed his empty glass to Sunny as the plane descended over the Potomac. As she bent down to retrieve it, Ben appreciated the youthful abundance of tanned flesh that was so richly revealed. Strapping herself into the jump seat diagonally ahead of him, Sunny smiled, her bright eyes dancing with good humor. Ben thought he detected a certain willingness to play and Ben liked to play, hard and often.

"The Mayflower," Ben quietly said to her as he disembarked. "About ten in the bar? I'll be wearing an American flag in my lapel so you'll recognize me."

"I already have a date," Sunny protested, blushing for the first time in years, much to her consternation.

"See you there," Ben smiled, glad it had been a productive flight. She'd break her date, he knew, as soon as she reached a phone in the crew lounge.

Ben grinned at the pilot as he exited the aircraft.

"Air Force, right?" he asked.

"Yeah, how'd you know?"

Ben only smiled as he made his way onto the jet way. Set, match, he thought. If only handling Washington, D.C. ad campaigns would be as easy as this.

CHAPTER FOUR

A Failed Russian Coup

June 23, 1992, 4:45 PM

"This is Peter Prescott speaking to you from the White House gates, where crowds of people have gathered in response to the news of a major coup d'etat in Russia. Ever since the Berlin Wall came down less than two years ago, the unexpected failure of twentieth-century Communism has been on the minds of people around the world. Now it appears that remaining elements of the old Soviet Communist regime are dedicated to returning Russia to its pre-revolution Communist domination. Details are scant, but we do know that Russian President Boris Yeltsin is on his way to Washington to sign a historical anti-proliferation treaty with President Rogers. His plane will land in minutes. As he arrives, we can only guess what is being done about the coup. We will keep you apprised of developments as we learn more. Back to you, Tom."

Tom Brokaw's tanned face immediately appeared on the TV screen and he began discussing the implications of the coup, while President Rogers and a group of his senior advisors watched in rapt attention at the White House. Sitting next to the President, National Security Advisor Janine Warden was solemn and quiet. The sullen expression on her face communicated all Rogers needed to know; no one had seen this coming. That was a most unwelcomed revelation, especially since Yeltsin would be joining him in just a few hours.

Ben's plane touched down at Dulles National Airport, ten miles south of the White House, just minutes behind Yeltsin's Russian turbojet. Meanwhile, in the steaming streets of Washington, DC, the late-afternoon summer sun baked down on the scores of tourists swarming toward the White House. As a growing number of tourists clustered noisily in front of 1600 Pennsylvania Avenue, they ignored the blistering heat in a vain attempt to glimpse President Rogers and other luminaries. They knew the President was inside the White House because the national political conventions were only weeks away and network news vans jammed the streets. Television, radio and Internet news broadcasts were full of interviews emanating from various locations throughout the Capitol. The crowd that stood behind the ironwork fence that framed the sweeping lawns and well-tended gardens of the White House were waiting to hear what President Rogers himself thought about a coup led by Russian Army generals.

Familiar faces of evening newscasters could be seen

lining the White House driveway amidst dense thickets of cameras, mike booms and other TV gear. In the afternoon heat, the tension generated by all the activity was electric. Other concerned citizens hovered around TVs and radios throughout the U.S., and people worldwide strained to hear the news. Many of them recalled the fear that the Cuban missile crisis had created during the Kennedy Administration and they imagined a similar threat of the use of nuclear weapons.

Inside the Oval Office, Chief of Staff Charlie Gaines discussed the latest CIA assessments of the coup with the President and key advisors. Ornate ceiling fans circulated welcomed streams of cool air. The breeze stirred a few hairs on Gaines's head but his smooth composure remained unruffled by recent events. He knew the President would consider his astute opinion and the advice of other key personnel before taking appropriate action, just as he had done consistently in the past. Rogers had always been a moderate conservative, and thus was tough on Communism, like his famous predecessor Ronald Reagan. There were many politicians who stood further to the right on national security issues and frequently pressed the President for more dramatic action, sometimes dangerously dramatic action.

Periodically, Rogers found himself forced to acquiesce to their requests in order to maintain harmony within the Republican Party. Given the frailty of Yeltsin's post-Communist power base in Russia, Rogers realized that this might be one of those times to take more decisive and forceful action, before everything the U.S. had done during the forty-year struggle to win the Cold War went down the drain.

"I simply don't believe it," exclaimed the graying, middle-aged President. "How could we not have known about another coup until it happened four hours ago? We spent decades bringing down the damn Iron Curtain, and we can't track the political aftermath? Russia and her satellites are wide open now, and we should have eyes and ears on everything that moves. Yeltsin got himself elected President against all odds, but they still can't control things over there. And we don't know squat!" His eyes bored into those of his powerful advisors, many of whom were on secure phones listening with one ear to distant voices detailing the unraveling of the latest events.

With a quick nod and several terse orders, the head of the Joint Chiefs of Staff, Admiral Robert Thompson disengaged himself from his call and addressed the assemblage. "It's now clear that the eight or nine key military leaders involved in the coup have broken ranks from the others. Once again, the army at large has refused to support these men and several rebel generals are urgently requesting to meet with President Yeltsin, most likely in an effort to save their own necks. Mr. President, the unthinkable has indeed happened. First the Berlin Wall was torn down twenty-one months ago with virtually no advance word from our security agencies; then an armed coup against Gorbachev failed, thanks to Yeltsin's intervention last year; and now the latest coup attempt against Yeltsin, who has been on the job for less than a year, has apparently, and fortunately, been brought down by military units faithful to him. We don't have to go to DEFCON 1, but what bothers me is this: we didn't see this one coming." His autocratic gaze settled on the heads of two key governmental agencies, the CIA and the FBI.

While the group reacted to this sobering pronouncement with measured tones of relief and optimism, one man standing off to the side continued his phone call, seemingly unmoved by recent developments. Speaking in hushed tones into his phone, he remarked, "I agree with the Admiral. The coup has failed, but Russia is rudderless. Even Yeltsin is vulnerable and will remain so." Alan Toland, the Vice President of the United States, grimaced to reveal bright gold fillings on several teeth as he continued. "They have tried mutiny twice. Now we must move quickly, before Rogers decides to dramatically step into the breach that has been broken wide open. It is time for 'the trees' please.'"

On the other end of the line, Chief Justice Blackstone, the dean of American jurisprudence, agreed, then severed the phone connection. While his mind raced with the news, Blackstone gazed with admiration at the small prototype mobile "pocket phone" that had recently been distributed to key administration officials to test. What a little miracle, just like in the 1940's Buck Rogers movies, he recollected. Chuckling over his familiarity with all things American, placed the phone in the pocket of his dark blazer, embellished with the seal of the prestigious Chevy Chase Country Club. Then he depressed the off switch on a tiny electronic proximity scrambler sitting on his mahogany desk. The small black box had been assembled in a suburb of Moscow only weeks earlier. Glancing again with pride in the people whose technological acumen was superior to their U.S. counterparts, the large, silver-haired man turned and rejoined the small group of distinguished guests who had gathered on the broad terrace behind his stately, white-columned Georgetown mansion.

"Just a small matter, my dear," Blackstone said as he smiled reassuringly at his regal wife, Alicia, while shrouding his own inner anxieties with a smooth patrician manner. She noticeably relaxed, and turned her striking green eyes back to a small group nearby that included Reginald Heathgow, a frequent visitor to their home and, Blackstone suspected, to the master bedroom of their country home.

"It appears no one can do anything right these days, not even conduct a successful coup!" Alicia said, with words slightly slurred from the effects of three gin and tonics. "They have had two tries, and I don't expect Mr. Yeltsin will give them the lux-shury of another."

Blackstone's brief irritation with his wife was quickly replaced with thoughts of what he must do soon, now that the long-dormant plan had been activated by events in Russia that even he and his associates never seriously thought would happen. First, East and West German citizens had unexpectedly dismembered the Berlin Wall. Then came the shocking demise of the Union of Soviet Socialist Republics, when Russia and several satellite countries rejected their Communist heritage and held free elections for the first time in history. Now another coup attempt aimed at reestablishing Communism in the Mother Country has occurred, led by dedicated ex-KGB senior agents, like him. Agents who were part of a larger, long-term plan to save Russian Communism should it ever come under siege, as it was now.

For nearly half a century, Lenin-inspired Communism had reigned in Russia, Blackstone reflected, and now it's about to become history. He was sure the U.S would take action to keep the old USSR permanently out of business. But what would they do? A "Marshall Plan" for Russia was the probable answer, Blackstone thought dourly, and most likely it would occur right after the presidential elections. Those elections were sure to be complete with gifts of Levis and Harleys for the Russian peasants in order to gain their favor and turn the historical tide against the remnants of Communism, Blackstone knew. He and his cohorts would have to act quickly to prevent such a U.S. response, because upon re-election, President Rogers would be pressured to take immediate action by his party's powerful conservative faction. The plan to save Communism that Blackstone had been preparing to activate for the past forty years of his life must be executed immediately, before matters got out of hand and they lost the advantage of surprise.

The usual buzz of "unofficial" official Washington gossip dominated the terrace conversation as the Chief Justice considered his options. He nodded pleasantly, appearing to be listening intently to Philip Webster, Dean of the Harvard Law School, who was an old friend and a verbose storyteller. Wait until Philip hears the real story, he thought. It has a pretty scary plot with a not-so-happy ending for Philip and his countrymen. Now that the much-anticipated week of early November was drawing near, things will be set in motion. And, my friend, you'll see that actions speak louder than law any day of the week. He grinned, then noticed his wife studying him closely.

The chink in my armor, Blackstone thought, but the hottie in my bed, for now. His real hottie was miles away, but she would be much closer soon, for good. Raising his thick glass to his lips, he pondered the pleasure of vodka, very cold, no ice; just a little reminder of the old country being enjoyed in the new country. Why would anyone drink anything else, he wondered? Vodka, without ice to dilute its rich, smooth taste. In his youth even children drank it that way. Never dilute anything worth having, he had heard someone say. Smart man, like me.

He mulled over the secret plan devised so long ago. It would work beautifully, he assured himself, taking another deep gulp of his drink. Yes, just perfectly. Why wouldn't it? Stalin himself had conceived the plot and had appointed me and my comrades to carry it out. Now I am in charge. We cannot fail.

CHAPTER FIVE

"Can't Get No Satisfaction"

June 23, 1992, 5:20 PM

In the limo Gaines had sent to take him to his hotel, Ben was surprised by the jitters he felt about the impending meeting with the President. I've never met a real president before, he reflected, just corporate ones, and they don't count. As usual, his response under pressure was to divert his attention to subjects that really interested him. This time, it was his three ex-wives. This little exercise always helped distract him from the rude demands of his profession, and as he eased back into the limousine's rear seat he let his mind wander back to those ladies.

All were blond and gorgeous, savvy, and clever. And all were, surprisingly, still his friends, albeit expensive friends, he thought ruefully. He knew people were curious about whom to blame for the failed marriages, but Ben knew the answer wasn't as simple as Jimmy Buffett's song about margaritas. For better or worse, Ben was a hungry man who attracted equally hungry and equally quickly bored women. It was the boredom they still talked about during periodic late-night phone calls. It was the hunger, still very much alive, that none of them would admit.

Ben had all but lost faith that there could be a permanent female partner for him. He expected to go on grazing among the vast sea of attached and semi-attached willing blondes until the restless roaming and hunger finally abated with old age, or a beating from a jealous husband.

Janet was his first wife. They grew up together in the wealthy New York City suburb of Rye. It had just felt right to be in love and, at first, he had been faithful. They dated all through high school and Cornell, using the deep winter shadows of snow-covered parking lots and frequent fraternity house parties to explore the rituals of lovemaking. Ben had no clear goals beyond college, but when he learned the Navy would let him fly airplanes if he survived their rigorous training program, his path was set. Crossed swords held over their heads by half-soused classmates, he and Janet rushed down the steps of the chapel at the naval base in Pensacola, Florida, and jumped into the schizophrenic lives of young couples chasing ever-shifting dreams of love, family, career and friends.

Ben survived two treacherous tours in Vietnam, but his first marriage failed to survive his reassignment to the Naval Air Station North Island on San Diego Bay in California. Karen was a fellow pilot's youthful wife. California-born, suntanned and spoiled, as only an Admiral's daughter can be, she decided Ben was a wonderful name to be uttered in the throes of passion. So convincing were her amorous talents, she succeeded in displacing Janet in his heart, mind and groin. Ben was surprised at his glibness when it was time to tell Janet her ship had left port. He also was truly surprised at her readiness to agree to a divorce without alimony or acrimony.

His preference for blondes remained, but the names were always changing. For some reason, most of the women that attracted him were married. Ben wondered why he was interested in other men's wives. It seemed he was more interested in them than their husbands were, and the wives liked that very much. They liked the careful yet confident way he took them, his willingness to meet their emotional as well as sexual needs. They couldn't say no to his grey-blue eyes and energetic dedication to carnal pleasures.

His last divorce, from Angie, was now six years ago. Although he had been with many women since then, he still didn't feel happy. He felt he could have written the lyrics to the popular Rolling Stones tune, "I can't get no satisfaction." That song was a hit when he was twenty-two and still going strong. Blondes, drugs and rock 'n roll. Some things never go out of vogue, he mused as the limo pulled up to an imposing building in the Capitol. He had always avoided the drugs part of that popular 60's war cry. Unless money and fame are drugs; then maybe he was an addict after all.

But now in his mid-forties, Ben was tired of being adrift, with little but his creative and sexual victories to show for his silver temple hair and the crows-feet at the edges of his deep-set eyes. He wanted, no, needed something, someone more. Someone he could always savor and enjoy. He was bored playing the hapless suitor of a constant stream of admiring and needy young New York "ad biz wannabes."

It was time to set a new course. Even though he realized this, he wasn't sure he was ready to leave the easy pickin's of breast-augmented graduates who seemed to line up at the end of the bar at P.J. Clarke's on Third Avenue. Perhaps he would find the answer to his dilemma during his new mission in the nation's capitol. He certainly hoped so. Fifty was only a few years away and it seemed he had better get something accomplished soon, something more than a bunch of ad campaigns for bleach, toothpaste and other stuff people thought they needed.

CHAPTER SIX

"The Trees, Please"

June 23, 1992, 5:43 PM

Blackstone would have been horrified if he knew his brief phone call had been computer-analyzed, along with millions of other calls, at the CIA facility only minutes away from his stately home. David Albright Blackstone had been Chief Justice of the United States Supreme Court for two years, appointed by President Rogers. He was a confidant to presidents, premiers, kings and congressmen. Had it not been for the phrase "The trees, please" his call would have been ignored along with millions of others.

As it happened, the massive Cray supercomputer located in the bowels of Langley, the CIA headquarters in Virginia, took note of the use of a signal scrambler, broke the relatively sophisticated code in less than two seconds, then noted a phrase it had "heard" before in nine previous calls made from this number in the past six years. It immediately printed an alert report. However, because the Cray failed to instantly crack the scrambler's code, it did not record the brief conversation that preceded the three-word phrase.

Within minutes, the report was being studied by several patient men in a windowless office four floors below the expansive lawns at Langley's sprawling headquarters facility.

"Sort of hard to believe, don't you think?" queried the youngest. "I can't believe the judge has a scrambler. Where'd he get that, and why such a short, cryptic conversation, 'the trees please'?"

"I suppose we ought to up this to Level Four surveillance," said another analyst. "It'll kill two birds if we learn more about his wife and her various international heart-throbs."

"Yes, put it on a Four," said another of the men, with a wry smile. "But, let's not make a big deal about this with Davenport just yet. He and the Chief Justice are old golfing buddies and he'd be hard-pressed not to tell him our concerns. Before this new coup settles down, everyone, including us, will be under some kind of heightened scrutiny. We used to know who the enemy was or was supposed to be. Now, no one knows for sure. Intelligence in the world at large is back to ground zero, or maybe sub-zero."

The others nodded at the familiar complaint and got back to work.

"I wish we knew where Blackstone got that scrambler," remarked one of the men as they left the computer room to go back to their gray-walled cubicles. "I've never seen that footprint before. I just wish we knew what the old guy was up to."

Back at their desks, each of the men was alone with

his thoughts. One of them finished entering the report into the CIA computer system and distributed it to a limited list of recipients. Before long it was the end of their shift, and while they rode in the elevator up to the parking garage, unbeknownst to them a special CIA unit code-named "Mind Cloud" was meeting in another wing of the vast facility. The small secret group had hastily gathered to discuss the alert report and its disconcerting upgrade to high-level surveillance.

If the President or the Director of the CIA, Paul Conover, had known of this clandestine meeting of CIA veterans and their dangerous purpose, the traitors would have been arrested for treason. But neither knew. No one did. Only the members of the group knew, and they weren't talking, except to each other. They must find a way to snuff-out the report fast, or nearly a half-century of planning would be shot to hell; and probably they, too, would be shot.

CHAPTER SEVEN

The Mayflower Hotel

June 23, 1992, 6:09 PM

Ben had traveled extensively developing advertising ideas and campaigns for numerous clients. He had lived well because he appreciated living well. He actually cared that the sixteen-year-old scotch he drank had aged four years longer than the stuff his friends drank. Ben had learned in his late teens that he could intuitively see, taste and smell the difference in most things more clearly than the average person. He saw things others missed. His penetrating power of observation and discrimination was what made him so good at his creative craft. It was what women smelled in his imported aftershave. It was what men saw in his confident demeanor. It was what had made him such a skillful pilot, with the ability to quickly locate and kill his target amidst heavy enemy missile fire, returning unscathed to the carrier with his flight team intact.

This hypersensitivity made things worthwhile,

worth drinking, worth driving, worth flying, eating, and frankly, worth loving. In short, Ben saw things more clearly and wanted those things more dearly than other men. It was what guided and controlled his view of the world, and was the one instinct he could rely on in a treacherous and demanding business of egos and money.

However, his first evening in Washington was to be even more unique than even he could have imagined. As soon as he arrived at the famous Mayflower Hotel, the name "Coleman" took on the cachet of a Hollywood star. The hotel staff seemed to surround him as he exited the limo, obviously briefed by Gaines's men to provide him with special VIP treatment.

"Welcome to the Mayflower, Mr. Coleman. Hans will take your luggage," the porter said. "Please follow me. I will show you to your suite."

"Thanks very much. You're making me feel like a potentate!"

Realizing he was in the sweet spot of luxury, Ben handed his black leather Mark Cross briefcase to the tall uniformed man and followed him through the ornate brass front door.

"We'll take the first elevator, sir. Your suite is ready and you have several messages," said the bellman, handing an envelope to Ben. "I hope you enjoy your stay. Don't hesitate to ask if we can assist you further."

"If this is politics, I'll take it," he said to himself as two porters led him toward the elevators. Ben walked easily, feeling eyes following him, the heady swirl of power. Like a fine brandy, he savored it. And like any intoxicant, he knew it could overwhelm him if he wasn't careful.

If anyone had asked, Ben would have estimated that creating a new campaign for President Rogers would take at most two months of hard work in his temporary home. As it turned out, Ben was going to call the Mayflower home for more than five unforgettable months.

CHAPTER EIGHT

Strange Bedfellows

June 23, 1992. 7:28 PM

The "Davenport" that the CIA executive had referred to while studying "the trees" data at Langley was Raymond Davenport, Jr., the son of a Seattle carpenter who had failed to pass on to his son his strong work ethic. "Junior" had selected a public service career because it looked easy and because several of his preppy college friends had chosen that direction. Due to the protection of those wealthy friends and to some astute political gamesmanship of senior U.S. government officials, he had advanced through the ranks rapidly. Three years ago had been promoted to Chief Assistant to the Director of the CIA, at the specific behest of the newly installed Vice President, Alan Toland.

Junior's crafty grasp of office politics, agile career management, quick wit, scratch golf game and polished social skills were his key strengths. However, among his many character weaknesses were dependencies on single-malt scotch and Asian women, developed during several years serving as a junior diplomat posted to U.S. Embassies in various capital cities in Asia. Had he known of the latest Cray report, he would have acted quickly to prevent the wrong eyes from seeing it, including deep-sixing the special CIA team that had just distributed it. He had arranged similar "disappearances" many times before, ironically under the guise of his sworn duty to protect the United States of America. The recent White House meeting about the foiled coup attempt and the phone call that followed ordering him to rendezvous at "the fundraising," were on his Ivy League-educated mind as the black CIA limousine raced to the secret meeting. How would these fast-breaking events impact their long-standing mission and, most importantly, his future, he wondered.

The limo eased to a stop outside the courtyard of AuBoir, a fashionable suburban Washington restaurant surrounded by mature maple fundraising. David Blackstone liked to hold their periodic meetings at the place, and also liked to use code words such as "the trees," even though the practice was outmoded and silly. Davenport went along with this and other more serious charades because he had no choice. His role as assistant to the head of the most powerful secret service organization in the world was thoroughly and irrevocably being manipulated by a small group of powerful men who had parlayed his weak character and dangerous appetites into an extremely useful senior operative.

Davenport suppressed the familiar feeling of helplessness and anger, realizing there was little he could do or, frankly, at this point in his life wanted to do about his bizarre situation. Well, fuck it, he thought, just keep working at it until something happens.

His long-time chauffeur, CIA Agent Roland Marcus, responded to his quiet directive to return in two hours with a brief "Yes, Sir." Davenport stepped out and strode rapidly into the quiet recesses of the restaurant. The place still reminded him of the wood-trimmed, silk-screened Japanese hotels so popular in the mid-seventies with young Foreign Service agents like himself, who had been safely posted hundreds of miles from the hell of Vietnam. He had escaped that duty thanks to influential political connections. It had been in one of these bamboo-embellished hotels that he had begun his affair with Kirin, a petite Japanese beauty he'd met at a reception five months earlier in the ancient city of Kyoto. That state department reception had been organized for a visiting group of California legislators, including a young David Blackstone. It was Blackstone who, with the help of several explicit photos, had patiently convinced Davenport to provide him with seemingly innocuous confidential information, for increasingly large payoffs. Later on, the hotel was where Kirin delivered the blood money to Davenport, money that allowed him to continue to afford her and the lifestyle he had coveted while growing up on the poor side of Seattle. Several years passed before Davenport realized the treacherous connection between the money and the intimidating Californian, who now was a powerful elder statesman. And this treacherous link, tied to his continuing need to keep Kirin in his life, had remained firmly in place ever since.

The "fundraising" was his own tragic Briar Patch, and he was thoroughly entangled in it. Chief among his duties was preventing the CIA from discovering the truth behind what they had always assumed was an odd, but insignificant relationship between himself, the Chief Justice, and the Vice President, who also was at today's meeting. Most people, if they cared, would have attributed the apparent long-term friendship to the fact that they all had attended Stanford University, and had become Young Republicans like Richard Nixon, their mentor and hero.

"Thanks for coming, Ray," Blackstone said, grinning widely and motioning Davenport to a curved leather chair situated in front of a fish pond and an impressive waterfall. "We're always fortunate to get this table on such short notice as it allows us some privacy amidst all of Mr. Toland's Secret Service retinue. It is reminiscent of one of the wonderful geisha houses in old Japan, isn't it Ray?"

The acidic tone of Blackstone's comment unleashed a second wave of queasiness in Davenport's gut. He knew Blackstone would never ease up on the tight leash that kept him linked to this evil mission. While Blackstone appeared to take his jabs at Davenport with light humor, the frequent insults he hurled at the Vice President seemed meaner and more personal. When Davenport had met them years earlier, the evident rift between the two other men had impressed him as nothing more than idle banter. But he soon realized their enmity ran deep and potentially threatened their mission. Obviously, the two had been tossed together by politicians from another era. At that time, people put little store in personality screenings and psychiatric match-ups, techniques that his organization now practiced religiously. Davenport didn't enjoy the verbal infighting; it was unprofessional and nerve-wracking. He also worried that it could flare into a conflagration that would engulf him, destroy his career, and possibly his life.

"Geishas were in my past, Chief Justice. Presently we have much to discuss, I imagine, given all that is happening here and overseas, yes?" Davenport had hoped to diffuse the highly charged environment and get to the business at hand.

"My dear Raymond, I will manage our agenda, as always, if you please. I have learned from studying Asian manners that one must ease into difficult matters with light humor and conversation. I am concerned we have gotten a little too soft waiting for our mission to activate. So, let us review where we are and how well-prepared we are to get underway, now that our crude Slavic countrymen have screwed things up so badly."

Alan Toland nervously adjusted his shaded gold-rimmed glasses, revealing a Rolex that appeared too ostentatious, even for a vice president. In contrast, the Chief Justice's blue suit was simply and elegantly understated. Davenport, in his light gray suit, striped red tie and heavy wingtips, was as different in appearance as the other two were from each other. It was a curious trio viewed through the eyes of the Secret Service agents assigned to the Vice President, who sat thirty feet away at a table near the entrance to the private dining room.

"This town makes for strange bedfellows," griped one of the younger agents, Vince Jenner. "It's a good thing we don't get concerned about that sort of thing like we used to. In the fifties, if a guy didn't wear a Brooks Brothers suit or have shined shoes, they figured him for a foreign operative. Nowadays, anything goes; even beards and tattoos, for Chris' sake."

Vince and his associates would have been more concerned had they realized the three men they were babysitting were core members of the group responsible for carrying out a complex plan first conceived over forty-five years ago by Joseph Stalin, the dictator of terror in Russia. They also would have been astounded to know that these three men and a small cadre of well-placed, well-paid ex-CIA and Russian operatives had succeeded in replacing the Mafia over the past seven years as the leading supplier of cocaine into the United States. Their achievement brought millions of dollars into the secret Bermuda bank account set up to fund their lethal mission in America's capital city.

"We appreciate your dedication, Raymond," Blackstone said, after their drinks arrived and the waitress departed. "I am particularly heartened by the rapid progress your team made in expanding our West Coast product distribution. It is the last link in our network, and probably will prove to be the most lucrative. Perhaps Alan and I will have to return to our adopted hometown of Fresno to gauge the impact of our flourishing distribution operation. It's been a long time since either of us were in 'raisin land.' I suspect the only thing of merit to have come from there besides Alan and myself are the 'dancing raisins,' God help us." He laughed quietly at the memory of the rock-and-roll raisin commercials that seemed to have been everywhere on TV a few years earlier. So trite, so very American, he thought, so typically stupid and crass.

"Dancing raisins were just one of the many proletarian outrages I had to put up with in the California farmlands," Toland said, grimacing and taking a slug of his drink. "The only things they talk about in Fresno are the damn rain or lack of it, the grants program that pays them to plant nothing, and the hookers at the local strip parlors. They deserve what they will soon get. They laugh at Russian peasants but they're worse because they have college educations and live on government handouts. What ignorant people."

"Alan, such rude observations of the people who put you in office," Blackstone laughed heartily, enjoying Toland's characteristic bad humor. "Well, the little fuckin' raisins seem to have left the building along with Elvis," Blackstone chuckled, priding himself on having so thoroughly learned American expressions. With the exception of his rough skin and wide cheekbones, he viewed himself as American as they came.

More drinks arrived along with the appetizers the Chief Justice always ordered, smoked oysters. He liked to think the shellfish lived up to its reputation as a mild aphrodisiac, but he was realistic enough to know it was wishful thinking. Fortunately he had access to all the medicinal help he needed to remain virile, compliments of his Bethesda Medical Center doctor. He should thank the U.S. taxpayers sometime, he mused, and glancing over at Davenport, so should Kirin.

Toland glared at Blackstone, irritated as always by stirring up his memories of Fresno that were for him anything but pleasant. His adopted family had resisted his need to attend college, nearly destroying his mission before it began. Only after using a shovel to threaten his surrogate father, who thought Alan was a foster child, had Toland succeeded in gaining his grudging approval to leave the family fig farm and attend Stanford University in Palo Alto, California, a "rich kid's school." His real ticket to lofty places had taken the form of Mary Ann Adams, the full-bodied, flamboyant daughter of a powerful rancher, and an active Republican. Within two years of graduation, the intense young Toland had married Mary Ann and had become ensconced in Washington, D.C. as an aide to Senator Cleary of California. Society unwittingly awarded a law degree and a Supreme Court clerkship to the earnest young man, years before he became a senator himself. Now fifty, he had been personally placed on the national ballot for Vice President four years earlier, primarily through Blackstone's influence. Toland had never liked him, but it was evident that Blackstone controlled both the covert mission and his political career. It also was clear to Toland that the vice-presidency was the last step towards his long-term goal of becoming President of the United States. And for that, he could abide Blackstone's nasty comments.

Toland's thoughts were interrupted by the arrival of dinner. He smiled at the petite redheaded waitress, noting her innocent beauty, short dark hair and large blue eyes. He wondered at her age. She appeared to be in her early twenties, the same age Debby would have been, he realized. His stomach suddenly lurched and he lost his appetite, feeling only deep loss and quiet rage. The country he was dedicated to destroying had been responsible for the death of his only daughter, an event that served to strengthen his resolve to fulfill his long-awaited mission.

"Alan, is there something wrong with your drink?" Blackstone solicitously inquired.

"No, I suddenly don't feel well, nothing to worry about."

Blackstone noted his associate's distraction with the waitress and knew the source of his sudden moodiness. Secretly, he was glad Toland had lost his daughter years ago in a freak accident only weeks after she had joined the Army Reserve in Sacramento. Anything that kept Toland focused on their mission and not on himself was good. Blackstone had never had children because their mission plan forbade it. The men in the Kremlin who had masterminded this daring far-sighted plot had insisted that the core cell of five young men avoid family beyond obtaining wives and living what appeared to be normal American lives. It was argued in heated tones over many glasses of vodka that having a family would expose the operatives to too many potential pitfalls, such as applying for their children's birth certificates. Authorities might instigate aggressive probes and the risk of discovery increased each time such questions arose. As it was, Blackstone resented the years of happiness that Toland had enjoyed with his daughter. Alan had always been crafty and he had found a way to skirt the restriction by adopting a young orphan, loving her as though she were his natural-born daughter. Pricking the latent scab of Toland's wound and enjoying the anger against the U.S. that it generated, prodded Blackstone

to incite verbal skirmishes that served to remind Toland of his control over him.

Blackstone's incisive, inscrutable eyes turned back
to Davenport. Here was a man who was easily compromised, more easily than almost anyone in Blackstone's experience. If he hadn't been so effective at
supporting us, I would have turned him in to the Feds
just for spite, he thought. But, I sponsored him and
ensured his swift ascent through the CIA ranks by
feeding him information that led to some spectacular
arrests around the world. The men arrested had been
people who Blackstone had wanted, for one reason or
other, eliminated.

"How are your dinners, gentlemen?" he asked as a
formality rather than out of concern.

"Terrific as always, your Honor," Davenport responded out of habit. He had never liked having to
referring to Blackstone in this way. The irony especially irritated him because he had never fully accepted the full horror of his own treason.

"It's almost as though we've done the country a favor, putting Gotti and the Mob out of the drug business. We did what Eliot Ness couldn't do, and we
don't even have a TV show," he laughed awkwardly.

"Well, Ray, perhaps we should look into that," Toland joked. The Vice President was someone who always enjoyed seeing himself on TV, in print, or even
on billboards, and his vanity seemed to grow larger
each year he was in office. Blackstone often remarked
that Toland was going to run out of space on his body
to hang expensive suits, shoes, and other spoils of his
success. If only the boys in the Kremlin could see their
Legion of Lenin lad now, he mused.

"Ray," Blackstone said. "Alan and I have some other things to discuss when we're finished here tonight, so would you bring us up to date on your end of things?"

As Davenport began to speak in crisp, thoughtful sentences, Blackstone considered the need to close this chapter of their work together, now that the long-planned mission was at hand. This bothered Blackstone somewhat, because Davenport had become a valuable resource. However, the plan specified that only the core members of the Communist cell be involved in the final steps. Davenport had mistakenly thought the group's primary objective was to enrich its members. Working under that assumption, he had a high level of success spearheading the design and implementation of a worldwide drug network, run by retired CIA and FBI operatives, who imported cocaine into the U.S. from South America via Cuba. Even the Mafia didn't realize that their major competition was a powerful cadre of senior U.S. government officials. Had they been aware of it, there would have been little they could have done. Davenport had even subordinated parts of the Medellin Cartel and other powerful international drug organizations to the plotters' purposes. While it appeared they were working for themselves, members of the Cartel had been allocating over fifty percent of their best cocaine and crack to the most powerful and secretive Communist organization in the world. Known by its limited membership as the Green Lake Duck and Skeet Club, the organization had fattened numerous offshore bank accounts in several countries.

Davenport had done well, Blackstone reflected,

even to the extent of controlling the Cuban drug re-connaissance data and photos that covert CIA opera-tives, members of the secret "Mind Cloud" group, had periodically prevented from getting leaked out of Langley. Yes, Davenport had done very well. In fact, due to his ability to manipulate the system, the FBI and CIA had never worked so unwittingly well with his "sleeper cell."

But that was the past, and now was the future they all had looked forward to, the Chief Justice reasoned. Anyway, he wanted Kirin back. All of her. He could certainly afford her, and where Davenport was going he'd no longer be able to enjoy her many charms.

"…and you've been calling all the shots and that has to stop," Toland grumbled. The accusation jolted Blackstone back into the present as he realized he was being challenged.

"I've been a key part of this deal from the begin-ning," Toland continued, "and I'm getting zero respect from you and the others, including those who aren't here. I will be President in a few months and if this group doesn't change its attitude soon, it sure will then!" he argued, taking another slug of his Manhattan and sitting up straighter in his chair.

"Hold on, Alan, of course you're a key guy in all this," Blackstone countered, grasping for time to assess what was bothering the Vice President to the point of his being so upset.

"People treat me like a second-class person every-where in the White House, right down to the Secret Service detail assigned to me. I only get five agents, and most of them junior agents at that. It's as if I'm expendable. That fucking Greenwood covers Rogers like a blanket with dozens of agents, but I get a platoon of college boys. Believe me, things will be different soon, and guys like Greenwood will be history. I'm going to have a detail of nothing but Swedish Vodka models packing Uzis in alligator briefcases," he laughed, suddenly relaxing with the vision of power that seemed so close at hand.

"Sounds like a great idea, Alan. And it will be yours to implement very soon. I just hate to think of beautiful women leaping in front of would-be assassins and taking a bullet for you, but that appeals to your imagination, no?" Blackstone joked.

"Well, perhaps not beautiful Secret Service agents, but really I wonder if Greenwood would actually take a bullet for Rogers, or any of us. All that expensive training and the only time it was tested was with Reagan. Maybe we·need a little more Secret Service training action around here," Toland muttered, glancing over at the other table. "Yes, a little more action might keep things working in our favor, right?"

"Wrong, Alan, very wrong," Blackstone warned. "This has been all carefully planned. Don't go off half-cocked just when we are finally underway. I don't want any screw-ups."

"Well, I just like the idea. Nothing wrong with thinking about it, is there?" asked Toland.

"Forget it, Alan. We have more important things to talk about. Ray, thanks for coming. Why don't you head out? Alan and I have some things to sort out," Blackstone commanded.

Realizing he had not been given the option of eating his dinner, Davenport slowly rose from his chair and said good night, adding with a wry smile, "I agree there is a lot to do now, so I guess I should get going. Thanks for the drink, Mr. Chief Justice. Keep an eye on that itchy trigger finger, Alan."

The two men watched Davenport exit the restaurant without a glance from the security detail.

"Fortunately, we are not as expendable as he is," Blackstone observed. "Too bad. He's done well for us. But, like a good bottle of cabernet, his time has come. Now, after years of waiting, we have to put everything into fast-forward my friend. Fast forward, right?"

Nodding into his second Manhattan, the Vice President found himself more energized than he had been in a long time. Whether it was the Maker's Mark bourbon or the prospect of finally achieving his destiny, he couldn't tell for sure, but it didn't matter. All that mattered now, as his despised mentor had said, was going fast-forward.

CHAPTER NINE

Welcome to the Circus

June 23, 1992, 6:27 PM

Ben answered the knock on his hotel door still dressed in his traveling clothes and holding one of the best glasses of scotch he'd had in years.

"Good evening, Mr. Coleman," said the conservatively-dressed man standing in the hall. "I see you still know how to break training!"

Ben opened the door further and grabbed the blond, lanky man in a bear hug. "Chet Greenwood. My gosh, it's been years!" Ben was thrilled to see his best friend from college. "You haven't changed a bit; still look like you just got off the gridiron."

Ben and Chet Greenwood had played football on opposite teams, Ben at Bucknell and Chet at Lehigh. The competition for Saturday afternoon touchdowns and Saturday evening girls had started in their freshmen year and continued until graduation day. Chet won the final prize, the beautiful Connie Chase, who had grown up with them in a New York City suburb. The three had continued their friendship in Pensacola, Florida, where Ben and Chet went through Navy flight training while Connie worked at the base hospital. Connie was one of the few attractive women in Ben's life whom he had never bedded, although since second grade, he subconsciously had compared every woman he met to her. They lost touch after the close of the Vietnam War. Ben had often wondered about them, but was too busy and distracted by his advertising career to locate them.

Chet was already walking to the small bar in the suite when Ben asked if he wanted a drink. "I'm on duty, but this is too special an event not to have a small drop. Here's to you and your tremendous success! Welcome to the DC circus," Chet said, helping himself to the fine scotch. "I had heard about you periodically, but it wasn't until this week when I learned you were going to join the campaign, that I realized this famous ad guy was the same chump I got drunk with in so many Philippine and Japanese bars."

"That's right!" Ben smiled. "R&R back in the 60s—those were the days."

Chet dropped his tall body into a large armchair, returned the grin, and smoothed his dark blue tie. Unconsciously, he adjusted his electronic earpiece, from which Ben could hear periodic transmissions crackling softly.

Chet raised his glass to Ben. "How did you get involved in the campaign? Tell me where you've been. I've read your dossier of course, but fill in the blanks." Chet took a sip. "Oh yeah, Connie sends her best. So do our two girls, who think you are a big deal. Boy, it's good to see you again!" he exclaimed, crossing his legs and admiring the dark amber color of the expensive scotch in his crystal goblet.

Ben freshened his scotch and sat opposite Chet. "Well, it's been a fast twenty years since we mustered out, but with a family, it looks like you've got more to show for it than I have. The best I've produced is a Porsche Carrera, a great set of fly rods, some tennis trophies, an accountant who makes all my alimony payments and keeps the taxman at bay. Then there's the office in Manhattan where I spin thirty-second stories about products, some that people need and others they don't, but they buy 'em anyway," he chuckled. "But what are *you* doing here?"

"I work for the President as his primary Secret Service detail head. His Chief of Staff tells me to go get you and I say 'Yes Sir,'" Chet laughed, draining the glass and putting it on the table.

Offering Chet another splash of scotch, which he refused, Ben said, "I couldn't miss that cannon under your jacket. Am I in trouble or are we filming a Dirty Harry movie?"

Chet laughed heartily, glancing at the empty glass on the table with a twinge of regret. "I joined the Secret Service right after we checked out of the Navy at Treasure Island. I was stationed in San Francisco and other places for years, moved here six years ago, and now run the Presidential Protection Unit. You're here to spend time with President Rogers and I'm here to make sure you enjoy yourself and don't get shot by a jealous husband."

"Well, smack me with a small world bat...it sure is great to see you haven't changed at all. Anyway, I'm supposed to meet Charlie Gaines; he was going to call me here."

"I'm your official guide to meeting Gaines," smiled Greenwood, standing up and walking to the window, where he surveyed the activity in the park across the street with a critical eye. "Get changed and let's go. They're expecting you at a reception for Boris Yeltsin. That'll give you a fast introduction to the powers that be in DC."

Minutes later, Ben, Chet and two young Secret Service agents motored to the White House. Ben was surprised to find that he liked the fairly new large black Oldsmobile. Its ride was surer than he remembered American cars having. He hadn't driven an American car in ten years, ever since a borrowed Cadillac Eldorado experienced a steering failure on the New York Thruway that had launched him and a date off the highway into an overgrown ravine. No, Ben preferred BMWs, "rocket ships with brains," as he called them. Later, he also had rewarded himself with a crimson 1989 Porsche speedster, with wide tires and awesome performance.

"Nice machine. I'm surprised!" Ben remarked and sat back in the sumptuous rear seat. He smiled at the built-in ashtray and lighter in the armrest, a holdover from another era. Maybe not so advanced, he thought.

Reading his mind, Chet told Ben that Oldsmobiles are used by the Secret Service and other government security agencies because they can be readily retrofitted with heavy-duty springs, special high-powered pursuit engines and other tricks of the security trade. Also, the trunks are large enough to hold the small arsenal of semi-automatic rifles, ammo and other defense gear that are staples of their profession. Most importantly, the cars draw little attention relative to the other luxury makes that populate the nation's capitol.

"This car can penetrate a concrete wall, outrun your Porsche, and along with several others can form a fairly impenetrable ground-level defense perimeter around the President's limo. It does the job. And I think it's great that it's made in Detroit," Chet said with pride.

"Always the All-American," Ben laughed. "Some things never change. Thank God!" He recalled that Chet's key value as his wingman flying over Vietnam was that he would boldly ignore the clutter of numerous SAM missiles and defending Russian MIGs to ensure he stayed tight on Ben's right wing as they destroyed their targets.

Greenwood's driver swung into an assigned parking space near the White House. The front car doors swung open as the two young agents got out to survey the immediate area. It struck Ben that even Secret Service Agents, in this case Chet, had security details. Ben had seen the lights of the TV crews and some half-curious faces had turned to inspect the Olds as it swept by the gated entrance. He wondered what all these people did when the political carnival was not in town. Probably line up at the unemployment office for their paychecks or spend them at the Off Track Betting parlor.

"C'mon, I'll locate Gaines for you, then I've got to get to work. This is a major diplomatic reception and I'm in charge of security. But let's plan to get you out to Bethesda to see Connie and the girls. Our daughters are both home from Columbia now, and they'd love to meet the big-time ad man they've heard so much about over the years," said Chet.

Ben gave him a "thumbs up" and followed him up the stairs into the White House. He even checked the shine on his shoes, aware he was resorting to an old Navy habit to look sharp.

The opulent surroundings were impressive. Quite a large house just for one family, Ben mused. With a glance of respect at the Marine sentries who seemed cast in impenetrable marble at either side of the wide entrance, Ben passed through their protective net with a sense of excitement and curiosity. Clearly, big guy, your life is changing right now, he thought. Better open your eyes and hang on tight.

CHAPTER TEN
Vodka, No Ice

June 23, 1992, 7:45 PM

"So what are we ordering for Tony?" Mr. Dade asked
his associates, whose large bodies were tightly packed
into the small chairs at the marina restaurant. The day
had passed uneventfully in the wheelhouse of the
docked yacht as the men patiently monitored certain
radio frequencies. Once again, Tony was ordered to
stay with the boat as the other four set out for dinner.
Their breakfast had been the highlight of an otherwise
tedious journey, and they were looking for a repeat
performance from the garrulous French Canadian
chef, whose specialty was large, greasy steaks and
mashed potatoes smothered in butter and dark mush-
room gravy.

"Make it steak and he'll be happy," answered the
man named Maurice. As it was, none of them referred
to each other with their real names. Being gifted primarily in the brawn department, their limited intel-

lects precluded their boss from allowing them to use their real names, with the exception of Tony who just looked like a Tony.

"I've never met a man who is as happy sitting on his butt as Tony is...unless he's chasing babes," joked another. "But even then, he doesn't run very fast."

The group, having enjoyed their first full day of relaxation in weeks, laughed easily at the exchange, all of it carefully spoken in English, albeit with strong European inflections.

Their trip from the yacht harbor in Maryland had been a strange one. So used to the freedom of the open sea, the men had found the confines and the placid nature of the Hudson River's inland waterway boring. Now that it was only a matter of hours before reaching their objective, the anticipation of completing their mission fueled their egos. They began to enjoy themselves.

"You're just jealous because Tony does so well with the ladies in America. It helps that he speaks English with that crazy Polack accent. I just hang around with him hoping for leftovers," laughed the tallest of the group. "With Tony's size, he'll need a thick steak. Make it rare."

"What's our ETA to the site, boss?" asked one of the men quietly.

Mr. Dade turned to him with a glint in his eye and scanned the room once more before replying. "Tomorrow afternoon as planned. We'll motor into Lake Champlain early tomorrow morning, cruise to Westport by noon and reach our anchorage at Basin Harbor on the east shore around 14:45. We've received confirmation that the people at the resort are expecting us and have several available dock slips that can take our length. The place is supposed to be very tranquil and classy. Wait until they see the early 4th of July fireworks we've got for them!" he snickered.

"Hey, too bad we can't wait until July 4th," Maurice said, "but it'll be close enough for government work."

"Yeah," commented Mr. Dade, "*our* government work."

The waitress was startled by the sudden raucous laughter that erupted from the corner table where the coarse men sat. The hair on her neck bristled with apprehension as she approached the table to deliver their drinks. Had she linked her instincts with the liquor the men had requested, she might have had more reason to be concerned. To a man, they had ordered short glasses of expensive chilled vodka, no ice.

Two hours later, the group staggered back to the yacht, aglow with liquor and the anticipation of tomorrow's events.

Tony removed the radio headset as the four entered the wheelhouse. "Well, it's on, Mr. Dade," he said, handing him a pad on which he had written the simple phrase, *expect a full moon soon.*

The short man picked up the pad and used it to salute the others. "It's official. Check all your equipment, then get some sleep. We'll be busy tomorrow."

"Yeah, and then on an Air France jet heading for home two days from now. That's the part of the plan I like. Get out of this muggy climate, back to the mountains, and get to ogle some cute French stews on the way," announced Tony, dimming the pilot house lights.

"All of you had better forget about that flight and those mountains until this thing is done," Dade commanded. "Take your mind off the mission and we may end up in a pine box packed in the belly of that airplane instead of enjoying a first class seat. Tony, get your fat ass below and get some sleep. And keep your mouth shut about anything other than driving this thing."

Slinking down the ladder into the lower cabin, Tony restrained himself from grabbing Mr. Dade around the neck, an impulse he had experienced all too frequently lately. He's right, dammit, he thought. Gotta focus or it's my ass, not theirs, that's going to be fried. There's always another day for dealing with Dade."

Turning away from the huge man, Mr. Dade glanced sternly at the others. He didn't have to say any more; they clearly got his message.

Within minutes, the yacht was silent, rocking softly against the pier as if it were sleeping in preparation for a particularly big day.

CHAPTER ELEVEN

Meeting the President

June 23, 1992, 8:20 PM

Before hurrying off, Chet introduced Ben to Charlie Gaines, who was no taller than five feet and was surrounded with young men and women clutching notepads and thick black binders emblazoned with the formal Presidential seal.

"Well, welcome to the fun, Mr. Coleman. Guess I'd better call you Ben. There's going to be too much to do to stick with formalities." Brushing back one of the few remaining hairs on his large, sun-tanned head, Gaines shook Ben's hand in a vigorous Kiwanis Club grip.

"Folks, this is Ben Coleman. He's going to help us get the President re-elected in a landslide," he quipped, his blue eyes dancing.

"Thanks, Mr. Gaines. Glad to be here. It was great to see Chet Greenwood. We flew together years ago in the Navy."

"Yup, knew that," Gaines said in the manner of one

who knows more than it appears. "And it's 'Charlie,' okay? Listen, we're headed for the Yeltsin reception, so this is as good time as any to introduce you to the President and get you immersed in our little business here."

Gaines's entourage of young men and women, who towered over their fiery little leader, proceeded down several long hallways before arriving at the ballroom doors, behind which Ben heard the excited voices of a large crowd. When they entered, Charlie gestured to him to follow.

As Ben surveyed the room, several fashionably dressed people standing in the receiving line glanced his way. Charlie spoke briefly to the tall, distinguished-looking man at the head of the line, who then extended his hand to Ben with a twinkle in his light brown eyes.

"Thanks for coming, Mr. Coleman," said the imposing man, whose attractive face, framed by thick hair with tinges of silver, was familiar to everyone who owned a TV or read a newspaper. "I was happy when Charlie told me you would be joining us on such short notice. And I was surprised to find how many famous ads you've written over the years, even the ones for my favorite diet soda, Now Cola."

"Thank you, Mr. President," Ben said, returning the firm handshake and sensing why President Rogers was such a successful chief executive. He exuded power, was comfortable with it. "Usually, people have less complimentary things to say about my work. But, it sell products."

"Well, Ben, we're all salesmen, and for better or worse the country runs on sales. Charlie, who's been my personal sales guy and a good one to boot, told me of your modus operandi, that you like to get to know your 'product' and I heartily approve. I'm looking forward to the whole packaging process. Although I'm a moderate Hawk, I'm open to negotiating with liberals. It's worked well to date, but the world is constantly changing. We need a big win in November, so we're glad to have you on board." The President beamed at his wife as he turned to introduce her to Ben.

Elaine Rogers, a woman obviously at ease in the power-charged environs of the White House and Washington, replied, "Mr. Coleman, so nice to meet you," as her gray eyes met his directly. "I have met a great many people in all walks of life, but somehow never someone in your profession. I'm so pleased."

"Well, thanks for the compliment of considering advertising a profession, Mrs. Rogers," Ben said, half-seriously. "We're an odd group, generally frustrated poets or novelists. Most of us can only write thirty seconds of acceptable prose, so we're stuck doing TV commercials."

Elaine Rogers laughed gently, her happy response causing a wide grin to appear on the President's face and on those in line nearby.

"Oh, come now, Mr. Coleman. May I call you Ben?" the First Lady asked. "After all, apparently you're to be part of the family for the next few weeks. It must take a great deal of talent and insight to decide how to convince people to buy certain things. Although the President would say that it doesn't take much to make me approach a sales counter." She laughed lightly, impressing Ben with her genuine warmth.

"Well, thank you. You're making me feel right at home, and yes, please call me Ben."

"I understand, Ben, that you're going to join us for our annual trip to Vermont," she said, pulling him aside to allow others to file past. "The Basin Harbor Club is quaint, but the golf course is challenging and the cabins are delightfully rustic and comfortable. Brad has gone there with his family since he was a boy. We were engaged there. It's a special spot for us, always a family adventure, and we are so looking forward to escaping for a few days. It'll give you a good chance to see him with his hair down, and thank God there's still lots of that left," she smiled, noting Ben's thick shock of reddish blond hair.

Ben was enjoying the idea of being part of the presidential family, a rather foreign concept given his lifestyle to date. He wondered why there had not been more women like Elaine Rogers in his life. She reminded him a little of his own mother, gentle and warm. The idea of family was one he had not fully confronted or accepted, yet he liked the notion—liked it a great deal.

"Well, that is a pleasant surprise. I haven't been to Basin Harbor in years and I appreciate the invitation," Ben smiled, feeling a little like a kid getting to be with the grownups—another strange sensation indeed. He was being caught up in a very different world of quiet but clear power, much different from the noisy Donald Trump brashness of New York, and he found himself looking forward to this "family adventure" with relish. But he also had deep reservations regarding what he could contribute to the apparent slam-dunk political success of Brad Rogers. This guy was not just another box of cereal or a new line of lipstick—a President, not light beer. This is a different game. So, okay, I like games, especially the games I have heard they play here.

"It's usually just family and close friends," Elaine continued, "but after years of watching your Pan Asia Airlines ads with that beautiful music and photography, I feel I've known you a long time. You also might want to meet a key staff member who will be joining us on the trip. She's the White House senior research analyst, Laura Sinclair. The redheaded young lady over there," she said gracefully pointing across the crowded room, "wearing the lime green dress, standing by the fireplace with the head of our security detail, Chet Greenwood."

Ben turned to follow her gaze, his eyes opening in immediate wonder. "Wearing" the green dress was an understatement, something Ben admired in women's clothing. Laura Sinclair was doing more than just wearing the dress. She was effortlessly emblazoning its remarkable light green sheen and subtle erotic profile on every set of male, and some female, eyes in the gilt-trimmed White House ballroom.

As he raised a hand to stifle a dry cough of surprise, Ben saw the First Lady had noticed his reaction and was nodding toward him with a sparkle in her eye. He found himself speechless and of all things, probably blushing, his brain working overtime to absorb the vision of Laura. Thank goodness she's yards away, he thought. Gotta pull yourself together, champ. He glanced back at the President's wife, now smiling in sympathy.

"Well," she said. "It's fun to see your New York
élan shaken just a bit, Ben. But, Laura certainly has
that effect, even in this jaded world of Washington. I
know, I used to have the same effect," she laughed
again, squeezing Ben's arm and gently turning him
towards Laura and Chet. "Have fun, Ben. Always remember that first."

In Ben's mind, the prospect of a stay in Vermont
had begun as a pleasant surprise. Now it had become
an exciting prospect. Ben tried unsuccessfully to remember the last time the rush of blood to his temples
had been this intense.

As he attempted to arrest his emotions and "remain
calm," an old Navy phrase that seemed especially appropriate in this situation, Laura chose that moment to
smile in his direction and start making her way toward him. Ben suddenly felt like a spotlight had been
targeted at him. Her beautiful eyes smiled hello as she
strode easily across the floor, people moving aside to
allow her energy and beauty to pass. Ben found his
heart racing, something that only happened when he
was racing for a backcourt save.

"Laura, meet a new friend of the family, Mr. Ben
Coleman of New York," said Mrs. Rogers, hugging
Laura in a maternal fashion. "He'll be with us for a
while getting to know the President, and hopefully,
some of the rest of us," she laughed again, amused at
her private thoughts. "Perhaps you'd be willing to
take him under your wing and introduce him
around?" The First Lady's question had the cool
authority of a command, but Laura didn't appear to
resent this in the least as she smiled again at Ben
through the most symmetrical line-up of brilliant teeth

he had ever seen. Perhaps, had he worked on a tooth-paste account, he might have run into Ms. Sinclair earlier.

Better late than never, he thought, still attempting to recover his composure. With a slight deferential bow, Ben took his leave of Elaine Rogers, who gave him a merry wink before turning to greet a short Indian diplomat and his wife dressed in a multi-colored sari. He allowed Laura to gently guide him to one of several bars arranged around the room.

"I'm so happy to meet you," Laura said. "My boss, Charlie Gaines, was pleased you agreed to join the campaign." She quickly looked back at Mrs. Rogers and, noticing she was engrossed in conversation with several people, stole another glance, this time taking in President's Roger's quick gaze her way. "I'm the re-election team's lead researcher. I've been here almost three years, after working for Yankelovich Research running their political division here in Washington. While I've never worked directly with advertising research, my work is similar. I track consumer or voter attitudes on issues of interest to the President and his aides, and I particularly like speaking directly to voters about their thoughts and desires. Whatever I can do to help you with your work, please just ask," she said as she handed Ben a heavy tumbler of scotch and took a small sip of white wine.

Ben realized, to his annoyance, that Laura was responding to him as she would to any new addition on the President's team of advisors and hangers-on. Crisp, to the point, she was letting him know that she knew his role, was aware of her turf, and would protect it at all costs. Ben had been in this position before many times, but found himself disappointed that she was reacting to their meeting in such an impersonal, professional fashion. She even knew what he drank. Okay, he thought, so there is a more insincere town on Earth than New York City. But she is gorgeous, and even though I can't think very clearly right now, I'm sure I've never met such an elegant woman or one so smart and focused on her job.

Rarely had a scotch been as welcome a steadying influence as Ben's eyes toured the lovely face of Laura Sinclair. He guessed the "background dossier" detailing his life that Chet had mentioned had made its way to her desk. Nice that she noted his preference for scotch—actually more than nice. She really does take her research seriously, he realized, finding that insight particularly intriguing. Maybe he should just pay attention and not pre-judge all of this. "When in Rome," he thought.

Laura completed her little speech that she had been preparing in various forms for two days. Gaines had made it clear he wanted her to "ride herd on the guy from New York" and make sure that he focused on the key areas of Rogers's political strength that Laura's research had identified. Gaines had joked with her about Ben's ribald reputation and had asked if she was up to babysitting such a notorious playboy. Laura's cool response reflected confidence in her ability to successfully "handle" any aggressive man. Indeed, four years ago, she had firmly shed herself of a two-year affair that had almost destroyed her with its wild passion and heartbreaking frustrations. Since then, she had been able to be around her one-time lover without yearning for a moment alone with him. And only lately had she accepted the fact that Elaine Rogers would remain the wife of Bradley Stuart Rogers III well after he had left politics and retired to his sprawling cattle ranch in Texas, or to his Palm Beach waterfront complex, complete with the gleaming 56-foot Hatteras yacht she knew so well.

"It's very nice to meet you too. Sorry my intelligence on you is so lacking, Ms. Sinclair," Ben responded, noticing how good it felt just being next to Laura. Her smile was blinding and caused a certain level of mental meltdown. He took a deep breath before he continued. "I've not been a close ally of market research, as my New York associates would attest, but I do like to read what people say about our products. I expect you must be particularly valuable to the President."

If you only knew how valuable I once had been, Laura thought, letting a devilish smile play across her full mouth. Surprisingly, her thoughts dwelled only briefly on her past lover as she found herself absorbed with the remarkable grey-blue eyes and thick dark eyebrows of her new acquaintance. Who did he remind her of? Her mind raced to find his Hollywood look-alike, quickly settling on a taller Spencer Tracy. Both men had the same strong and intelligent eyes, eyes that reflected the deep warmth of a very intelligent man. But enough of that; let's keep this professional, she concluded.

"Well, we do a great deal of research and you're right, the President is quite interested in what we learn, she replied. "Mr. Gaines is even more interested, and he certainly knows what to do with the data." Privately, she was often suspicious of Charlie, who often seemed to want to meet with her only to admire her voluptuous thirty-five-year-old figure. But he was one of many men she'd met in Washington who had similar goals, and she was no longer naive.

"Well, what have you learned lately?" Ben asked, buying time and her presence. He was still attempting to regain his normally nonchalant deportment, but Laura's presence continued to short-circuit his efforts. She just seems so fresh and lively, Ben thought, catching Chet's eye as the Secret Service agent quietly scanned the room. Ignoring his friend's brief "thumbs up," Ben thoughts returned to Laura. And she's not even blonde, he realized. Maybe he was going through a sea change, but he'd never before been intrigued with a redheaded woman. Also, she seemed so unlike the upwardly mobile young ladies whose forced hilarity surrounded them in the crowded room. But, no, it was something more.

In fact, he had just noticed the color of her hair, which was tossed up carelessly in what Ben had learned from his fashion accounts is called a French twist. On New York models the hairstyle seemed contrived, but on Laura it seemed as if a random gust of wind had wrapped her luxuriant tresses into a soft knot. That's it. I'm actually looking at this woman directly, rather than being interested just in the size of her breasts or the length of her legs. What a novel experience, he mused.

"...and it seems he's a shoe-in for the nomination and re-election, but the Chief Justice and Charlie want a major landslide, so that's why you're here." Laura finished her response to Ben's question, but he hadn't heard most of it.

"That's terrific, Laura. The President is lucky to have you on his side, and I hope to have you on my side. I'll need all the help I can get being the new kid in town."

"Ben, you don't strike me as being a kid, but I will be glad to be your guide here in the big, bad city."

"Well, I'd certainly like to learn more about what you're doing," he said lamely, trying to keep the conversation moving.

"You will. You and I are going to Vermont tomorrow with the President's party. I hope you play tennis, because they have great clay courts at Basin Harbor. My boyfriend used to take me there once in awhile," she added, grinning at having alluded to her presidential affair without detection. Little did she know that the Secret Service agents had changed her code-name from "Snow White" to "Madonna" during her intimate relationship with Rogers, when she had accompanied him on numerous official trips around the world when he was a congressman. While "Madonna" was perhaps an overstatement, it provided an exciting image that helped the President's imaginative palace guard while away boring nocturnal shifts.

"Obviously, you've just received some good news, Ben," Chet said playfully as he put his arms lightly around the shoulders of Ben and Laura, observing Ben's unwitting shit-eating grin. "Laura, Ben is best friends only with tennis pros, Porsche mechanics and New York bartenders. He'll only break your heart and walk into the sunset," added Chet with a chuckle.

"Hey, that's not true," Ben protested, taking Chet's arm firmly in his grip, for once wanting very much not to have earned such a checkered reputation.

"That's okay, Ben." Laura flashed him a brilliant smile. "Chet is always trying to keep me away from men. He thinks they're all up to no good."

They are, Ben thought ruefully, but only returned the smile.

Laura took a sip of her wine and shrugged elegantly. "His wife Connie and I have taken some graduate courses together in anthropology at George Washington, so he thinks I'm his little sister or something. Many of my male friends know he's capable of physical harm, so I've led a very sheltered life here," Laura said, smiling again and letting loose a warm easy laugh.

Ben watched in awe as her throat contracted smoothly. What's going on here? Not even CJ was able to get to him like Laura had in only a few minutes. I'd better have another scotch, it's getting warm in here. Maybe something to eat would be smart, too.

"Aren't you two hungry?" Laura read his mind as she placed her empty glass on a passing tray, lightly took his arm and Chet's, and guided them in the direction of the sumptuous array of delicacies prepared by the White House kitchen staff. Ben let himself be guided, as Chet threw him a conspiratorial wink. "C'mon, I haven't enjoyed the company of two such handsome men in a long while," Laura said. "And with two Navy men, I'll be doubly safe."

As they moved across the room, the looks on the faces of many of the men present indicated they would have given their lucrative careers for the opportunity to escort Laura to dinner and participate in whatever events might follow.

"Jesus, who is that babe with Greenwood?" asked a

dark-suited young man speaking to an associate who was similarly attired. Both sported unique lapel pins and earphones with cords running under their shirt collars. The latter adjusted his miniature earphone, over which he monitored a constant stream of situation reports from various Secret Service agents stationed throughout the building.

"Kevin, you must be the only guy on the team not to know 'Madonna.' She is Sky Chief's research assistant and, until he became President, his favorite aide on unofficial retreats. Used to be called 'Snow White' but that changed rather quickly. She's also a close friend of Greenwood's wife, so watch your ass and not hers."

Kevin grimaced at the thought of being bounced back to Des Moines for having pissed off the Washington station head. He knew that private relationships could seriously affect duty assignments in the Secret Service, so he turned his attention to the wealth of other female attendees at the reception. Every attractive young senate and White House groupie was wedged into the ballroom hoping to catch a glimpse of guest of honor Boris Yeltsin, the boisterous and volatile newly-elected President of Russia. Most of them were there to partake of the free booze and great food and, he mused, most likely would enjoy a slow ride home afterward with their latest acquaintance. This new duty station will work out just fine, if I can keep my nose clean and my weapon well-oiled, he thought, patting his hip pocket with a confidence-building touch.

At that moment, a contingent of American and Russian security agents firmly cleared a path through the crowded room. Behind them, effusively shaking hands and bellowing hellos to those gathered nearby, a large and vibrant Boris Yeltsin strode toward the waiting American president.

From his vantage point, Ben was impressed with the obvious confidence exhibited by both Rogers and Yeltsin. With the cold war waning in the public consciousness, relations between the two countries had moved from the White House and the Kremlin to the boardrooms of worldwide corporations, whose highly paid executives were endeavoring to grab their share of the potentially enormous economic bonanzas that resided—in the form of coal, oil, gold and other abundant mineral deposits—deep in the barren vastness of Russia. Rogers and Yeltsin were both being forced to learn how to play more directly to the business leaders of their countries, rather than only to their respective political parties. This pleased American conservatives immensely, but greatly irritated the numerous Russians who refused to let go of old Lenin ways. Since the Nixon years, U.S. conservatives had been out of favor, in spite of Reagan's efforts to mollify them. Now they were back in the driver's seat, and being pragmatic men they realized they must decisively grasp the opportunity. Therefore, it wasn't long before they had managed to generate increased presidential support for various trade agreements and federal grants that had been targeted to support their efforts to dominate the fragile emerging economy in Russia. These modern day carpetbaggers, with help from Russia's mafia, the KGB, aimed to wreak the same kind of economic havoc on Russia in the coming months and years that their U.S. Civil War-era brethren had brought to the southern states a hundred years earlier.

But for the moment, American industry was enjoying the shakeup their Cold War machine had achieved. Yeltsin's current task was that of attempting, through his unique and colorful brand of statesmanship, to prevent Russia from being completely humbled and treated by the U.S. like a bankrupt S&L. Little did he know that a small group of deeply embedded fellow countrymen were at this moment endeavoring to accelerate his noble effort. Yeltsin had seen and caused his share of bloodshed in his home country. However, he would not have condoned the brutal methods that this cadre had planned as the means to achieve a revised world order, one that once again would favor their vast homeland and their own personal interests.

"Well, Ben, what do you think of all this?" Laura asked quietly, aware of the intensity with which Ben had been studying the two world leaders. She could almost sense the physical and mental energy he exerted while taking stock of the two men.

"They remind me of two Sumo wrestlers," Ben answered, "enjoying the attention of the crowd, but completely absorbed with appraising one another, now that they're face-to-face. There is nothing like a first-hand meeting to get a true sense of your adversary, and that's just what's going on here."

Laura felt a prickling of the hairs on her neck realizing how accurate Ben was in his astute observation. No wonder he's so successful in his work, she thought. He's certainly got a different way about him than most DC men…more alert and somehow more insightful, in a low-key fashion. Hmm, this is going to be an interesting couple of months. I may just learn something from this man, perhaps many things, as she grinned to herself. He's older, but since he's not as old as Brad, he's younger. Older and younger, she mused, bringing a full smile to her luscious mouth, causing Ben to glance at her curiously. Let him wonder a little, it will be good for him. And maybe, who knows, good for me, too. I need some "good for me" soon.

CHAPTER TWELVE

The Chief Justice Looms

June 23, 1992, 9:10 PM

After their brief dinner, Chet excused himself to tour the room and Ben spent almost half an hour alone with Laura in a corner of the ballroom. At her insistence, he told her a little about his career and his interest in classic 356 Porsches.

"In the advertising business every day feels like another flight over Vietnam, full of exciting challenges and threats. The objective is to beat the competition with better weapons, in this case, words and pictures that convey convincing stories about our products. As for the Porsche, it just seems to be the right jet for me now, built by experts who want nothing more than creating the best road machine on the planet. Year after year they continue to improve, based on that fundamental principle. I like that simplicity of purpose. I try to apply it to my work."

Laura had dated enough Porsche owners to have a

structured defense in place when "the damn car stalled again," usually on a darkened roadside or in a half-empty parking lot. Her self-defense consisted of a White House-issued portable radiophone and the numbers of local 24-hour repair shops. It never failed to amuse her how quickly the driver was able to get the car moving again.

As the two talked, Laura suddenly grew pale and grasped Ben's arm. He was surprised but pleased at her gesture, but then sensed a large presence behind him, soon accompanied by the rumble of a gravelly voice and a wave of bad breath.

"So, you're our Great White Hope, Ben Coleman," the man exclaimed boldly, extending his large hand to shake Ben's. "We should have this election in the bag, but we can't assume anything," boomed Chief Justice Blackstone. "What kind of ideas do you have for us, and when do you think we can see something? Soon, I hope. The convention is just around the corner."

Ben, too, felt himself recoil from the tall, domineering chief jurist of the United States. His flippant attitude toward what Ben knew would be the lengthy and arduous process of developing an advertising campaign to re-elect the President sounded exactly like many of his obnoxious, uninformed clients.

"Your Honor," Ben replied, hoping he had used the appropriate title, "As I explained to Mr. Gaines, my work requires a period of getting to know the President. If it could be done overnight, my position would be staffed by a newspaper reporter who thrives on meeting tight deadlines. As it is, a successful ad campaign will depend on our ability to determine the most important needs of the voters. That's where Ms. Sinclair's work will play a key role," he smiled reassuringly at Laura. "Then we must find a unique and provocative way to express how our 'product,' the President, will satisfy those needs. Generally, the final ads seem simple and obvious, but getting there is anything but fast and easy."

"Mr. Coleman, I appreciate the time needed for preparation. As an attorney, I require the requisite time to prepare for my court," said Blackstone, in a slightly cooler tone of voice. But as he continued, his dark eyes projected a quiet threat. "However, our goal is a landslide victory for President Rogers, and we cannot and will not settle for less. This gala is the calm before the storm of activity that will begin next week in preparation for a most dynamic convention in Dallas in mid-August. Every piece of the campaign must be perfect, and must ensure the result that I, er, we demand. Not just victory, but total victory, do you understand?" Blackstone didn't wait for Ben's response, but plowed ahead. "I certainly hope so, because your name was not the only one given to Mr. Gaines as a top ad guy. We could have had Hal Riney or Jay Chiat, who do the Saturn and Apple ads that are so effective. This sort of opportunity knocks only once for most of us, Mr. Coleman," he concluded with a "catch my drift" lift of his bushy gray eyebrows.

"Your Honor, I intend to give the President the best campaign possible. You can count on that," Ben said, his back stiffening with the familiar anger he felt in the presence of an overbearing client.

"Good. Keep me posted. I want to see everything," ordered Blackstone, before nodding a slight goodbye to Laura. Ben watched him walk to the bar, like a pig

to the trough, he thought. He wasn't surprised to notice the bartender pouring vodka into a crystal de-
canter without being asked. Now, he'll stuff his fat self
with free food, Ben predicted and laughed when he
saw Blackstone do exactly that.

"Well, now I've witnessed the separation of the ju-
dicial and executive branches at their all-time worst,"
Ben said to Laura. "This place is a zoo. All I see is
power being sought, given and paid for around here,
and it stinks! At least in New York, the most damage a
jerk can do is to shortchange his clients, not an entire
country."

Laura nodded sympathetically then looked up and
winked at Chet, who had returned after touring the
room again. "Your friend here is not as sophisticated
as I would have imagined, Chet. He has the expecta-
tion of a child at a magic show. What does he think
Washington is…the Land of Oz?"

"For all his charm and swashbuckling ways, this
guy," Chet said placing his hand on Ben's shoulder "is
really the last Boy Scout, Laura." Chet recalled how
proud and idealistic Ben had been in his Navy days,
when he was so thoroughly convinced his jet squadron was doing the right thing by blasting holes in the
tropical forests and rice paddies of Vietnam. "He's
really just a good guy who is clever at out-thinking,
out-talking and out-maneuvering the enemy, no matter who that turns out to be. When I last saw him, the
enemy flew MIGS. Now they fly desks at Nabisco and
RJR, and evidently, also at the Supreme Court."

Ben had to laugh at his friend's vigorous defense
before coaxing them back to the bar. He was already
starting to feel better. An old friend and a new woman

was a heady combination.

"That's not the first time Chet has come to my aid, Laura," Ben said. "He used to do that fairly regularly when he was my wingman during the war. It appears his current assignment is another opportunity to keep me out of the flak." He looked toward Chet with a surprising catch of gratitude in his throat and said, "I just hope you have someone riding wing for you, my friend."

"No sweat," Chet reassured him. "I've got nine lives, although I've lost track of how many I've used up."

Later, after the President and Yeltsin had departed and the reception had wound down, Laura urged Ben to stop by her office in the morning before their afternoon flight to Vermont. "You can't miss it, I'm in the only office without a door...sometimes I feel it's a plot or something."

Ben couldn't suppress his disappointment at her departure. Laura seemed to sense his feelings. With a lingering handshake and a quick hug for Chet, she was gone.

"She is something else, Chet," murmured Ben. His friend simply pointed to the exit doors and said, "Probably a good time for us to leave before anyone else breaks your steely-eyed composure, buddy. And frankly, Ben, she's a little young for you, don't you think? Or are they all still fair game, my man?"

Ignoring Chet's remark, Ben glanced once more in the direction Laura had taken. Moments later, he and Chet were in the Oldsmobile heading back to the hotel through a warm, late-evening drizzle. As they slowed to a stop at the Mayflower, Ben saw the beautiful

young stewardess he had met on the plane being ushered into a departing cab by the doorman. To his
amazement, he didn't hail her. Instead, he thanked
Chet.

"Keep it in your pants," said Chet as Ben shook his
hand.

"Turns out I am."

"Talk about déjà vu, I seem to have told you that
same thing many times a long time ago!" Chet
laughed.

"At this time of night, I won't have much choice. I
just let my main chance to get lucky tonight slide. I
have to tell you, Laura certainly has clouded my
mind."

"I don't blame you. She has a big fan club, and not
only because she's gorgeous. Class with brains is
something that's gone out of style in this city with a
few rare exceptions, and she's one. But, again, be sure
she doesn't see you as a father figure rather than a
dashing New York dude, or dud," Chet chuckled
again, enjoying Ben's discomfort.

Ben stepped out of the Olds and tipped the doorman, who held his passenger door open and offered
an umbrella to shield him from the drizzle. Once inside, Ben was surprised at the large number of people
still milling around the lobby. He briefly surveyed the
bar crowd before opting for a rare full night's sleep. As
he proceeded to the elevator bank, he failed to notice
two heavy-set men who rose from richly upholstered
lobby chairs behind him and made their way to the
street through the revolving front door.

The man in the light trench coat spoke quietly to
his partner, "So that's the guy and we're the team, ac-

cording to Central. We split eight-hour shifts and can eat all we want. Got it?"

"As these folks say, 'no sweat,'" answered the other man, opening his umbrella and accompanying his comrade down the street to a waiting car.

Only minutes earlier, Ben had been in the company of the world's foremost security detail. Now, as he took off his jacket and tie preparing to mix a nightcap at the full bar in his room, he was alone, more alone than he had felt in years. And in a strange city at that, where the decisions made were ones of life and death as opposed to just an increasing share of the market.

The drink tasted good, but Ben realized something was missing. And it wasn't the drink that was lacking; it was him and what he had become. Downing the drink, he made his way into the bathroom for a hot-and-cold shower before bed.

CHAPTER THIRTEEN

Breakfast with Sunny and Laura

June 22, 1992, 10:12 AM

As Ben stepped out of the shower early the next morning, the phone rang. Tucking a thick towel around his waist, he answered it to hear the familiar voice of Helen Mayfield, his secretary, calling from New York.

"How's my favorite Park Avenue beauty?" Ben teased.

"Oh stop, Ben. You know it'll never work," Helen joked back, for the umpteenth time.

"You love me for my money—or is it my break-dancing?"

"DC is already getting to your head, isn't it?"

"I did get to shake the President's hand and met the First Lady. What's up? Is everything calm at the office?"

"Actually, no! That's why I called. Everyone here keeps asking me what you're doing, and *Ad Age* and

Adweek have been calling every day to learn more."

"You can tell the magazine editors that they'll get their story with the rest of the media."

"Of course." He could hear Helen scratching notes on her steno pad, and he waited for her to say more. There was always more. "Ben?"

"Yes." He smiled. Here was the "more." The advertising merry-go-round wasn't going to stop just because he left town.

"Dan Roth wanted me to tell you that the product group at General Household rolled over when they heard your comments; they've agreed to shelve the research and focus on the creative. He said you'd want to hear about that." He could sense Helen was grinning.

"Well, justice finally wins out," he said. "Most likely cooler heads at Gen. Household reconsidered the wisdom of making such ridiculous claims in the first place. It's always dangerous to make big changes to a product that people have come to know and like.

"Yes, Ben, we know." she joshed.

"Helen, I think I'm going to be here for awhile, and I want you to ask Roth to do me a large favor. Have one of his account guys, preferably someone who knows sports cars, drive my Porsche to DC this week. I've got my work cut out here and that car is the best way I know to keep my brain limber and happy, short of a fast handball game. In fact, have him bring my tennis rackets and shoes, too. Tell Roth the guy can use my room here at the Mayflower. I'll be in Vermont for several days. Also mention that Waylon Jennings and Dolly Parton-Dolly Parton are staying here and I'll try to arrange tickets for their show."

Ignoring what she knew to be a crude reference to the country singer's impressive claims to fame, Helen assured him she would talk to Dan and promised she would forward any important mail via FedEx every day. Making a mental note to buy some FedEx stock, Ben thanked her and hung up.

He stepped to the window, feeling the rising heat radiating through the glass. It was going to be another scorcher, for the eighth day in a row. Remembering that Chet was due to pick him up in an hour to go to the White House, he walked to the closet to select a few items for the trip to Vermont. Fortunately, he had brought slacks, shirts and a dark sport coat. He would have to buy some tennis whites and other articles later. He packed his Ralph Lauren slacks and polo shirts and Adidas tennis shoes, noting his penchant for brand names. It was an expense he justified with a belief they were worth the premium he paid. Ben knew Ralph Lauren personally and admired him, both for his designer savvy and for his fabulous classic auto collection. He appreciated that Lauren's entire line was made using richer, thicker fabrics. His designer name promised total customer satisfaction, and that was what marketing was all about. As long as that promise was delivered he would remain a fan and a customer.

The phone rang again.

"Hi Ben, it's Laura. Chet called and he's picking me up on the way in. Let's all have breakfast at your hotel in an hour, traffic willing, if that's okay with you."

"That would be terrific!" Ben exclaimed, pleased at the prospect of seeing Laura so soon.

"Wonderful. I truly enjoyed meeting you last night. You seem different from so many of the people I work with here. I have to admit, you kept me up after I got home just thinking about those differences. I think I will learn a great deal from working with you, at least I hope so."

"Well, I'm flattered, Laura, and sorry about the loss of sleep. I tossed and turned a bit myself," he admitted, aware that the room was getting warmer.

"So we're even. Good. See you soon."

Ben hung up the phone hoping Laura was less interested in learning about advertising than she was in experiencing something much more exciting. There was a light knock on the door, thirty feet across the beautifully-appointed room. Dropping the towel and donning a plush hotel robe, Ben looked through the peephole and asked who was there.

"It's Sunny. You stood me up for drinks, so now you owe me breakfast," she laughed through the door. When he opened it, Sunny pressed Ben back into the room. Stronger than her small, buxom frame would suggest, she pushed Ben onto the large bed, pulled his robe aside, and grasping him intimately with her soft, long fingers, kissed him with an open mouth. A familiar rush of energy suffused his body as he found himself quickly rising to her clever ministrations.

Thirty-five minutes later, Ben was relieved to learn he had arrived at the hotel coffee shop ahead of Chet and Laura. Ordering coffee to help him recover from the intense sexual bout with Sunny, who fortunately had to depart for a flight, he marveled at her ability to bring his body so rapidly to readiness. He hoped there were no obvious vestiges of his recent activities, guiltily feeling his face for signs of the pleasant struggle. He had managed to smooth Sunny's quick exit by promising dinner and a tour of the White House some-time soon, a promise he had no idea how he was going to fulfill. But, hey, he was the President's personal ad guy; that must mean some perks, right?

His thoughts were interrupted by Chet's booming "Hello!" and the sight of Laura sweeping across the dining room with an expectant smile on her lips. All thoughts of Sunny evaporated as he shook hands with Chet and offered a quick but firm hug for Laura. Ben held her chair as she glided into it.

"You really *are* different, Ben," Laura said, as Chet laughed at her.

"My momma made me do it," Ben countered, pleased that she was pleased.

"Watch out, Laura, he's only trying to impress you with his prep school manners. I swear, everything Ben does has a purpose and he's the only one who knows what it is."

"Thanks, Buddy," accused Ben. "Why does being polite have to be part of a strategic plot?"

"Because it does, my old friend. It has been years, but it's just like yesterday with you, Ben. Connie was so happy to learn you're here and wants you out at the house when we get back from Vermont, no excuses accepted. And bring Laura, too!" Chet smiled, know-ing that Ben wouldn't object to a home-cooked meal, especially with Laura present.

"Chet, I am going to be doubly busy the next few weeks with my New York clients plus my new Wash-ington client. Hell, I have never sold a person before, only household products like detergent, hairsprays, automobiles, television sets and airplane seats. Selling a President is new to me. I'll need lots of time to myself," Ben pleaded, half-heartedly.

"Sorry, the wife said no excuses. And Laura already agreed she could make it."

Laura's vivid smile and velvet laugh melted any further excuses Ben could think of, so he happily consented to Chet's invitation.

"Now, that's settled," Laura said, reaching for her menu. "I'm famished. I think I'll get their special 'Omelet de Lafayette' to ensure I have all the energy I'll need to keep up with you two." Ben beckoned for the waitress to take their order, but the process was interrupted by a large rumbling of chairs moving on the floor above, resembling the sound of a gathering thunderstorm.

"Sounds like rain and maybe some lightning coming," Chet joked. "I love thunderstorms as long as they're generated by nature and are not man-made. I never could tell whether bombs or monsoon storms made more noise in 'Nam, and I certainly don't want to go through that kind of experience again. Washington is just the nice quiet little capital of a nice quiet country, right?"

"Yeah, it must be really quiet over at the White House with the President and wild Boris swapping power trips," Ben quipped.

Chet and Laura smiled at Ben's innocent joke and enjoyed their breakfast.

As it would turn out, these would be their last quiet moments for many weeks to come. Over the course of the hot summer ahead, Ben was about to learn the consequences of a real battle for power. At the moment, as he glanced around the spacious dining room, his primary concern was whether he would play a decisive role in the campaign or just be a cog in the world of politics—just another mouthpiece.

CHAPTER FOURTEEN
Ben's New Shadow

June 24, 1992, 10:20 AM

"He went straight to the elevators last night, boss," said the heavy-set man into the pay phone. "Contacted no one. Didn't even go into the bar like we thought he would, but we had someone waiting in there. Good looking dolly, too. She would have spent the night with him, given his reputation, but she never got the chance." The man pulled his tie away from his rumpled collar, hating the Western-style clothing he had to wear for his work. Fifteen years of espionage, which included entrapping Americans with hookers who could bleed information out of them after providing sexual favors, was beginning to catch up with him. His trainers back in Moscow would have been proud of him, he thought, but to hell with them. There's a lot they don't know about the real world of intrigue in the Capitol of the West.

"What's next?" he asked. "Right now, he's having

breakfast with a guy and a good-looking woman who works on the President's staff. The guy is Secret Service, name's Greenwood, been around for years. The woman is Laura Sinclair, Roger's research hotshot. Our target looks like he slept well. There were two calls to his room this morning, nothing out of the ordinary. We didn't stake out his room…too risky."

Listening attentively, the man tugged again at the knot of his tie. "All right, we can certainly do that…we've had enough practice," he agreed and hung up.

Returning to a lobby wing chair sitting just outside the coffee shop, the man picked up a fresh copy of *The Washington Post* lying on the end table. With his target in sight, he turned to the sports section to see how his adopted baseball team, the New York Yankees, was faring. He had made more money betting on the Yankees than the sizable payments he received regularly at various drop points around the city. "Go Yanks," he thought, laughing at all the dumb expressions he had learned studying American lingo, primarily through sports.

He glanced again at the trio having breakfast, and wondered if this guy Greenwood would ever become a hot target at some point. He'd always wanted to take out a cocky Secret Service jerk and Greenwood is a nice big bulls-eye. Then the folks back home would have to transfer me back, he thought, and fast. Yes, home is a nice idea—almost as nice as that redhead in there. Maybe I'll take her with me. Sure don't have women like that back home; but she's a little too skinny, never make it through the winters. Shit, what happened to my Yanks last night?

He threw down the sports pages in disgust and read the front page, which was full of fast-breaking political news, as always. Democracy, he groused, what a joke. Two parties, hell; it's all run by the rich guys, just like home. Just like anywhere, he griped. Well, at least there's work for guys like me and it pays well, he consoled himself. I just need a chance to get back home and spend it. Be one of those wealthy oligarchs, get a yacht, live it up.

Moments later, Ben and the others walked briskly past the heavy-set man slumped in his chair. Laura's presence was so distracting to Ben that his normally heightened skills of observation failed to notice the unkempt man, so clearly out of his element in the ornate lobby.

After they passed, the man moved out of the chair and followed them out of the hotel, still pondering why he was shadowing Ben Coleman, what he was supposed to do with him, or when. Then he recalled he wasn't supposed to worry about all that. Just don't lose him, he told himself.

As Chet climbed into the Secret Service limo, he glanced back to see the hefty man who had followed them out walking briskly toward a waiting nondescript Buick. Who is he tailing? Chet wondered. I guess time will tell. Most likely my driver got his picture. He doesn't look familiar, but they never do; probably just another Russian spy, in spite of the supposed new reign of peace in the world.

CHAPTER FIFTEEN

Presidential Visit Preparations

June 24, 1992, 10:38AM

Twenty miles south of Burlington, Vermont, a thirty-man Secret Service advance team was fanning out over the acres of lawns, pools, tennis courts and golf courses that comprise the exclusive Basin Harbor Club. As the annual site of the President's brief Fourth of July holiday, several command posts already had been discreetly set up, the guest list combed for names of possible threats to the President, and key employees interviewed and advised that they would be accompanied in their duties by government agents. The employees took it in stride, glad that one of their favorite visitors was on his way.

Ralph Watkinson, the head of the security detail and an ex-Marine major, called Chet Greenwood to report that the site was 'clean and clear.' "Looks like a great place for a fireworks display," Watkinson said. "Bring the sparklers, boss!"

"Will do!" Chet said from the secure radiophone inside the Oldsmobile, promising to call later when they were inbound to the resort. Chet hung up the phone, grinning at Ben and Laura.

"You're having too much fun," Ben said, smiling back at Chet. "I thought being a Secret Service agent meant being serious 24/7."

"I was just thinking how I always caution my daughters against playing with sparklers on July 4th. 'You can hurt someone with those things, kids,' I tell them, just like every other dad."

"I knew it! Being a dad is serious business so you're in the Secret Service to have some fun."

Glancing out the bulletproof tinted window at the crowded sidewalks, Chet answered softly, "Well seriously, Ben, it's great to be able to work with the same kind of professionals you and I served with. It does make this job almost fun."

Back at the Basin Harbor Club, Watkinson called to his team to gather together by the brightly painted Adirondack chairs spread across the freshly trimmed lawn. "That was the boss, guys. He said not to play with any sparklers. Particularly you, Jackson," he joked, pointing to a large, black agent who was swatting mosquitoes from his sweat-drenched face.

Jackson was the team's primary firearms expert, capable of firing semi-automatic machine guns with both hands at the same time. Generally he scored near-perfect clusters on the targets at Quantico, where agents underwent periodic training. Moving or stationary, he could be relied upon to put people, weapons or small trees permanently out of business.

Jackson donned his big, easy-going smile and continued fighting off the early-summer black flies and mosquitoes.

"These are worse than Potomac flies. I'm surprised this high-priced place doesn't pay these critters to fly across the lake to New York."

Watkinson turned to his second in command, Larry Grant. "Is Davison back from sweeping the harbor yet? There are a lot more yachts out there than I've seen in years. We've got to check 'em all, and be sure the photo series is in place by dinner time so we can check that none of them move around without us knowing it."

Grant nodded affirmatively and looked across the lawn to the harbor where a small Boston Whaler containing three agents was circling the wide variety of anchored yachts. He spoke into his radio and one of the men waved in response.

Watkinson watched, but privately was wondering where all these people get their money. Those stinkpots are all sixty grand or better, he observed, and not a scratch on any of them. Must be an annual competition among these dudes for whose got the biggest boat, best golf clubs, blondest wife, foxiest daughters, smartest sons and best club tie. It sounds to me like too much work to be cool, he thought, but then, I wasn't born on the Main Line of Philly like those guys. Of course, when Sky Chief lands, all bets will be off. Sky Chief holds all the chips these days.

The Secret Service detail continued their preparations to provide a safe environment for their one and only client, President Rogers. Just about the only precaution they did not, and could not, take was sealing off the harbor to new arrivals. This had been a direct order of the Commander in Chief himself, who had grown up with many of the guests and did not want to irritate them or more likely, lose their votes.

That particular oversight was critical to the plans of six men who were headed north just fifteen miles away, where their yacht was cruising beneath the out-croppings of Fort Ticonderoga, the stone fort that had played a key role in defending this rural part of the infant country over two hundred years earlier.

President Rogers, an avid history buff, always vis-ited the fort on this holiday. When he was young, he and his sisters would find old Indian arrowheads along the shore of Lake Champlain. As an adult, he would observe with awe the fort's strategic location, situated high on a promontory above the lake, where its unmatched complement of cannon controlled all travel on the lake below. Later the President would comment that had the fort been as active on this day as it had been in its heyday, things might have gone dif-ferently for him and his presidency.

The Secret Service agents and hotel staff continued their urgent preparations. As the region began to bake with humid heat, the guests began clustering in the water at the beach or taking cover under the large, striped awnings near the bar.

Watkinson scanned the area once again, appreciat-ing the fact that the heat was keeping people relatively immobile and docile. Makes our job much easier, he thought, less to worry about.

CHAPTER SIXTEEN

On Air Force One

June 24, 1992, 1:15 PM

The highly polished custom-designed 747-200B aircraft rose swiftly from the high-security runway at Dulles International and turned on a northerly course, while being tracked closely by a triple team of veteran FAA air traffic controllers. Inside Air Force One, the President and his wife were briefly visiting with each of the ten guests and members of a small press contingent before retiring to their private quarters in the middle of the plane. As Rogers approached Ben and Laura he seemed, from Ben's point of view, particularly glad to see his research assistant enjoying herself.

"Well, I'm happy to see you two have met. Laura, I expect Ben will need a lot of your time and research support. Be sure your group provides him with everything he needs. And Ben, perhaps we can play some tennis. Chet tells me you are something of a terror on the court, and it will give us some time to talk about my administration and things that are important to me." Noting the high color of Laura's face, the President beamed, assuming he was the cause.

"I'd be glad to, Mr. President," Ben said. "Thanks for the opportunity to use the club's clay courts to practice. I could easily get used to the benefits of this 'account.' Your corporate jet certainly beats the hell out of the ones RJR and General Household send for us."

The President chuckled. "We're a bigger corporation."

Turning to continue down the aisle, he patted Laura's shoulder. Laura realized she was still blushing, maybe for two reasons rather than one, she thought. If Ben noticed, he didn't show it.

"Well, the President said you'd take care of my every need," Ben said smiling. "Should I start a list or are you going to continue to read my mind?"

"I'd love to see your list, as long as it is strictly professionally inspired!" she responded with a grin so brilliant it competed with the sunny horizon beyond the aircraft's oval windows.

"Absolutely, Laura," Ben said, realizing how good her name felt on his lips. "Remember, Chet told you I'm a trustworthy Boy Scout, right?"

As the plane leveled off at 31,000 feet, Ben was pleased to note that his wine glass barely rippled with the easy motion of the plane. "Must be Navy-trained folks up front," he murmured to Laura, although he knew that flying the President's private jet was a plum assignment limited primarily to Air Force pilots. Well my assignment beats theirs all to hell, he thought. Eat your hearts out, you guys up front.

Ben raised his glass to Laura's saying, "Cheers" softly as they clinked their crystal goblets together. "I wonder when the vacation stops and the work begins."

Looking at him directly, Laura replied, "I have a sneaky suspicion you have been hard at work since you got to Washington. You just make it look easy."

Little did they know that far below and further north, on a yacht crossing a sun-speckled lake in the Adirondacks, six men were preparing to instigate an incident so violent it would put Ben and a great many others suddenly hard at work.

CHAPTER SEVENTEEN

Fireworks

June 24, 1992, 2:45 PM

From his vantage point in the Whaler skiff, Secret Service agent Davison was the first to notice the large yacht approaching the mouth of Basin Harbor. Gesturing to his pilot to intercept, Davison noted the large beam of the boat and wondered how someone could afford the gasoline required to keep a yacht that large underway hour after hour.

"Pull up close and we'll hail them," he ordered. "If they're not on the dock manifest, they'll have to move on."

Mr. Dade strode up the port deck watching the small officially marked Whaler move closer. He was dressed in an immaculate white yachting outfit that he had worn only twice: once in the fitting room in a Wilmington, Delaware, hotel room where he and his men had been thoroughly briefed on their mission, and again last night in order to put some creases in the trousers and scuff the white shoes a bit.

Dade waved to the small boat, hoping his relaxed pose and ridiculous outfit would reduce any chance of suspicion. "Ahoy, what can we do for you?" he called out as the small boat drew close to the Hatteras.

"Who are you?" responded the agent standing in front of the wheelhouse.

"I am Derek Dade with two friends and my crew. We're meeting our wives and spending the next few days playing golf and enjoying ourselves."

"They're on the guest list, boat and all," one of the agents said to Davison, who then instructed Dade to follow them into the main dock. "Have your entire crew, with the exception of your pilot, stand out on deck. We're agents of the Secret Service and must search all vessels in the area. Keep your speed under five knots and follow us."

Dade waved his understanding, called an order to Tony, and both boats began moving slowly toward the dock.

"Well, 'here goes,' as Americans say," Dade told his cohorts. "Each of you knows your job. Just remember, if you're caught, use your wallet grenade...hold it in front of your face with both hands. That'll make any identification efforts useless. Don't forget, what they'll do if they catch us alive is much worse than a grenade. But I've got a strong feeling we'll make it through this one, just like all the others, right?" Dade smiled at his comrades.

They all nodded confidently.

"Mr. Dade, are you sure they won't find the graphic-gun?" asked one of his men.

"No problem, Alexis," Dade said using his real

name for the first and only time to reassure the youngest of his team. "The gun mount looks just like a standard smokestack. They probably won't even look at it closely. And if they do, the graphic-gun looks like its part of the workings of the radar power system. No problem."

Two of the crew hustled to man the bow and stern lines as the yacht began its docking maneuver. At the helm, Tony adjusted the twin throttles and the boat lightly touched the dock bumpers. Several college-aged boys in bright green polo shirts grabbed hold of the lines and secured them to the dock's shiny brass cleats. Grigori and Hasbad, dressed as rich visitors, accompanied Dade down the ladder to meet the Secret Service agents and begin the final phase of their long-planned mission. Dade put on his best smile to greet the wide-shouldered agent walking up to him.

"Hello, my name is Special Agent Watkinson. I'm in charge of security for President Roger's arrival later today, and we are verifying the identity and length of stay of each guest. May I have some identification please?

"My associate in the Whaler led me to believe that you might not be aware the President is going to be here today. Most of the regular guests know he comes here each year before the July 4th weekend," Watkinson drawled, while carefully watching the reactions of the three men. They don't look like yachtsmen, he thought to himself as he scrutinized their driver's licenses, but the thug in the wheelhouse handles this thing like a toy. Watkinson knew many foreigners had discovered the favorite retreats of America's elite in the last few years, with the help of Robin Leach's *Life-*

styles of the Rich and Famous TV show. Handing their licenses back, he continued to be concerned about the men despite their valid-looking documentation.

"This is our first visit. Our wives are driving up from Albany Airport because they didn't want to interrupt our fishing trip," Dade admitted, glancing with mirth at his two friends, who joined in his laughter.

"They don't like how we fish, if you understand my meaning, Mr. Watkinson," Dade disclosed with a wink.

Chuckling at the small man's infectious humor, Watkinson waved off his men and suggested that the visitors find a buoy to anchor to overnight before they were all taken.

"We have permission to remain at the dock, Mr. Watkinson," Dade responded. "This yacht is too big and clumsy to anchor in small harbors."

"Okay, have a good visit. We'll be back in a few minutes to do a full security search of your boat, so ask your pilot or someone to hang around," Watkinson announced.

"No problem," Dade replied. "Tony, the big fellow in the wheelhouse, will stay."

Watkinson made a mental note of the size of the man named Tony, and was surprised at his agility climbing up the ladder to the roof of the pilothouse as he made his way around the large radar mast.

Thirty-five minutes later, the four Secret Service agents completed their search of the yacht. "My only question, gents," Davison said to his men, "is what special additions or customized installations did you see? It seemed to be a fairly 'off-the shelf' yacht. Usually these things have been more gussied up by their

Daddy Warbucks owners."

"Nothing special like you said, sir, but it seems these guys are overdressed for the trip."

"Well, I suppose they're aware the club is pretty picky about their guests, so they came prepared," Davison suggested. "You checked those storage units forward?"

"Yes, but I can check further."

"Maybe later," Davison responded. "I just talked with Greenwood. Sky Chief has landed at Plattsburgh and his ETA here is twenty minutes, so let's go."

After the agents left, Dade turned to Grigori and Hasbad and nodded toward the parking lot.

"There's the green Jeep Cherokee, up by the entrance to the lot. We each have a key, but remember to drive moderately so no one notices us. I don't know how the agents will react when the balloon goes up, but that's the purpose of this little trip: to burst their cocky little balloon and watch how they respond."

Dade and his associates walked back into the yacht's lower salon, where Tony and a deckhand were making adjustments to an innocent-looking control panel near the map table.

"How's it calibrating, guys?" he asked.

"Just fine, boss. The computer is loaded with individual multi-angle photos of the entire Secret Service detail. We're selecting six of them to be our big winners."

"Good. The three of us are leaving now," said Dade. "ETA for the big fish is less than thirty minutes, according to those jokers who just questioned us. We've got our video cameras. You guys do your thing, then leave the boat. We'll see you at the Jeep after the fireworks. I can't wait to show our client the videos. He'll shit a brick."

The others laughed, shook hands firmly, and went on with their individual responsibilities. Dade and his two associates walked down the dock with their overnight bags and video cameras strapped over their shoulders. Dade even had the audacity to wave at several Secret Service agents, who ironically, returned the seemingly innocent gesture.

CHAPTER EIGHTEEN

Basin Harbor Arrival

June 24, 1992, 3:20 PM

"What spectacular country!" exclaimed Brad Rogers from the copilot's seat of the VH-60N helicopter soon after it lifted off from Plattsburgh Air Force Base. Located on the western shore of Lake Champlain, the base had been named after the first French military agent to venture south along these murky waters from Montreal many years earlier.

The enthusiastic outburst of the 41st President of the United States continued. "That's what I like most about being President...getting to see everything from an eagle eye's perspective."

From her seat behind him, his wife remarked, "You're just like a kid, Brad. You just have bigger toys."

Ben, Laura, Chet and another staff member were sitting behind them, squeezed in the aft sling chairs into which two Marine staff sergeants had carefully strapped them minutes before. Looking out the window, Ben also found the view impressive. The mountains were lush and thick with green pine trees and rock outcroppings. Ben remembered climbing many of the peaks as a boy, including Mount Marcy, visible in the western distance.

The base disappeared behind them as the jet helicopter climbed east across the lake heading toward Vermont, just five miles away. Ben marveled at the ribbon of deep blue water stretching two hundred feet below them as they flew above sailboats, waterskiers and windsurfers.

"This is my favorite trip of the year," Rogers shouted to Ben over the noise of the chopper's rotors. "It is the only place where I can dress up for dinner and enjoy myself. I've been coming here since I was a kid and I know every blade of grass on the golf course and every crack in the clay tennis courts. During college, I caddied here. That's when I met the love of my life," he said glancing at his wife affectionately. "It's the only place where I feel I'm not the President, just Brad to my old friends from Princeton and Penn. Jeez, I'm really looking forward to this!" Both Rogers and his wife then put on headphones to listen to the chatter between the pilot and the controller.

"That's one of his major strengths with voters," Laura said to Ben, speaking closely into his ear. "He has a very attractive boyish quality to his public self." Due to the cramped seating arrangements, Laura's hand was resting innocently on Ben's leg. As she continued, he was keenly aware of the warmth of her hand and how right it felt there. "People feel he can be trusted," she said. "They feel he's really interested in what they want and need in their lives. God knows he can be a convincing politician, but no one can match him for voter sensitivity."

Ben shifted his weight slightly, which brought his leg firmly against hers. Laura didn't budge. "I've been to Vermont with him before," she divulged, "and it's a great opportunity to really see Rogers in the raw, so to speak," she almost blushed and quickly glanced toward the President's wife to see if she had overheard her indiscretion. But Elaine and her husband had put on their headsets.

Ben smiled at Laura's discomfort, not realizing the full implication of her remark. He squeezed her hand lightly. "My uncle's family used to vacation here, too, so I know it's a perfect getaway spot for busy people. I haven't played on the tennis courts in years; should be fun. But you and I also have to get to work soon. Maybe meet at the children's beach around five when the kids will all be at the horse stables? At least, that's how it used to be up here."

Minutes later, the glistening helicopter began its gentle descent toward an oasis of green fairways and a large, blue harbor teeming with boats of various types and shapes.

"I'll have to make amends to the owners of those yachts all weekend," the President shouted above the engine's whine. "Sorry, Chet, but the guests don't enjoy the search procedures the Secret Service agents must conduct. I guess I'll just have to lose a game to some of them on the first day of golf. That way they can brag to their cronies back home about bagging the President, and the memory of the imposition will blur into oblivion. Right, dear?" he said to Mrs. Rogers.

With her headset askew, Elaine had heard most of his comments and she kissed his cheek, telling him she had never known him to accept defeat in any kind of competition, and certainly not a golf game.

"Well, I'll make them think they have me on the run," he replied smiling. "That should make up for the inconvenience."

The harbor loomed up quickly as the chopper settled down toward the grassy landing area, identified with a large white circle and an orange windsock, which hung limply in the summer heat. Ben assumed the President and his wife would land first, but he noticed a second and third chopper descending past them. "I didn't see them take off, but I guess they were with us all the way across," he said to Chet, who sat opposite him.

"We always have at least two other birds carrying other passengers and some press people," Chet explained, peering down. "They fly with us as a distraction, to help confuse any potential threats. They will land first and set up a secure perimeter for the President's aircraft. We'll land as soon as they are in place."

"I've been with some pretty impressive people who liked to make grand entrances, but this one takes the Dutch chocolate cake," Ben quipped.

Laura laughed and squeezed his leg. "If you want to get used to this kind of thing, you'd better start writing some dynamite ad copy. Otherwise, it'll be back to New York and the subways for you and back to Ann Arbor for me." He was about to protest that he actually liked subways, but the helicopter suddenly set down softly on the thick lawn. The twin engines whined down to prevent onlookers and exiting occupants from being blown by the force of the prop wash.

Ben watched as dozens of hotel guests pointed and talked excitedly about the arrival of the choppers. He assumed many of them had witnessed Roger's arrivals on previous occasions, while others were relishing the novel experience.

Perhaps the only onlookers who were not impressed were the six men, standing separately at predetermined locations. Not only did they observe the aircraft's arrival but, like many guests, they were videotaping the action compliments of Sony and Canon. However, unlike the vacation videos the guests were taking to show to friends later that summer, the men's videotapes would soon be shown to faceless men with little interest in summer vacations.

Within seconds after the President's chopper set down, dark-suited men encircled the landing zone, intent on scanning for possible trouble. As the rotors glided to a stop, the main hatch opened. Getting a thumbs up from Watkinson on the ground, Greenwood stepped nimbly down the stairs. Rogers followed to a large applause from the crowd. He smiled and waved, then held out his hand to the First Lady. "Thank you, dear," Elaine said, exiting cautiously as Rogers and Greenwood assisted her to the red rug at the foot of the stairway.

Through his dark sunglasses, Chet intently surveyed the area while Ben departed the aircraft. Reaching for Laura's hand, Ben marveled at her grace getting out of a helicopter.

Suddenly, the unmistakable sounds of automatic gunfire rang out. Ben pressed Laura firmly back into the chopper cabin. At the same instant, Chet grabbed the President and carried him bodily back up the stairs and into the rear area of the chopper. Another agent hustled Mrs. Rogers back inside, where he and Greenwood instantly laid spread-eagle on top of the First Couple. Ben instinctively covered Laura with his body, hugging her tightly while holding onto one of the seat frames to avoid being bounced around inside the chopper.

"Rapid ascent!" Greenwood barked into his lapel mike, causing the pilot to immediately rev the engines for takeoff. Within seconds, the chopper was airborne, skittering low over the waves to avoid exposing it to any incoming rounds. Looking down through the open door that the enlisted airman was closing, Ben saw people racing towards the harbor, some falling, some dodging, and others firing. Neither of the other two choppers lifted off.

"Code Red-One. This is Greenwood. Sky Chief and Lady are clear and unharmed. Arriving at base ten minutes. Request immediate air cap, all air response, all Federal services ASAP!" Chet rasped into his hand-held unit, while simultaneously checking the President and First Lady to confirm they hadn't been hit. "What is our condition?" he yelled to the pilot, who was busy gaining altitude over the lake, heading west to the Air Force base.

"No apparent hits, no impacts I can see; flight controls and all systems operational," the pilot shouted back. "We'll be landing in five minutes, so be sure everyone is strapped in."

"Mr. President, are you okay?" Greenwood asked, pulling his weight off him.

"Yes. It was so fast I don't think I even saw anything," the President said, hugging his wife. The First Lady looked bewildered, but was quickly regaining her composure.

"Darling, are you alright?" she asked, feeling his face and neck for any signs of damage. "How is everyone else?" she said looking around.

"Fine. Looks like we're all fine," Ben said.

Laura hugged him, with tears of terror still in her eyes. "Yes, I'm okay, but it all was so crazy."

The helicopter, now closely surrounded by four drab green Huey Cobra gunships, dipped over the western shore and began its hasty approach back to the VIP sector of the base, which was rapidly filling with Military Police and other personnel.

"Well, it looks like we made it. I'm not sure what happened, but I'll be learning some answers quickly," Greenwood said to Ben. "Kind of feels like old times, doesn't it, hotshot?"

Ben, still holding Laura tightly, nodded. "Guess we'll have to play that game of tennis another time, Mr. President."

"I guess we will at that, Ben. Thanks for taking such good care of Laura. We should put you on Chet's detail, you've got the right instincts for it!"

"We can't afford him, Sir, and anyway, he's got another job to do. And I imagine what happened back there won't make it any easier," Greenwood said. Cuffing his old friend on the arm he added. "I think you can get off Laura now, Ben."

While President Rogers laughed aloud, joined by the other much-relieved passengers, Ben found himself totally activated in a way he hadn't been in many years. As strange as it might seem, the heat of the danger had felt really good to him. Whatever had taken place back there was exactly the kind of thing that had caused him to fly his Navy jet straight into the mouths of artillery and missiles in Vietnam. He might be a successful New York City ad man, but all of a sudden he felt he was back in his F4 fighter seat—and it felt good. Perhaps he never should have left it.

As Agent Watkinson would report later, the large yacht tied to the Basin Harbor dock had suddenly erupted with automatic gunfire. The smokestack on the yacht had opened like a clamshell, revealing some sort of high-powered gun or cannon. Throughout the manicured lawns, guests and employees had run for cover, while six widely dispersed Secret Service agents lay lifeless on the ground. One of them, Agent Davison, had realized at the last minute that this type of yacht doesn't have a smokestack. Gesturing at the yacht, he yelled for everyone to hit the ground as the full menace of the boat's gun became clear to him. Too late for him, as he was one of the first to fall, his life draining into the rich carpet of bluegrass.

Dozens of other Secret Service and State Police agents aimed their automatic rifle fire at the yacht and two weapons specialists trained their rocket launchers on the hull and pulled the trigger. With a combined whoosh, two missiles struck the boat, lifting it several feet in the air with a massive explosion. The automatic fire from the stack abruptly ceased as the huge vessel, with large holes in its waterline, sank in several feet of water.

Screaming "Find those guys now!" into his field

radio, Watkinson sprinted from his station near the landing zone, headed to the dock. "There were six of them, all dressed like they just shopped at Barneys! They were walking around with video cameras, and couldn't have gotten far. Grab 'em NOW!" he commanded. As he ran, he looked over his shoulder to see the presidential chopper winging west rapidly while the other choppers burned on the ground. He heard Greenwood's transmission indicating the President was safe.

Thank God! Watkinson thought to himself. Shit! I can't believe this, he fumed. How did these guys get past us; who were those people on that yacht? When we did the database check, none of them had a record. Running at full tilt as he reached the dock, Watkinson wondered why all that gunfire hadn't hit the President and his bird.

Suddenly, he was knocked down along with dozens of other people as the yacht exploded into a huge fireball. "Damn! Explosive charges on board, too!" he exclaimed as he got back on his feet. The shit will hit the fan over this one, he thought ruefully. Look at the thing. It's white hot!

"They're frying the evidence," Watkinson called out to several of his men, who were picking themselves up while straightening their tattered clothing. "Nothing will survive that fire. Get some hoses on it, fast! We've got to salvage as much as possible!"

Walking purposefully across the parking lot, the six men from the yacht looked inconspicuous, having already shed layers of clothing to leave only their blue jeans and "Welcome to Vermont" and "I Love New York" t-shirts in place. With all the commotion, no one noticed them make their way to the parking lot and climb into the green Jeep Cherokee. Several carloads of guests were racing out of the Club's compound, so the men simply joined the convoy that carried them away from the terror and carnage they had so expertly crafted.

The six agents who were struck by the bullets fired from the yacht were all Secret Service medics. "All dead of direct facial wounds," cried one of the remaining medics over his chest mike. "Shot right in *both* eyes Sir!" he told Watkinson. "No other injuries. That is the most accurate gun I've ever seen; identical shots in each eye to each of our men. Davison tried to warn us and was shot. I've never seen anything like this, even in Iraq."

Watkinson answered, "No one was on the yacht at the time, so it must have been some sort of automatic gun, programmed somehow to fire at these men. The President and his chopper were not hit." That's what is really strange, Watkinson thought to himself. Why kill some agents and not kill Sky Chief? Why did they go to all the effort and expense of the yacht if they only wanted to kill some agents?"

"This must have been a dry run," Watkinson guessed. "No windows shattered, no innocent people hit, only these men. I want to see that gun," he stated emphatically, hurrying across the charred dock to oversee the inspection of the burning remnants of the yacht.

Speaking into his lapel mike, which was now patched into the Secret Service headquarters in Washington, D.C. and his boss, Colin Waters, head of the agency, Watkinson reported: "We've got a mess up here, Chief. Six agents dead, all of them shot in *both eyes*. No, I repeat, no collateral damage; just the six agents. Sky Chief has probably already landed at Plattsburgh and we're prosecuting the yacht, which appears to have been the source of the automatic, highly accurate gunfire. No sign of the perps. We can't launch the other two choppers as their engines were shot out and are still on fire. The yacht was taken out by our men's missiles and suffered secondary explosions, which seem to have been purposely rigged. We are endeavoring to board it as soon as the hull cools down from the explosions.

"A lot of the guests are leaving in cars," he continued, "so we are going to have trouble identifying the escape vehicle the perps used. Roadblocks are going up, but there are dozens of small country roads anyone could take." Watkinson listened for a minute, hearing on the same frequency that the fire on the yacht had been extinguished.

"Yes, Sir. I will keep you posted with developments," Watkinson said obediently.

"Agent Watkinson," Waters added, "you had best provide me with a much more complete report within one hour, or consider yourself suspended from duty. Get the post-op going and report here by 1800 tomorrow."

Watkinson's normally light complexion blossomed like a hydrogen bomb. "Yes, Sir," he said again, before continuing his brisk jog toward the charred yacht. "Wrong place, wrong time," was all he could think as he tried to decide how he would break the news of his obvious early retirement to his wife, Lynn.

When I was a Marine major commanding a company in Vietnam, he thought ruefully, I only had to worry about myself and trained soldiers. Now there are Lynn and the kids, innocent bystanders to this horror, along with all the people here at the Club. As he arrived at the smoldering hull of the yacht to take charge of the investigation, he snapped out of his lament and pressed on, duty first, as always. He would worry about the fallout later, he decided. At least, the President and other people are safely out of harm's way.

CHAPTER NINETEEN

The Great Escape

June 24, 1992, 4:45 PM

The green Jeep careened along the narrow farm road, veering south, away from Basin Harbor. Tony kept the Cherokee tightly positioned behind a silver Mercedes sedan and several BMWs speeding away from the harrowing events at the Basin Harbor Club. As he muscled the car around an abrupt turn in the narrow road, Tony joked, "I bet none of those pansies checked out of the hotel properly. They probably shit their Brooks Brothers slacks!"

"The country store is right up there," Dade said coolly from the front right seat, "so get ready to pull over, Tony. They're going to meet us in cop cars for the rest of the trip. What a great idea," he laughed. Turning toward the seat behind him, he said, "Give me the videotapes. I'll put them in this bag. The safe delivery of these tapes is worth another fifty large ones to each us so let's not lose them."

Prior to the arrival of the President's helicopter, the six Russians had wandered around the grounds of the Club. Each had a pre-assigned position where they acted like tourists videotaping the event to show to friends and families back home. But unlike other guests, these men continued taping after the gunfire broke out. Dade had filmed the activity on the yacht while another camera focused on the landing zone and others recorded how the Secret Service agents responded to the gunfire. Walking away from the boat, Dade had pressed the second button on a remote control in his jacket pocket. Instantly, the periscope-like mechanism swiftly rose out of the engine room stack on top of the yacht, and he videotaped the action as the three-foot-long telescoping gun barrel started swiveling and spraying bullets. Other videos captured the killing of the two Secret Service agents on the landing zone and of the four agents standing guard in other areas of the Club. The explosion of the two helicopter engines and the Secret Service protective units' gunfire and bazooka attack on the yacht was also recorded. Dade had been surprised by the bazooka response, but was glad to have it on tape.

As he continued walking toward the Club's parking lot, Dade had pressed a third button on the remote control, immediately igniting an immense cache of plastic explosives that had been secretly woven into the fiberglass decking of the yacht.

All together, the videotapes chronicled—in brilliant color and vivid sound—the most sophisticated assassination attempt on a U.S. President in the nation's history. Soon those tapes would be viewed, not by conspirators in a foreign country but by traitors in a non-descript office building in Washington, D.C., twenty minutes away from White House.

"Pull in behind the store," Dade ordered, and Tony slowed the Jeep to a stop as the fast-moving caravan kept going down the road. Just as they arrived, two green-and-gold Vermont State Trooper cars raced around the corner, sirens wailing. "Don't sweat it, guys, they're with us." Dade said. "Get ready to get out when they pull up."

The police cars screeched to a stop thirty feet away from the Jeep and four uniformed officers leapt out with compact UZI sub-machine guns pointed at the Jeep and the men inside.

"Great acting!" Dade commented, but as he started opening the car door he watched the men with growing concern. Before anyone knew what was happening, the state troopers began pouring dozens of rounds into the Jeep, causing it to bounce crazily on its all-terrain tires. Once they were sure all the men were dead, one of the troopers rushed up to the bullet-riddled Jeep and grabbed the black bag from Mr. Dade's lifeless hands.

"Blow it!" he yelled, running back to one of the police cars, while another trooper dropped a foot-long silver canister into the shattered rear window of the Jeep and raced to hop into the second patrol car as both vehicles sped from the lot. Once inside, the trooper pressed a remote unit, looking back to watch the white-hot explosion destroy the Jeep and its passengers.

"The only remains of those guys that they'll find are their car keys. Maybe not even those," said one of the phony state troopers. "Nothing can stand that kind of heat. They're history, along with their fingerprints and dental records." Grinning at his cold-eyed comrade sitting next to him, he continued, "They'll probably think this was done by Castro or the Mob, like Kennedy. That should help the President get re-elected because assassination attempts always build sympathy for the target. Plus, we got a chance to test that incredible computerized gun system on the boat."

"Well, we're not supposed to know all this," countered one of the others. "And the more we talk about it, the more chances we have to end up like our friends back there. So shut up."

"Fuck it, Frank. We helped plan this operation from the beginning, so we should get some of the credit. The Cartel, Castro, the Mob and all the usual suspects, even those Mideast maniacs, are going to come under a lot of Kennedy-at-Dallas scrutiny, which is good; makes our own operation less noticeable." Then he said to the driver, "Go ahead and radio home base with an all-clear." Immediately the driver pressed a button on the radio and was greeted with a three-second hum in response to his message.

The two patrol cars raced east with sirens blaring and lights flashing, appearing to be emergency vehicles going about urgent business on that hot summer day. Their destination: a small private airport minutes away.

Thousands of feet above them, the bright silver contrails of Air Force One were the only evidence of its rapid return to Washington, D.C. This time the President's plane was closely guarded by four Air Force F-15 Interceptor jets, and two more followed a mile behind with pilots alert and missiles set to respond to any further threats.

Inside Air Force One, Ben sat with his arm around Laura, whose head was nestled on his shoulder. While he enjoyed her warmth, Ben's mind burned with the fact that, after twenty years of fat living, he was back at war with people who threatened his country. Somehow he would do his part to thwart that threat, even if the weapons he used now were different. But just as he had known how to handle the murderous capabilities of his powerful jet twenty years ago, he now knew how to effectively employ the influential persuasive power of his current weapons: ideas, words and images. He felt ready to unleash his unique talents on behalf of President Rogers, his country and his friends. The tough part would be deciding how and where to begin.

CHAPTER TWENTY

A Successful Production

June 24, 1992, 4:59 PM

"The production was successful, boss. Even HBO couldn't have done better," the caller reported. "We have the videos en route to you and, as planned, the cast of characters has been reduced to cinders, with nothing left to connect them to us."

Placing the handset down on the secure phone in his home, the pleased recipient of the call switched off the unit's scrambler and walked to the window of his large study. He glanced down at *The Washington Post* newspaper lying on the windowsill and read the headline proclaiming "Hot Fireworks Promised in Town!" above listings of Fourth of July firework displays throughout the Capitol. "Hot indeed," chuckled Chief Justice Blackstone.

Several miles away at the CIA's Virginia headquarters, the vigilant Cray supercomputer noted a scrambled call made to the Chief Justice's home from an office in the Smithsonian Institution, located just across the river. Had a scrambler not been used and had increased surveillance not been recently placed on the Chief Justice's home phones, the computer would never have caught the call. As it was, the notation of this garbled transmission was among hundreds of other exception reports spewed out for subsequent review. Level Four surveillance didn't require notifying the duty agent, so it was effectually useless. In the months ahead, that procedure, like others that had failed to protect the President, would be revised. But for now, it apparently was just one more random event in Washington's complex, frequently sinister world.

CHAPTER TWENTY-ONE

They Got Away, Boss

June 24, 1992, 5:50 PM

"It's going to take days to unravel all of this, Mr. President," Chet said to the most powerful man in the world, who was seated in his oversized desk chair aboard Air Force One. "We think a Jeep SUV was likely the car used by the perps. Luckily one of the guest's cameras caught a glimpse of it on videotape as it joined the caravan of cars escaping the resort. They probably rented it in Burlington, but we don't have any rental records yet.

"Other evidence includes six burned bodies found inside an incinerated Jeep parked outside a restaurant ten miles east of the resort. It's the same SUV model, according to the VIN placard that survived the fire. Because most of the guests fled the resort soon after the attack, we are having trouble re-constructing what occurred or even developing a list of suspects. Our best guess is that the six men on the yacht with the graphic-guided gun acted alone; if there were any other accomplices, our investigation, while much hampered, should identify them."

As the Air Force staff sergeant steward brought more coffee, he announced, "Mr. President, we are due to land in Washington in ten minutes."

"Thank you, sergeant," the President replied.

Turning his attention back to Chet, and to Ben and Laura who were seated on a leather couch nearby, the President explained, "Gaines has gathered together members of my Cabinet and other appropriate people at the White House. We'll work out a game plan for the next forty-eight hours and prepare to go on the networks at eight tonight." Reaching over to hold hands with his wife, who was still wearing the disheveled slacks and blouse that revealed evidence of being crushed against the floor of the helicopter, he said, "I'm amazed there were so few casualties in what seemed like a pitched battle. Did any agents take videos?" he asked Greenwood.

"No, Sir. Since this was officially a holiday for you we normally would not record any video. But many guests at the resort filmed your arrival and we hope to learn more from those tapes."

Ben noticed Chet's grim expression at the arduous task that lie ahead for Secret Service agents to reconstruct what had happened and helping the FBI and CIA identify who was behind it. Watching him talk with the President, Ben could see Chet was as cool as ever. Wish I felt as calm, he thought.

"Well, Chet, your team certainly did everything we ever rehearsed, shocking as it was for all of us. Please give them a 'well done' from me and Mrs. Rogers," the

President said, squeezing his wife's hand. "And, Ben, once again, Bravo Zulu, as you Navy types like to say. Well done. I still can't believe we escaped that hell."

Laura glanced at Ben, who seemed lost in thought. She smiled at him and said, "Thanks from me, too, Mr. Ad Guy," trying to lighten the mood and bring Ben back into the present. She noticed his hardened jaw and the deep creases around his eyes, which continued staring out the window at the distant sunset. Realizing that this may be his focused mode under stress, or any kind of challenge, she softly removed his arm from around her shoulders and sat back to think about this new man and the new mystery in her life.

Air Force One began descending from 33,000 feet over Pennsylvania, and as it did, a leased Learjet with four passengers simultaneously began its descent in order to land at Dulles Airport within minutes of the President's plane. On board the Learjet, safely tucked into an inconspicuous black briefcase, was the evidence President Rogers, Greenwood and a great many officials in Washington desperately sought: six digital "photo-sticks" containing a comprehensive visual record of what had transpired at the Basin Harbor resort.

The technologies used to invent the photo-sticks, and the sophisticated high-powered gun on the yacht, as well as other weapons used in the attack, had been developed at a top secret U.S. government research installation located just a few miles outside the nation's capitol. Conceived and fabricated at great taxpayer expense, these weapons were not only designed to be used in the assassination attempt, but were planned to be used directly against those taxpayers, their elected officials and, in fact, against the very way of American life. Investigations into how the development of these tools had been diverted by foreign operatives to their nefarious purposes would, in the months ahead, be the subject of numerous meetings among top-level U.S. defense and security officials and intense debates in Congressional hearings.

To Ben, it all seemed part of the continuing chronicle of man's ability to kill using increasingly creative and dramatic methods. But what if words, simple but carefully crafted words, could once again be employed as an effective weapon? It had happened many times before in the history of the American people, he recalled. Hell, if Lincoln's "Gettysburg Address" had helped mend a nation and if Churchill's speech could energize a beaten British population against a Nazi maniac, it could be done again. Putting his head back against the back of the seat, he closed his eyes for a few moments before Air Force One landed. As the jet engines whined down and the giant aircraft eased toward the runway, Ben pulled out the pocket notebook he always carried with him and began jotting down notes earnestly, momentarily unaware of Laura sitting close by.

CHAPTER TWENTY-TWO

The President Speaks to the Nation

June 24, 1992, 9:00 PM

The President stood at the podium under the hot Klieg lights in the Press Briefing Room at the White House.

"My fellow Americans, today our country was attacked by unknown assailants at a small Vermont resort called Basin Harbor. The immediate threat appeared to be to myself and my wife, but ultimately the attack was against you. Over two hundred years ago, this area on Lake Champlain was the site of many of our forefathers' efforts to create this great nation. Today, it was the site of a treacherous and failed attempt to radically undo those brave efforts and the decades of freedom we have so fortunately enjoyed.

"I want to reassure you that Mrs. Rogers and I are safe and fine, as are others who were travelling with us. I also want to extend our condolences, and those of all of the American people, to the families of the six Secret Service agents who were killed in the brief but violent battle. Their professional and personal dedication to their country and the fulfillment of their duty mirror that of the patriots who came before them, who gave their lives to protect future generations of Americans."

The President looked down for a moment then said, "I have met with my Cabinet and the Security Council, and tomorrow I will address Congress. This is the first time in modern times that Americans have been attacked within our borders. Every person in the defense and security communities is now on DEFCON 1 emergency readiness, and our allies around the world have responded with full support and similar security actions, including President Yeltsin, our honored guest, who will soon be returning to Moscow.

"My purpose in speaking with you tonight is to promise you that every effort is being made to identify and capture the people responsible for this heinous and callous act. I also want to encourage you and your fellow citizens to be part of this effort. If you know or become aware of any information that could help us ferret out these terrorists—and yes, I use that word purposefully because terror is obviously their goal—I want you to contact your local police or the FBI. Please do not take any action on your own.

"In closing, I want to again express my sincere appreciation of the brave sacrifices made today in response to this horrific event. God bless you and this great country. Good night."

As soon as the President ended his address, all three major networks, Fox, and CNN turned to their anchormen and commentators to try to make sense out of this unprecedented event in the nation's history.

Ben and Laura watched the televised speech with several White House staffers in the office wing. The speech instilled in Ben a growing sense of mission and increased respect for the President. Handing him another cup of coffee, Laura sat down next to Ben. He thanked her with a smile and said half-seriously, "For a guy who was the target of an assassination attempt, he certainly is a cool customer. I know this may sound crass, but won't this hurt his chances for re-election? I should probably just broadcast that speech as a campaign commercial."

Laura sipped her coffee; her hand still slightly shaking. "It certainly was surreal. All that shooting, yet the only people struck by bullets were the six Secret Service agents; all killed in an identical brutal manner. What kind of weapon was on that boat? It certainly wasn't one I have ever seen before," she said, shuddering involuntarily.

"You're right. The gunfire sounded like a string of nonstop fireworks but only a few agents were hit and killed. It's weird, but I'm sure Chet and his people will figure it out. I don't envy Chet. He was never a good loser and it sounds like the shit has hit the fan for the Presidential protection business.

Ben stood up and looked around the room. "I'm not sure how to get my job done now," he divulged. "What do you think, Laura?" he asked, realizing it was one of the few times in his career that he had turned to a research person for ideas, or to a woman for that matter.

"Thanks for asking," Laura responded, almost blushing. "All I can think of is somehow we let down our guard. Rogers is a great President, but national security has not been a top priority because of the success of his international diplomacy during the last four years. Laura crossed her legs, which caught Ben's eye as always, but this time he controlled himself. "Rogers has always been more proactive than reactive, more confident than cautious," she continued. "Maybe we need to think about upping our vigilance. Someone out there hates us immensely and seems capable of operating openly and easily within our own borders."

"Do you mean 'More vigilance, danger never takes a holiday' or something like that?" he asked, appreciating Laura's clear line of thinking. "That's a great kernel of an idea and I'm going to sleep on it. Our President may have to begin speaking along those lines given the dangerous situation he just encountered."

Flattered by Ben's response to her ideas but exhausted, Laura said, "All of the President's staff have been assigned cars and armed drivers until further notice, so if you would like, I can drop you off at your hotel and we can get back to all of this tomorrow."

"Perfect. I'll get my stuff and meet you outside. And by the way, I hope I didn't hurt you in the helicopter. It looks like your chin is bruised," Ben said, softly brushing the rough red spot.

Laura smiled for the first time in hours, feeling his strength and concern. Much to her surprise, she reacted in kind. "Ben, I must admit this has been the most eventful twenty-four hours I can recall. And because of you, I survived it," she smiled, "and at times even enjoyed it!" She squeezed his hand then departed to retrieve her luggage.

Ben rubbed the hand she had softly touched thinking everything about her just felt right. Here he was in the midst of an assassination attack on the President and his first thought was for Laura. Not for the President; not for himself; but for her.

Ben walked to his small White House office to check messages. There were several. Glancing again at his hand, still warm from Laura's touch and black-and-blue from the attack, he listened to worried messages from his New York staff and a few close friends who had gotten his number from Helen Mayfield. They all seemed a million miles away, he realized, so he decided to call Helen later and let her follow-up with them. Then he left the office to join Laura for the ride back to his hotel. He knew it would be a sleepless night spent starting to shape the re-election campaign, but now he understood it was needed, not only to help the President but to help heal the nation.

CHAPTER TWENTY-THREE
Walter Cronkite Returns

June 25, 1992, 8:01 AM

After finally falling asleep around three in the morning, Ben woke up abruptly from a frightening dream. He recalled flying high above a white desert in a silent aircraft that seemed to run on electricity. He was flying over a deep crater covered by miles of molten red lava, when suddenly he was floating under a large yellow parachute, watching his plane slowly drift down into the flaming cauldron. He too was being swept towards the crater. Twisting the cords on the parachute with all of his strength, he tried to steer away from the fire, but still he could feel the heat intensifying. With one final tug, he awoke with a start, one of the hotel pillows twisted in his sweating hands.

Slowly recovering from his first nightmare in years, Ben sat on his bed rubbing his shoulders, bruised and sore from the day before. He reached for the television remote, turned on the morning news, and was surprised to see the long-retired legendary CBS anchor-man Walter Cronkite speaking in urgent tones.

"...and while I had intended to retire fully with the exception of doing a periodic documentary and work-ing on my books, recent events have returned me to this desk. It was Dan Rather's decision to board an airplane bound for the Russian capitol. We at CBS want to do all we can to honor President Roger's call for all of us to do our part in responding to the recent cowardly attack on this country. At CBS, my tempo-rary return as New York anchor and Dan's new role as worldwide anchor is, in our view, the best way we can track events and report them with as much accuracy and depth as possible. As events unfold in the wake of yesterday's assassination attack and the recent unsuc-cessful Russian coup, events that may or may not be connected, we at CBS join in President Rogers's bold promise to do everything possible to make this terrible chapter in American history as brief as possible. Now, on to the news.

"Early this morning, President Rogers met with his Cabinet and the Joint Chiefs of Staff, and a full report of that meeting will be made to the nation at the Presi-dent's press conference at 6:00 tonight. We will be there with you to learn what actions are being planned.

"Now we turn to the site of yesterday's assassina-tion attempt and Peter Prescott on location in Basin Harbor, Vermont...Peter?"

The familiar, comforting face of Walter Cronkite gave way to that of a prematurely silver-haired vet-eran *Washington Post* and CBS News reporter, Peter Prescott, standing next to an elderly woman and several trim young men.

"Yes, Walter, we are standing on the lawn of the Basin Harbor Club near Burlington, Vermont, on what would otherwise be a tranquil morning. However, it is anything but. With me are Robert Beach, the fourth-generation owner of this beautiful resort with his mother, Elisabeth Beach, and several Secret Service agents led by senior agent Ralph Watkinson.

"Agent Watkinson, what can you tell us?" Prescott asked as the camera panned to a tall, white-shirt clad man holding a large folder in one hand and a pocket-sized radio in the other. His grim expression conveyed the fact that he would rather be anywhere but where he was. But Watkinson knew that speaking to the news media might help the effort to solve this heinous crime, so he took a deep breath and replied to the question with his eyes never wavering, his voice strong.

"Larry, we are still piecing it together. What we know is that when the President's helicopter and the two protective helicopters were arriving here yester-day afternoon, gunfire of a highly accurate nature broke out from a yacht moored in the harbor. The en-tire episode lasted less than five minutes, but I can tell you it felt like a lifetime. While we estimate over two hundred rounds of ammunition were fired in the at-tack, only six people, all Secret Service agents, were killed."

"Isn't that strange, all those shots and only six peo-ple hit, no one wounded?" asked Prescott.

"Yes, it is highly unusual, and it has no precedent. Two things sit heavy on the minds of all of us, and I'm sure on the minds of your viewers. Each agent was shot precisely in both eyes, something we have never seen before; and none of the shots appeared to be directed at the President or his helicopter. Most of the shots were fired over the heads of people and trees, most likely just to create a chaotic scene. Also, several shots were accurately fired at and disabled the engines of the two accompanying choppers, but avoided any other casualties. Everyone on the presidential helicopter was unharmed and that helicopter was untouched as it escaped the area.

"Shot in both eyes. What kind of weapon can do that?" Prescott inquired about the grim reality.

"Frankly, we have little to go on. The yacht is in cinders and the assassins most likely got away in the panic that ensued. Almost half the guests fled in their cars and the perpetrators probably used one, too. However, soon after the event Vermont State Police discovered a burned vehicle with the heavily charred remains of several dead occupants in the parking lot of a restaurant not far from the resort. We are endeavoring to identify the remains to learn if any of those people may have been involved. The yacht, with the unusually accurate gun mounted on top, was completely destroyed by an internal bomb, so it has yielded very few clues so far. No one has ever seen a weapon of this kind, and we are doing everything possible to determine exactly what it was, where it was manufactured and how it got on that yacht."

"If it turns out your assassins and the weapon have been virtually destroyed, what are the chances of solving this crime?" asked Prescott.

"Exactly. That's what I want to know," Ben said. "That's what everyone wants to know."

"Right now, we are interviewing the guests and sifting through the boat's wreckage. I'm not sure what we'll find, but we do know that all aspects indicate this was professionally planned."

"Thank you, Agent Watkinson, and good luck from all of us.

"Mr. Beach, you and your family have owned and managed this wonderful resort for over fifty years, and the President and his family have been long-time guests. How will yesterday's events affect you and your resort?" Prescott asked as the camera zoomed in on a handsome middle-aged man, attempting to smile.

"Mr. Prescott, this is a family resort. Many families, including the Rogers, have come here for several generations. So many of them have come up to me and..."

Ben turned the sound off as the broadcast continued. *Glad it's not my job to make sense out of this mess. Bringing Cronkite out of retirement—that is something*—he thought, walking to the bathroom to turn on the shower. *I just have to figure out what we're going to say next, and that's not going to be easy. Maybe I can ask Cronkite for some help*, he mused, stepping under the bracing cold water. *At least, he might help me figure out how to deal with the media zoo, which is going to seriously eclipse the effectiveness of any early advertising in the campaign.*

Minutes after finishing his shower and getting dressed, Ben was answering the phone ringing next to his bed.

"I'm downstairs, Flyboy, with a car," Laura cheerfully announced. "We'll get breakfast at the office, so snap it up, Lieutenant! You have to save the world again."

CHAPTER TWENTY-FOUR

Our Day Has Come!

June 25, 1992, 10:05 AM

"It's time to play the Castro card, my friend." Chief Justice Blackstone said, holding the phone while fussing with a gold cufflink, a recent anniversary gift from his wife. He glanced around his opulent dressing room, still amazed at the lavish lifestyle of a senior U.S. government official. A "senior government traitor," is more like it, he mused, but we all have our missions, and so be it. On with the show.

"Do you have any questions?" he asked.

"No, I don't," answered a harassed Ray Davenport from his government car, "but we always maintained that this kind of terror stunt was going over the top, you know?" Fortunately, the privacy of this unusual conversation was guaranteed secret by a sophisticated scrambler and the heavy glass window separating its driver from the angry overweight occupant sitting in the back seat of the long black Cadillac.

"Just do it, and do it well, as you have always done." Blackstone commanded. "Castro needs a little shaking up to get him back in line and to pay his bills. Now is the time for action and for major cash...our day has come! Plus, we're going to need that money in our Swiss accounts until more millions pour in from our South American friends in the next few months, so move on it!"

As they hung up, several miles away the Cray supercomputer at Langley once again noted a scrambler being used on a call from the Chief Justice's residence, and once again it filed a report. This time, however, the report met with a heightened level of scrutiny. After the assassination attempt, every detail was being looked at more closely all over Washington.

Don Garrett, a twenty-year CIA veteran, read the brief report and dialed a number he knew by heart. "Frank, it's Garrett. Got something for you. Yep, I'll be in your office in five."

Meanwhile, Davenport angrily threw his handset at the glass partition separating him from his driver. Agent Marcus slowed down, moved to the right lane and lowered the glass. "Sir, anything I can do for you, or just business as usual?" he asked grinning, his teeth gleaming brightly against the dark interior of the limo.

"Sorry about that, Marcus," Davenport said, glancing up and thinking Marcus's expression looked just like his favorite comic actor, Eddie Murphy. "Nothing unusual, only sometimes these assholes are bigger than normal. Let's just get back to the office."

"Yes, sir," Marcus said crisply, wishing he could pull over and talk with his long-time boss. For months now, he had a lot he wanted to tell him, but had been unable to find the right time or moment. Pulling back into the passing lane, Marcus activated the red flashing lights on the front of the Caddy and increased his speed to over eighty miles per hour thinking, "At least, I'm still a good driver, if not a faithful CIA officer. Fuck it, a man's got to do what he's got to do, doesn't he? And so far nothing's gone wrong, right?" he asked himself. However, he did not like the accusing answer that flashed back at him in the rearview mirror.

CHAPTER TWENTY-FIVE

Clueless

June 25, 1992, 11:00 AM

The soft blue and ivory walls of the Oval Office glowed with the midday sunshine, in contrast to the dark topics scheduled to be discussed by its occupants.

"It's Ray Davenport, Mr. President. The Special Assistant to the CIA Director," one of Roger's secretaries related. "He and his boss want to meet with you and the Security Council as soon as possible."

"Tell him one o'clock and notify the team. And please get me some lunch, Betty. I don't think I've eaten since last night."

"Yes sir. The regular?" she asked, knowing the answer would be yes, and that meant a Cobb Salad, a glass of Husch Chardonnay and chocolate cake.

"But hold the wine...I'm going back to drinking Now Cola for awhile. Our friend Ben Coleman would be pleased. At least someone will be pleased about something around here," he groused before turning to talk with Janine Warden. His national security chief and old college friend sat across from him in an antique blue wing chair. Janine had always been a straight "A" student, he remembered, but for once she didn't seem to be totally on top of her game. Her dark eyes were clouded with deep concern.

"Janine" he said, looking intently at the short black woman, "the CIA wants to come over here. It must be something important. I certainly hope there's an early break in this situation because the American people want—no they deserve—a speedy resolution. There may be domestic aspects, so get the FBI over here too," he ordered.

"Yes, Mr. President, but I don't think what has happened will become clear for awhile. Nothing we have 'gamed' on the Cray or in concert with the FBI, the CIA and the military has ever looked like this. It doesn't even make much sense. They missed you or intended to miss you; killed six agents almost as though the gun was three feet from their heads; the perps disappeared or were eliminated shortly after the event; and we have heard nothing from any of our normal sources anywhere in the world to explain any aspect of it. What is really strange is that the weapon fired direct hits into both eyes of each victim, which is almost impossible to do, much less several times. We know of no weapon capable of that precision."

"A weapon of terror, no doubt about it. I've never seen or heard of anything like it," Rogers said, putting a small stack of papers to the side of his large oak desk. "We're stumped, I'm sorry to say," he mumbled. "But even so we have to get clear on this and fast. Tell me more about this weapon. What does the FBI think it is?"

"They're betting it was an automatic 50-caliber rifle guided by some sort of computer that somehow used photos to target the six agents and the choppers. The gun was programmed to find, isolate and shoot only those six men, and to destroy both choppers' engines. We believe this is an accurate assessment although according to sound recordings at the scene, more than a hundred rounds of artillery fired from the yacht were shot above the grounds of the Club and over the lake. The noise made people think the end of the world was at hand," she said, smoothing the skirt of her dark suit over her legs.

"I think the whole thing was some sort of warning or drill, or perhaps a test run of the gun and its unique video-driven guidance system. We had considered developing similar technologies for a few years with Kodak and Lockheed, but this looks like a state-of-the-art weapon, and we don't yet know its country of origin."

"So, we didn't design this thing? Who did? Was it developed under our own noses?" The surprise and anger in the President's voice unsettled his close friend and advisor.

"We don't know, Mr. President, and frankly we don't know why we don't know," she replied, realizing how arcane her comments sounded.

"It almost seems as if they are saying, 'next time it will be you, Mr. President,'" Rogers said crossly, reaching for his phone. "Make sure Officer Gilman is at our one o'clock meeting. Davenport is fine and so is the Director, but I like Gilman. He's a friend of Greenwood's and a tough-minded pro from past deal-

ings. I know he has his hands full, but this is important.

"And the treaty signing is still a 'go' with Boris before he returns to his own mess," the President reminded Janine. "So please make sure things are set up
for five sharp tonight." Then his tone lightened and he
asked his old friend, who had been instrumental in his
passing several tough courses at Harvard Law School
and continued to be one of the most important people
to his career, "Join me for lunch?"

"No thanks, I had better get together with my team
before one. See you there, and in the meantime stay
away from the windows, even if they are rocket-
proof," she smiled, hugged him quickly and left.

Two hours later, ten anxious senior government officials watched as the President's lunch was cleared
from his desk. With a terse word of welcome, the
President and his Chief of Staff led the group through
an intense hour-long discussion of recent events and
the few random pieces of evidence. It was a sober-
faced group of people who filed out of the office afterward, having been admonished to get something on
the table, and quick.

CHAPTER TWENTY-SIX

Rogers and Yeltsin Sign the Treaty

June 25, 1992, 5:00 PM

Never before had the Oval Office been used for a diplomatic event of such magnitude. In recent years, the President's personal office was increasingly used as the site of photo ops marking everything from National Spelling Bee winners to the passage of major civil rights and educational legislation, as well as announcements of military actions and diplomatic achievements.

In many ways, this hub of America's government was being promoted worldwide as the center of the universe of Planet Earth. So it's not surprising, although it was known only by a small cadre of government construction experts, that the Oval Office was also one of the most bomb and missile-proof aboveground edifices in the world.

Before the landmark nonproliferation treaty between Russia and the United States was to be signed,

Betsy Rogers, wife of the President's famous diplomat father, Bertram Rogers, spoke to reporters on the terrace of the White House Rose Garden. The reporters listened as she summarized the changes leading up to the agreement. Years of heavy military spending by the U.S. had slowly bankrupted the Soviet Union, culminating in the fall of the Iron Curtain and other Communist setbacks in the 1980s. Realizing victory, the U.S. government tried to avoid embarrassing the Russians outright by endeavoring to "put a good face on things," as she told reporters. Betsy Rogers had always been a plain-spoken Iowan farm girl, and today reporters were looking to her for the simple humor and frank honesty that had made her a household name. She did not disappoint them.

"These 'Ruskies' are just people like us, you know. So what if they are a little larger and heavier than most of us, they strike me as nice folks. They just want a decent life and to enjoy their families. I applaud what my son and his team have done. Treat the Russians nice now that they have decided to stop building nukes and submarines to bomb us. I'm all for it," she said, smiling her broad smile at the hovering cameras. "It's the right thing to do, and we Rogers always do the right thing."

Standing inside in front of an Oval Office now stuffed with officials and on-lookers, President Rogers whispered into Yeltsin's ear something everyone in the room would have killed to hear.

"I swear idiots in both our countries are going to do all they can to undo what you and I are building today." Yeltsin, understanding the thrust of the comment, nodded in firm agreement.

The two smiled for the cameras and traded ceremonial pens, one an antique American Scripto that had been manufactured early in the Cold War and the other, a large silver artifact created by a famous Russian artisan and purveyor to Czar Nicholas II. Then they carefully signed their names to the scrolled treaty containing the historic words, "…and pledge to reduce to pre-1960's levels, all strategic and tactical weapons with the exception of submersible combatants."

With a handshake and friendly smiles, Rogers and Yeltsin turned to the assembled crowd and raised their hands together in an American "high five." The crowd cheered and the two men looked delighted. Everyone was well aware they were witnessing an event no one could have predicted a few years ago, and certainly not thirty years earlier.

As the setting sun illuminated the salt and pepper hair of President Rogers, he looked around the room realizing that there was little he might do in the future that could match this moment. Maybe things will be a little easier now, but will this guy standing next to me keep his word? Who knows? I guess we'll find out in the next few acts of this play, which I plan to stay in office to see unfold. November should clinch that.

Off to the side, standing further down the hall, Vice-President Toland smirked at the incredible irony of the moment, realizing only he and a few chosen others knew the true meaning of this event. They knew its actual impact would likely delay any U.S. response to the internal events beginning to swirl throughout the USSR as the old Communist state yielded to the birth of democracy and capitalism. We need to buy time to get our new act together and rebuild what our comrades back home have screwed up so badly. And this treaty does the trick, very neatly. And these guys will never realize that. What fools!

Thinking of Joseph Stalin and the foresight of brilliant Kremlin conspirators many years ago, Toland thought: "You really understood history, Joe. You knew we might lose the Cold War just like Germany lost the Second World War, because America's ability to spend and build its war machine was, and still is unbeatable. But you also saw a way to avoid losing Mother Russia to the capitalists, appearing to play into the hands of the U.S. by creating the Yalta Treaty. America has always loved making treaties with people, including their own Native American Indians. But America has never understood how to nurture and promote relationships with new allies. In this case, just signing the documents with Russia without any follow-up to keep the agreement active and meaningful. No, America made weak, thoughtless treaties within her own borders and now is paying the price with the Indian casinos springing up all over California suburbs, untouchable by Federal gaming laws. Well, they will learn their lesson with Russian Communists too. We are not going to bow to the Americans. We are going to simply adjust where we must to these new developments, and continue to be the socialist powerhouse we always have been. It's just a matter of employing different methods and, soon, different leaders.

Toland's reverie was broken when he noticed President Rogers waving at him. Walking toward him, the lyrics of an old American tune Toland had learned as a young boy while studying the American language in the secret KGB enclave in the Ural Mountains, popped into his head. "There'll be a hot time in the old town tonight," he mused, knowing he would soon be right in the middle of it. Finally.

Approaching to shake hands with both presidents for the cameras, Toland reached for Yeltsin's first, thinking tersely to himself, "You are no Joe Stalin, Mr. Yeltsin, and today, we are no USSR. But, just wait, you bombastic fool, just you wait!"

Ben and Laura watched the proceedings on the small TV in her basement office. Turning from the screen, Ben remarked, "As I said, it seems we have won the big one, at least for a while. No telling what will happen back in Russia, but Yeltsin seems strong enough to handle a couple of platoons of bad guys all by himself."

"It's been a long time coming for the President, Ben. He always liked to be in the spotlight. The stakes in this game are the highest he's experienced, but he's holding all the chips now."

"Well, if he's not a little weary, I am, and hungry, too. How about dinner at the hotel?" Ben asked. "I haven't eaten in the main dining room and maybe we could get some work done in peace," he said, hoping to have another opportunity to be alone with Laura.

Gathering her notebook and purse, Laura smiled radiantly, "I thought you'd never ask! How about seven?"

Seven in heaven, Ben thought happily.

CHAPTER TWENTY-SEVEN

High-Fiving in the Oval Office

June 25, 1992, 5:28 PM

In his eighteen years with the CIA, Jeff Gilman had never been in the presence of a senior Communist official. From the rear of the Oval Office where he stood with his friend, Chet Greenwood, he could not help but sense the historical significance of the signing of the treaty. It would have been almost unthinkable a few years ago, but events in recent months had cascaded, bringing the uprising and dismantling of the Berlin Wall in East Germany three years ago to a crescendo. He and his CIA confederates had totally missed many signs that, in retrospect, abounded in all corners of the Communist State: the Wall coming down, the sudden warming of relations under Gorbachev and his Politburo appointees, and now Yeltsin signing a major arms treaty with the U.S. in his first year as President of the Russian Federation.

"Lenin must be rolling in his grave cursing all of

this," Gilman said to Chet. "Signing a nonproliferation treaty right in the White House, much less high-fiving the President! It's almost too much to believe!"

"I've been with Sky Chief for four years, and everything he has touched has turned to political gold," Chet agreed, "but you're right, this really takes the cake."

"Rogers makes it look easy, and I've been around a lot of Presidents. Then you have the Veep, or 'Numero Dos' as you guys call him. He looks like he wears someone else's fancy suits and Hollywood personality. How did these two ever get hooked up together? Look at him, standing off to the side, lost in thought. He always seems distracted, like he's off in limbo, planning, thinking," Jeff said, realizing he never really liked Vice President Toland. "Hard to imagine how he got this far."

Chuckling at his friend's concern, Chet watched the historic meeting come to a close with cameras flashing and smiles glowing with accomplishment. "We'll see how all this plays out. I imagine you're going to be even busier now, tracking the impact of the Communist implosion on other Central European states. Looks like they all bailed on the old USSR. But don't forget dinner at my house this Friday; the twins won't understand if you miss their birthday. And Ben Coleman, the ad guy, will be there. I flew wing on him in 'Nam."

"I wouldn't miss it. The twins are more important to me than any of this, and it'll be interesting to meet your flyboy buddy. He's got a big job I hear. Please tell Connie I'm bringing Donna, the woman she introduced me to last Christmas at your church. She has become a great friend. Puts up with all my absences and seems to like me, which is no small feat!"

"Great!" Chet said enthusiastically, then grew serious. "My team is still investigating last week's attack, but we haven't got a clue beyond what was found at the scene and the fact that the perps might have been foreign-born. All had accents. Beyond that, it's a big fat zero. Let me know if you guys get any info that might shed some light."

"Will do, but so far, we're just as clueless and it pisses me off," Jeff admitted. "First we missed any indication the Berlin Wall was coming down, then the attempted coups, and now this attack. The Company is on 24-hour watch at DEFCON 1, like the rest of the defense folks, but we've got nothing. I have a meeting tonight at 7:00 at the ranch and I have a hunch we'll find that the attack, the treaty and Yeltsin's visit are somehow connected. We just have to figure out how, and who is pulling the strings," Jeff said, turning to leave. "Let's stay in close touch, Chet. I may need some help as we go along."

"No sweat, will do. See you soon," Chet said, slapping the shorter man on his broad shoulder.

Neither Chet nor Jeff realized the Vice President had been watching them. Toland was gloating to himself about the two cocky men being put unknowingly smack in the middle of developments they could neither imagine nor most likely would be able to effectively deal with. At least that was part of the plan designed many years earlier, which was now being executed by many faceless conspirators in major cities around the globe. Give us a few months, Toland thought; you won't forget our faces then.

Never did like Greenwood, Toland concluded as he studied Chet's all-American looks. He never gave me the kind of respect he gives Rogers. My Secret Service detail is always a lot smaller, and has too many Blacks and dikes. Well, if he thinks he's heading up my detail after the post-election fireworks, he's in for a big surprise. Maybe that's what he needs. Maybe some more Vermont-style excitement is needed to boost our re-election chances and to make this mission the big success that Blackstone, the bastard, wants. Maybe good old Greenwood can play a starring role and "catch a bullet" for the President, as agents always brag about being so ready and willing to do. Got to speak with my guys and, for once, leave Blackstone out of it. Why not, he smiled. I need to assert some VP, no, Presidential, control here.

CHAPTER TWENTY-EIGHT

Back at the CIA

June 25, 1992, 7:00 PM

Ray Davenport surveyed the crowded Operations Room five stories below the ground level of Langley's CIA headquarters. Packed tightly into the massive electronic nerve center were over a hundred intelligence officers, the largest such gathering he could remember. Davenport could almost taste the anticipation among the men and women as they shared information about recent events. A great deal was riding on the Agency's response to these events and it was also clear that this briefing was pivotal to the U.S. government's successful response. He glanced at the large screens behind him, depicting the political affiliations of major world cities in various colors, ranging from red in Washington, New York, Los Angeles, London and Moscow to yellow and light blue in other cities. As he looked again at the map, Paris and Madrid changed from yellow to red, followed by several other European capitals.

"Thanks for being here on short notice, folks" Davenport began, as the room quickly quieted and almost everyone in attendance turned their newly-issued cell phones toward him. For several months government agents worldwide had been using the new, specially designed, high-security Motorola Cell Phones to quickly inform field personnel and headquarters of key international developments. While it was novel technology, the cell phones soon became indispensable to keeping everyone equally informed. Using a highly secure network nicknamed the C-Net, the brick-sized units provided the means of instantly communicating with headquarters from the field. Better than radiophones, which had limited range and battery life, the cell phones could transmit entire meetings and ensured all pertinent information could be communicated to team members deployed anywhere in the world.

"You all are keenly aware of the events of the last two days. The data is already resident on your Motorola Cell Phone under the code name Tiebreaker. The name refers to what appears to be a substantial shift in US-Soviet relations, indicated by the Wall coming down, member states withdrawing from the USSR, and today's historical nuclear treaty agreement. Forty years of Cold War tensions have finally been decided, seemingly in favor of the West, the U.S. in particular.

"Most recently, just prior to Yeltsin's arrival here to sign the treaty, we have what appears to be a failed coup in Russia. Frankly, no one in this room saw any of these things coming, and that has to change. Starting now!"

Jeff Gilman, seated in the third row with members of his special Russian desk team, allowed his mind to wander as the Special Assistant to the Director went into his standard "we have to get serious" pitch. He had heard it before, not only from Davenport but from other senior executives at the Company. He didn't have much respect for Davenport anyway. How the overweight unhealthy-looking career operative had risen to such an influential senior CIA position had always eluded Gilman. Whose ass was Davenport kissing in Washington, he wondered, concluding the CIA was just like the Marines, with loads of smart, qualified people serving under a few middle-management misfits who somehow rose to power in spite of their weaknesses. The fact that Davenport was a Princeton graduate was one reason, like so many old CIA operatives raised in the "Ivy League" mentality that had prevailed in the Office of Strategic Services (OSS). Gilman recalled that the OSS was originally the World War II secret service led by "Wild Bill" Donovan. In the fifties, when the OSS became the CIA, it was initially staffed with a good-old-boy network of Yale, Harvard and Princeton graduates who trusted few others outside their elite fraternity. During the intervening years, a broader range of bright young people had found their way into the organization, even though it was especially difficult for women, Blacks and other minorities to be accepted into the hallowed halls of the Langley campus. Most, however, had served with distinction, succeeding through brains and courage equal to if not surpassing that of their blue-blooded associates.

Like many Vietnam War veterans, Gilman had

been wooed by the FBI, the CIA and the Secret Service, and the Marines wanted him to re-enlist, based on his sterling military record. Within weeks of arriving in Vietnam, he had led a small tactical squad deep into remote mountains, capturing key North Vietnamese commanders and bringing them back for interrogation. The information extracted from the prisoners would have turned the tide of that badly managed war if the generals and officials in Washington had used that intelligence to make the right decisions. Disgusted with what he had experienced in Vietnam, Gilman decided to leave the Marines, but not the service of his country. The CIA's worldwide mission intrigued the young twenty-five-year-old and he opted for the life of a covert operative. His parents, who had been proud of him as a Marine, were less supportive of this decision. They viewed his new role as shady and underhanded, almost illegal, and they expressed their concern with unusual fervor. Even his friends, many of whom had flocked to Berkeley and New York during the anti-war peace riots, were confused and upset that their high school football-star friend would defect to the dark side and become a spy. Unlike his family and friends, Gilman had seen the threat of Communism up close and personal in Vietnam, having had his position at Khe Sanh in the Central Highlands of South Vietnam overrun several times by North Vietnamese units. Barely surviving these and other harrowing battles during two tours of duty, Gilman was convinced that America had to use every tool within its grasp to contain and defeat what he felt was a dedicated Communist effort to destroy life as Americans knew it.

Bringing his attention back to Davenport, Gilman

realized that most of the key points the man was es-
pousing were lifted directly from his own briefing to
Davenport and other top executives at Langley earlier
this morning, and then to the President. The major
threat to the U.S. continued to be from countries that
had comprised the USSR or the Soviet Block. Gilman's
career had carried him into the deepest reaches of espionage in these and other Communist countries, including Cuba and several South American states. In
briefings in which he had been a key participant,
Ronald Reagan had become convinced to continue
putting pressure on the Soviets by upping the military
budget to levels the "Ruskies" were unable to match. It
required years of massive U.S. spending on aircraft
carriers, sophisticated jets, and other instruments of its
military complex. Finally the threat of a "Star Wars"
style anti-ballistic missile shield brought the Russians,
particularly Mikhail Gorbachev, to their senses. The
resultant period of detente culminated in the remarkable destruction of the great wall that had separated
East Berliners from their families and friends in West
Germany for over forty years. The dramatic clawing
down of the Berlin Wall, symbolic of the "Iron Curtain," as Churchill had so aptly named it, and the collapse of the USSR, had been in no small measure due
to the efforts and the work of many dedicated people
on Gilman's Russian desk team.

Gilman recalled with resentment that it was Davenport, and kiss-ass fools like him, who had been purposely cut from the team, who had done all they could
to undermine the group's efforts, sometimes through
internal backstabbing and often with outright criti-
cism. After Davenport had been promoted into posi-

tions that gave him access to CIA budgets, he had almost succeeded in convincing Jimmy Carter's Director of Central Intelligence, Stansfield Turner, to disband the team because of alleged "misuse of government funds." Fortunately, Turner ignored Davenport's obvious political posturing and reassigned him to field operations in the Asian sector, an embarrassing assignment for Davenport. In the years that followed, however, Davenport had slowly found his way back into the mainstream of Langley operations, having become astute at working the system, like so many other incompetents at the CIA.

Reflecting on Davenport's surprise promotion two years ago, Gilman remembered wondering at the time if Davenport had a direct line to the White House. He recalled the rumor that Vice President Toland had played a key role in his appointment, which had dismayed his associates and the security community in general because no one could recall any aspect of the Vice President's background that would have given him the necessary insights into CIA operations that could justify such an appointment. Gilman understood it probably had just been politics as usual, but he had always sensed Davenport was a little off-key, even if he hadn't been able to figure out exactly why. Looking up, he turned his attention to Zak Baker, the senior mission advisor, who was now briefing the group.

Months later, in extensive Congressional hearings, Gilman would publicly acknowledge his negative impressions of Toland and Davenport in connection with the horrific events that preceded the 1992 Presidential Election.

CHAPTER TWENTY-NINE
Nothing is *That* Perfect

June 25, 1992, 6:45 PM

Ben arrived at the Café Promenade in the Mayflower Hotel and ordered a Balvanie Scotch on the rocks. He was pleased that Laura had accepted his invitation to dinner, and grateful that the wardrobe Helen had sent with Chuck May, who delivered his Porsche, included a black blazer and gray flannel slacks. Seated near the entrance, Ben surveyed the large, gracious dining room, crowded with attractive people busily judging others in the room. He realized this was just one more power center in this powerful city. The old-world culture of the restaurant was reflected in the white-jacketed waiters whose aloof manners reminded him of the staff at his favorite restaurant, The Palm, in New York City. There you found yourself at the mercy of the man at the front desk and the cocky waiters. But the food was worth the noise. Suddenly, Ben noticed a number of the diners turning their heads towards the lobby, and his eyes followed theirs. Stunning in a tailored sky-blue suit, her red hair framing her exquisite face, Laura was confidently walking toward him, preceded by Alfred, the maitre d', who seemed particularly anxious to safely guide her through the throng.

"Sir," he said nervously to Ben, "had I known your dinner companion was Ms. Sinclair, I would have selected a special table for you." Before he could answer, Laura gave the slim little man a quick hug, explaining that "Mr. Coleman" was in fact, a very special man in Washington now, only no one knew it yet. Giving Ben her hand in happy greeting, she sat in the chair offered by Alfred, who handed them large menus with a flourish and flashed Laura a grateful smile.

"Nice," Ben said to Laura, surveying the richly decorated surroundings and the busy, noisy New York-style ambiance.

"So, you like the Café? It's one of my favorites, but I haven't been here in months. It's a nice place to relax, especially since we have a big job ahead of us, maybe bigger than we thought."

"Well, the little I know about politics suggests that the President must be at the peak of his popularity after that little number in Vermont and tonight's extravaganza. You can't plan that kind of news," Ben observed, noticing that Laura's presence continued to be the object of attention for numerous diners who were busily trying to figure out his and Laura's identity.

"The President has enjoyed a very high and sustained level of popularity," she said, even well before he was elected four years ago. Charisma and its accompanying power seem to come naturally to him. I think it's because he genuinely enjoys his role as the leader of the free world, and knows he's doing a good job. That kind of confidence is infectious; people can see and taste it, and they love him for it. My favorite performer was Elvis. He was the same kind of potent personality. He was good and he knew it. People idolized him and he adored the attention. Funny, the President's Secret Service code name used to be 'Elvis' but his wife scotched it, telling them to find a better name. They settled on 'Sky Chief,' as you must have heard by now from Chet."

Ben watched Laura, realizing that he was actually listening to her with more focus than he had listened to anyone in years. What was different about Laura? Her natural beauty and canny intelligence were things she took in stride. Clear blue eyes framed by dark eyebrows and rich long lashes, a pert nose and full lips, she radiated happiness and sexuality in her fluid gestures. She made him feel special and that was something new in Ben's life.

Ben was lost in her beauty, but also curious about her remarkably nimble mind. "I look forward to learning more about the work you do for Sky Chief. You can't begin to sell something without 'the facts, ma'am, just the facts,'" he laughed, enjoying Laura's mirthful response.

She reached across the table, briefly squeezing his hand. "You may be the only person I know who remembers Jack Webb and *Dragnet* besides my father. I like it when you're funny," she said, realizing Ben's humor was only one of many things she liked about him. "It's going to be fun helping you. More fun, I hope, than work."

Although he appreciated her touch and comments, Ben felt a small prickle when she put him in the same category as her father. Well, hell, he thought, I am older than she is, and it sure feels more like respect than any possible love interest. When did I suddenly become the older guy in women's eyes? Nuts! Ben thought ruefully as he took a moment to look around the room again.

Laura gazed at Ben's profile, realizing he was very handsome and pleasantly relaxed, in contrast to recent hectic events. He is unflappable, she thought, just like my father. Same light blue eyes. Same kind of man as Dad, except Daddy was a pilot in the Air Force, not the Navy. That's alright. I always did like the Navy uniform better, especially the whites that fit so snugly, she recalled with a small catch of her breath. Quietly she began mentally reviewing other details of Ben's background document that had been compiled by Gaines, but she concluded Ben was so much more than what that backgrounder revealed. And he is actually interested in what I think! That makes me think I will enjoy this assignment, she told herself with a smile. Maybe he'll help me find a great opportunity in New York. Maybe I had better be nice to him and keep him out of trouble here. A little quid pro quo, she decided, would go a long way with Ben. However professional her intentions, Laura's thought of what "being nice" to Ben might mean stirred up conflicting, but pleasant, emotions about their professional relationship.

Noting the slight blush spreading across Laura's alabaster cheeks, Ben felt a strong tug in his chest and thought: This feels like being seventeen and actually getting to talk to the head cheerleader, only better.

"How about a drink?" he asked. "When it comes to liquor, I'm a broken record. Scotch and soda. It's a great song and a great drink, and it's kind to your stomach and the morning after, too," he said.

"A 'Congressional Cosmo' would be wonderful. It's something of a signature drink here."

The waiter was at his side before Ben could even call him over. Taking their drink order, the waiter was struck by what an attractive couple they were, a thought many people seated nearby shared. Several were struck by a comparison to Spencer Tracy and Katherine Hepburn, which was certainly not unreasonable.

Lounging in a small booth across the room with a clear view of Ben and Laura's table, two large men ordered "Stoli, no ice," while one of them carefully aimed a small camera, disguised as a pack of cigarettes, in their direction. Nodding confirmation of the clarity of the photos he had just taken, the larger of the two men smiled and sat back to enjoy one of the most luxurious stakeouts of his career.

Ben moved the menu aside and reaching for his second scotch said, "Laura, now that we have some breathing room, I want to learn more about your research work. It must be fascinating."

"I appreciate your interest," Laura said, "and frankly, I'm a bit surprised. Your reputation as an extremely independent creative person precedes you."

That was true. Unknown to most people, much of Ben's success as an advertising man was based upon his strong interest in market research, particularly consumer focus groups. Unlike many of his creative peers, Ben was intrigued with the innovative research tools agencies used to probe the minds of consumers on a range of issues associated with the products he advertised. One of the few senior executives who actually attended focus groups and listened in on telephone surveys, Ben had found rich veins of insights, which he wove into his ad campaigns. He had learned to creatively use consumer feedback in TV and radio commercials and print ads. Probably half the headlines for which he had received awards were inspired by quotes from consumers. He was recognized for his gift of authentically capturing consumers' feelings and beliefs about everyday household products in a few carefully chosen words.

"I work hard to have clients and agency folks think I'm not interested in their opinions. For some reason, I am not feeling that way with you. Maybe it's because you seem less self-absorbed. I learned pretty early that most business people don't know how to market their products because they only listen to themselves and people who think like they do. I am interested in what everyday people say, think and want, not in my clients' opinions about what their customers say, think and want. There is a big difference. People like you, who use one-to-one consumer interviews, really understand that and get the right information."

Laura found herself smiling with delight. "Yes, I love the work and I'm glad you understand its value. A lot of people at the White House don't. They think it's too simple, too pat. But it's the simplicity of political polling that makes it such a wonderful planning tool. I did my graduate work at NYU and never looked back. President Rogers hired me eight years ago when he was a Congressman. He uses polls like other Congressmen use perks: often and with abandon," she laughed, enjoying Ben's attention and steady gaze.

"Well, tell me what you've learned about him," he urged, noticing Laura was just radiating happiness. I can almost taste it, he thought; in fact, I would love to. He realized then that he wanted to be with her somewhere else, like Bora Bora or Martha's Vineyard. Just the two of them getting to know each other. His reverie was interrupted by Laura's answer to his question.

"President Rogers has enjoyed an unparalleled popularity profile, never dipping below a 58% approval rating. That's unheard of in politics, especially since he's been President for four years now. It's an almost perfect track record, increasing monthly in small, but clear increments...almost as if by magic. Everything he has done, from convincing Congress to adopt his universal educational programs and Wall Street initiatives, to negotiating with the Soviets, Chinese, British and French on disarmament and trade issues, has worked like a charm. Unlike his predecessors, he always seems to come away with favorable results, which gives the public tremendous confidence in his diplomacy. He's a natural-born leader who gets results." Blushing, Laura realized she was suddenly stumping for Rogers, and she caught herself feeling some unbidden emotions from five years ago on a sunswept yacht in Bermuda. Surprisingly, in Ben's presence she was able to quickly put those thoughts out of mind.

Ben suspected her flushed face was caused by something other than himself and he felt intrigued, but he was also confused by her comments. "I'm surprised at your description of the President's 'perfect track record,'" he said. "I've never seen a consumer approval rating survey with an unbroken ascending line. There are always ups and downs; it's just the nature of the beast. I would think that would especially be true in politics."

Impressed with Ben's canny insights, Laura was reminded of her early misgivings about surveys taken while Rogers was a Senate leader. She also had considered the unbroken record suspect, but had remained faithful to the research results, no matter how curious they might look. She also recalled that Rogers himself had expressed concern with the tracking results of his popularity once he was in the White House, and over time had ceased to focus on them as heavily as he once had. The person who continued to express interest, and in fact insisted on receiving copies of all the studies, was the President's chief counsel at that time, David Blackstone. Imperious and guarded, even in those days, Blackstone had asked her numerous questions about the studies, as well as about studies she ran on other politicians' ratings. Blackstone never expressed any point of view about the reports, he only seemed interested in seeing the latest information. Even after Blackstone's appointment by Rogers to the Supreme Court two years ago, he continued requesting copies of the research surveys. Laura had assumed reviewing the studies was a hobby of his.

"I actually sent copies of the approval ratings to numerous experts in the field, including my GWU professors. Beyond expressing some level of surprise, they weren't concerned. The general view was that Rogers was a particularly commanding and popular individual and unique in his capacity to be unaffected by negative events and opinions—bulletproof, they said. Which is a good thing for a President to be, in many ways. I guess I got used to the unusually consistent survey results, especially when they were always supported by verbatim records of the respondents' comments. Never a dark cloud over our man's head," she smiled, causing another rise in Ben's libido as well as his curiosity.

"Well, Laura, nothing in nature is that perfect, nor in business or I imagine, politics, but I appreciate the man's strength. I can feel it and it's powerful. For example, when he stood next to Yeltsin, who is a pretty powerful guy himself, he just portrayed success. Part of that may be due to his tailor, but good clothes can't hide a loser. I would like to read some of the recent research reports, especially the verbatim responses. Can we do that?" he asked.

"Sure, everything is at your disposal. We can start tomorrow." Laura was alive with anticipation of their working relationship. She enjoyed Ben's intensity and wondered about other ways in which he might manifest that unique energy.

Turning their conversation to the twenty-page menu, the two were unaware of anyone else in the Café, including the two men sitting across the room who periodically glanced their way.

CHAPTER THIRTY

The Ad Campaign Starts to Jell

June 26, 1992, 9:10 AM

After breakfast, Ben was escorted into the West Wing of the White House by his old friend Chet, who was delighting in Ben's evident surprise at the bustling environment: the hallways and lobbies filled with people speaking urgently and staff members hustling to deliver envelopes and briefing documents. As they strode through, Ben was struck with the high level of intensity and dedication he witnessed among people of all nationalities and races who appeared to be working together in one seamless operation.

"Looks just like my ad agency at ten in the morning, but there are fewer coffee cups. And I thought ad agencies were zoos!" he exclaimed as Chet gestured toward a bank of offices on the right. "I certainly hope they know what they're doing," he joked, "because what gets done here really matters."

"Don't worry, Ben. They march to an extremely focused drummer, Charlie Gaines. He drives more activity than a Marine Corps Drill Instructor, a position he actually held a long time ago."

This last comment surprised Ben, remembering the highly trained Marine instructors in Pensacola, Florida, who had converted him from a spoiled college graduate into a lean Naval Officer and candidate for flight training in just sixteen weeks. Noted for their icy calm and unmatched skills at making young men forget everything they ever knew about civilian life, Drill Instructors, or DI's, were often viewed as second fathers by their young charges. Thinking of "Tuna" Taylor, the imposing black DI from Memphis who had been in charge of his forty-two member Officer Training Battalion in early 1967, Ben smiled. He recalled the time Taylor chewed out the group and subjected them to an afternoon of arduous running over sand dunes after learning about his new nickname. One of Ben's classmates had thought up the name, but rather than reveal the culprit, the entire class proudly shared the punishment. Unknown to them, Taylor had taken immense satisfaction in teaching the class the most important lesson of being a military man: always work as a team and never leave anyone behind, ever. Ben also remembered the sadness he felt a few years later when he learned Taylor had been killed while leading a squad of Marines into a Viet Cong ambush. The memory still rankled after two decades. What a waste of a good man, in fact, a waste of thousands of good men, including the veterans who survived, but still suffered from complex mental and physical wounds.

"Well, Ad Man, here's your office," Chet said, "and meet Marie Jacobs, your administrative assistant. She's survived three Presidential administrations, so there isn't anything she doesn't know about getting things done around here."

Smiling at Marie, Ben extended his hand, which was warmly shaken by the attractive forty-year-old woman. "I have heard so much about you and I'm really excited to be helping out," she said. "I love advertising, watching the commercials and wondering how you all come up with those clever ideas. I never guessed I'd get so close to it all!"

Ben welcomed her enthusiasm and realized her positive attitude would be invaluable to him in the coming weeks. "Well, we're going to need a whole lot of 'clever' to make sure we don't blow what looks like a winning race for President Rogers. He seems pretty unbeatable to me. In any event, I'm glad you're in my corner because this definitely is unfamiliar territory for me. I'm just an ad guy from New York," he said modestly, putting Marie more at ease.

"I've gotta head out," Chet said to Ben. "Good luck, and I'll pick you up at the end of the day so we can get to the house. Your personal fan club is anxious to meet the great ad guy." With a friendly slap on the shoulder, Chet turned to leave for a meeting with the Chief of Staff in the Oval Office.

"Marie, please show Ben his office and familiarize him with how to operate the phone and all. He never was too mechanically inclined."

Following Marie inside the office, Ben was pleasantly surprised to find Laura sitting at a round table in the corner. Surrounded by stacks of folders and reports, she still managed to stun him with her youthful beauty.

"Well," Ben said, glancing at Marie then Laura. "Looks like it's time to get to work with my small, but awesome team!"

"I thought you'd want to get started right away," Laura said, causing Ben's libido to momentarily go ballistic. He quickly regained his composure as he lifted his briefcase and placed it on the large desk.

"Absolutely. Thanks for being here, Laura. Guess there's no time like the present, so let's begin by reviewing some of the research, then the three of us can meet later to identify what we'll need to do to build President Roger's ad campaign.

"In the meantime," he turned to Marie, who held a pencil and pad ready, "please call my assistant, Helen Mayfield, in New York and get to know her. I imagine you two will be joined at the hip for a while," Ben said. "And ask her to have my creative group gathered around the speaker phone in my office at 11:00 tomorrow morning. We'll want to get them started on some campaign concepts."

"Right away, Mr. Coleman. And I'll bring some coffee and Danish for you two to fuel your efforts. I'm so excited. This is more thrilling than anything that goes on around here!" Marie exclaimed.

"Call me Ben please, Marie. And thanks for thinking of the coffee; it's one thing I cannot live without," he responded, even though that was not entirely true. But enough, he thought. Get to work. You have to start earning your million dollars, hotshot.

Taking a seat next to Laura, the two began reviewing the research that Ben hoped would contain the seed of the President's re-election campaign. Just remember, he told himself, Rogers is just another client, just another product. No big deal, just follow your tried-and-true methods and things will be terrific. "A walk in the park" like they say. This is just a much bigger park.

By lunchtime, Laura had briefed him on the primary aspects of the research she had gathered for three years, and had highlighted key phrases voters had used to describe why they liked President Rogers. More to the point was a smaller list of phrases she had organized of responses to the question, "Why would you vote for President Rogers again in 1992?"

Intrigued that the question suggested voter intention, Ben was keenly interested in several of the reasons stated. The most frequent centered on Rogers' strong commitment to national defense, his consistently effective negotiations with Russia, and his adeptness in maintaining strong relations with traditional U.S. allies, including England, Germany, France and Japan. Words such as strong, trustworthy, reliable and decisive flooded the verbatim quotes.

"So, our man is a moderate yet diplomatic Hawk, and perceived as having more character than even he might imagine. When I first met him, Laura, he described himself as, 'a Hawk with a conscience.' Sounds like he projects a much stronger, more credible image than either he or Gaines realizes. I'll have to think more about that. So far, 'strength with flexibility' looks like the basic advertising theme. Perhaps headlines along the lines of 'Always On the Alert,' 'Never Drops His Guard, but Keeps an Open Mind.' It's almost like those old World War II posters that helped FDR galvanize backing for his efforts to support England and France."

"You're right about the President, Ben. He is so comfortable in his own skin that he doesn't think about how he got where he is. He just considers his options and keeps moving forward."

Continuing to explore the research. Ben periodically wrote notes on a whiteboard next to the worktable. When Marie walked in to deliver more coffee and sandwiches for lunch, she was impressed with how much progress the two had made in such a short time. She also couldn't help but notice how Ben and Laura seemed so happily content to be working together.

CHAPTER THIRTY-ONE
A Strange Vice-President

June 26, 1992, 3:00 PM

Later that day, the President invited Ben to play a quick set of tennis. It was a welcomed surprise and Ben was ready for a break. As it always had been his habit to immerse himself in the products he advertised, he figured that included the President of the United States. Laura laughed at the idea, saying Rogers was just looking for a tennis adversary who could cause him to break into a sweat. A high school and college athlete, Brad Rogers moved quicker on the tennis court than most men thirty pounds lighter and fifteen years younger. A keen competitor, he made everything he did look easy, including tennis. Putting the data aside, Ben decided to learn more about the subject of the research.

Minutes after Ben nodded to Marie indicating he agreed to the game, she produced a complete tennis outfit in his size. "No wonder we're the world's most powerful nation. This place is an efficient machine," Ben said smiling at Marie. "And Christmas is still six months away!" he exclaimed, boyishly enjoying the presidential seal emblazoned on the items, including the Nike tennis sneakers.

"This brand of racquet is the one the President uses, just to keep things fair," she quipped, taking pleasure in playing Santa to Ben with such enthusiastic results. "I'll take you to the courts. They're not far away."

Laura, knowing two of the most attractive men in her life were about to face off on the courts, briefly fantasized about being the object of their combat. To the victor would go the fair damsel, she laughed to herself.

An hour later, stinging from a 6-2, 6-4 drubbing by a man six years older, Ben vowed to get back on the courts with the President again. "That was a tighter game than you realize, Ben," the President told him on the way to the locker room. "I haven't worked this hard since trying to decide what to get my wife for our anniversary two months ago. Great game. Let's finish this set soon." After graciously introducing Ben to the aging gym attendant, Henry, the President turned toward the small elevator they had arrived in, obviously planning to change elsewhere in the White House.

"Thanks Mr. President. You've given me some great insights into your style, which is probably the same whether it's tennis or diplomacy. I hope to have some initial campaign concepts for you early next week."

"Great!" Rogers said, turning back to face Ben. "Charlie should see them first and I know Laura will be deeply involved. They're my eyes and ears in this campaign," Rogers smiled. "One of the few things I admit to doing well is picking smart people. And it looks like you're one more feather in my cap. If your game is any indication, you may be a workaholic like Charlie. Try to enjoy yourself and forget Vermont."

"I'll try, but selling a President is all pretty new to me. So far, though, I have to admit it's been interesting—and fun," Ben said.

Rogers took another appraising look at Ben, wondering just how much fun he was having, and with whom. Hell, my relationship with Laura is behind me, he reminded himself, and Ben seems like a good guy. Good luck to them if anything exciting is going on.

"Take care of Mr. Coleman, Henry. Maybe a quick massage would be appropriate, unless he's getting that handled elsewhere," Rogers joked, easily reverting to his guy-to-guy style. "See you soon for another game when we can fit it in."

Returning to his desk twenty minutes later, Marie handed Ben a small envelope from Laura. Inside, he found an old-fashioned buff-colored card with a brief note: "Had to run some errands. Enjoyed today. Glad you seemed so interested in the research and I think your ideas are intriguing. See you later at Chet's. Warmly, Laura." Interested in the research! If she only knew. Placing the card carefully in his shirt pocket, he told Marie she could take off and suggested they get going by nine o'clock tomorrow morning. Before leaving, she informed him that Chet had left a message about picking him up at six for their dinner date at his home. Then she wished him good night, reached for her stylish purse and left.

Ben stepped outside of his office, noticing that the frenetic tenor of the morning had subsided only slightly. Suddenly, a contingent of serious-looking young men rounded the far corner, alertly surrounding the slight, dark-haired Vice President. Seeing Ben, Toland stopped with a curt hand signal to his phalanx of security men.

"Mr. Coleman, welcome to Washington. It looks like you're settled in," Toland murmured so softly Ben had to lean toward him to hear clearly. I assumed all politicians were big and loud, he thought.

"Hello Mr. Vice President. Yes, I am getting my bearings with the great help of your staff."

"Not *my* staff," the Vice President said sharply. "In fact, none of my staff has been contacted about your activities here. As one half of the team to be re-elected, I expect to play a big role in shaping and starring in the campaign. I take great pride in knowing how to address the American public, and I want to have a lot of exposure. Considering a vice president as an afterthought is narrow-minded these days. Remember," he said, his voice growing stronger, "I'm only a maniac away from becoming President, so the electorate needs to know me better. I expect to play a key role in the campaign and I better see your name on my appointment calendar soon," he insisted, looking directly at Ben. Then he smiled a crooked smile, revealing several gold inlays, and abruptly resumed his brisk departure from the West Wing.

Recoiling from the brief but acidic meeting with the second most powerful man in the world, Ben thought, "American public." Toland uses the phrase as if he's speaking about a group apart, like we're foreigners or something. Ugly son of a bitch, too, he fumed. What's wrong with this picture? Poor social skills, unattractive, blunt, impolite and obnoxious to boot. Hopefully, Gaines can keep him at arm's length from our work. He's exactly the kind of client who gets in the way by asserting his biases and ignorance, wasting time and money and contributing nothing but confusion. He doesn't even look like an American with those elephant ears and gold teeth, Ben thought, realizing his anger might be causing him to get carried away, as it often did with difficult clients. Just then he heard his phone ringing, so he went back inside to pick it up.

"Ben Coleman," he answered more formally than normal, aware that he was a new person in the White House organization. Hearing Chet's salutation, he smiled and arranged to meet him in ten minutes at the entrance to the building. As he hung up, Ben's thoughts returned to the strange encounter with the Vice President and he decided to mention it to Chet. He knew he would have his hands full with the Vice President and the Chief Justice, both of whom were accustomed to wielding power to get what they wanted. And I thought I had tough clients before! Ben realized with a bit of apprehension. This is pretty fast company and a brand new game for you, Ben Coleman. Better get your game in shape, and maybe reactivate Chet's support as your wingman. This is new airspace and right now you're flying blind.

CHAPTER THIRTY-TWO

Dinner at Chet's

June 26, 1992, 7:45 PM

"Ben, it's so great to see you. You're even better looking now, and staying in shape I see," Connie said with a smile and a wink at Chet, who was sitting next to her across the table from Ben, Laura and Jeff's attractive date. The home-cooked dinner had been a treat for Ben, and he particularly found it fun to meet the twins, Annie and Abby. They were seniors at Bucknell University, where one of the subjects they were avidly studying was advertising.

The twins were awed with Ben's star-like status in the profession and, enjoying their obvious adulation, he kindly invited them to visit his agency when he returned to New York. Chet smiled his appreciation at the gesture, and Connie squeezed the girls' hands in delight. Jeff simply rolled his eyes, finding the fawning over Ben a bit obnoxious. He had little reason to share their admiration. In his eyes, Ben was just another highly-paid consultant who wastes the government's money and then heads back home to spend it. Unaware of Jeff's derision in the glow of the warm reunion with old friends, Ben felt more relaxed and content than he had in a long time.

"Thanks for being so gracious to the twins," Chet said after dinner, when the three men had repaired to his oak-paneled study. "It was nice of you to take an interest in them," he commented, raising a glass of fine cognac in salute.

"Well, being in a family setting is pretty rare for me," Ben replied, returning Chet's gesture before taking a sip of cognac. "My life after the Navy included everything but kids, and now I see how much I've missed. I hope they will take me up on the invitation. We need bright people in the advertising business, and women are taking the industry over from the men—for many good reasons."

When Ben joined the advertising business in 1972 it was strictly a male-dominated society. He still remembered the freezing day in November when he started looking for a job in advertising, based on a decision primarily inspired by reading David Ogilvy's book, *Confessions of An Advertising Man* in college, and his experience serving as the public affairs officer in his Navy jet squadron. After five years of active service, during which time he was awarded three air medals, a Distinguished Flying Cross, and other colorful ribbons of warfare, he was ready for a new adventure. Wearing his one good Navy-blue suit, handmade for thirty dollars in Hong Kong, he had convinced a series of account executives at Barry, DelGaldo & Fredericks that while he knew little about what went on in the agency business, he could learn quickly and would prove himself worthy of their trust. Unlike younger applicants with MBAs from top schools, Ben was more concerned with the agency's success than with the size of his office or potential bonuses. Beginning as an Assistant Account Executive, he was quickly transferred into the Creative Department as a copywriter, where he became adept at understanding how to motivate people to buy the brand being advertised.

He was good with ideas and words, the vital underpinnings of great advertising, and unlike other creative types who resorted to overstatement, outlandish claims, wild promises or silly theatrics, Ben understood that consumers wanted a simple and honest story about why they should buy a certain product. People liked stories and Ben was a gifted storyteller, able to capture a product's core benefit and explain it clearly and persuasively. He spent hours listening to consumer groups discussing what they liked or disliked about everything from cars and airlines to coffee and aftershave lotion. He found success reiterating consumer's own words in attractive scenes with believable spokesmen and spokeswomen. As the impressive sales results of his methods became recognized in the late 1970s and early '80s, the entire industry endeavored to copy his straightforward technique, but rarely succeeded. "Get me someone who can write like that bastard, Coleman, damn it," was the battle cry in many a New York corporate executive suite.

One underpinning of his success was that most of the voiceovers in his TV and radio spots were not done by professional announcers, but by Ben himself, in his warm and whiskey-smooth voice with Walter

Cronkite-like calm and conviction. This technique helped create a new industry of voiceover talent who tried to emulate his persuasive delivery. But the combination of his astute sense of what to say to consumers and how to say it was never quite duplicated.

Now here he was, charged with selling a President. He must find the right words to say to the American public on behalf of President Rogers. Clear, simple, strong-minded points to be said over vivid video action and powerful music would hopefully produce one more satisfied client and another successful TV campaign for his personal reel of commercials, the "video scrapbook" of a life's work that creative people cherish.

Ben's recollections and resolve were interrupted when Jeff and Chet returned from checking their phone messages. "Well, all is calm on the Potomac, which is surprising given the last few days," Chet related. "No word on the perps, or other information about Vermont, but that's up to you, Jeff, and your buddies at the CIA and FBI." Settling into the large leather chair in his study, Chet turned a stern face to his two guests saying, "The whole thing is scary: the style of the gun, whatever it was; taking out discrete targets rather than spraying an entire area, which is typical of terrorist attacks; and the use of what appears to be a trained team rather than a lone assailant, like Oswald and the attack on the Pope a few years ago. Whoever they are, they are rewriting the terrorism book and we had better catch up quickly. I've scheduled drills tomorrow with the entire protection detail. I'm also recalling several retired agents because I need to bulk up the team and don't want to rely on new hires at this point. In fact, hiring will have to be discontinued until we have this figured out."

"Will it be necessary to reduce the President's visibility during the campaign?" Ben asked, knowing that exposure to as many voters as possible along with heavy TV and radio advertising, would be essential to successfully marketing his client.

"Probably, and that's a real problem. If I was paranoid, I would imagine some flaming liberal Democrats ginned this up just to keep Rogers' head down. He is the most effective politician in history and he has them stumped. With Lincoln's oratory but not his rough looks, Reagan's presence but not his polarizing conservatism, Kennedy's charisma but not his religious baggage or liberal leanings, he's way out front as a classic politician, but only to the extent he can be seen and felt by the people. I guess reducing his visibility will make things tougher on you, Ben."

Jeff almost choked over his cognac, but said nothing.

Sensing Jeff's discomfort but agreeing with Chet, Ben turned the conversation to Toland.

"You know, Rogers is such a powerful man from so many standpoints, how did Toland get into the picture? I ran into him earlier tonight in the West Wing and he was anything but my idea of a popular politician."

"Toland is an enigma to all of us. And, I think to Rogers too," Chet replied. "I don't think he likes him. He certainly doesn't give him much to do except travel around the world on diplomatic junkets." Glancing at Gilman, who nodded reluctantly, obviously feeling uncomfortable exposing Ben to too much information,

Chet continued.

"Toland grew up in California with deep conservative roots. He did all the right things: went to Stanford;
married well; earned his law degree at Cornell; ran for
office and built a war chest. Most importantly, he
hooked up with Blackstone in law school. Both their
background files are somewhat slim but show both
made all the right moves to scale the power curve."

"Well, he turned me off, just like Blackstone did the
other night," Ben protested. "You know, Toland
doesn't even seem like an American to me, and Blackstone seems to hail from another planet," Ben said
bluntly, watching Jeff's and Chet's faces for any reactions.

"I have a similar response to Toland and I've been
around him for years," Chet disclosed. "But he's just
as strange as Nixon was or any number of other politicians I could name.

"You have that right, Chet, but I'd rather not get
into it with a civilian, if you get my drift," Jeff said,
glancing at Ben.

Ignoring Jeff, Ben pressed Chet. "You don't see
something weird here?" he asked him intently, setting
the brandy snifter down abruptly. Alert now and sensing the same sort of danger he felt in the dark skies
over Hanoi, Ben said, "From day one, I've been curious about Blackstone. When Gaines enlisted me in this
job, he said the Chief Justice was very interested in my
joining the team. Where is it written that a guy like
Blackstone gets so close to a politician of Roger's stat-
ure without anyone getting curious?"

"Hey, cool your jets, Ben," Chet said, smoothing his
dark hair. "Your creative mind moves a lot faster than

mine, I know, and maybe mine should be faster, but when you are protecting a President you aren't normally concerned about Chief Justices and Vice Presidents. I worry more about the guy in the tan jacket across the lobby who seems transfixed by his newspaper. We've gotten a lot better than Joe McCarthy in ensuring that undesirables don't get into government positions. Not perfect, but much better. Also, Blackstone has been an advocate and strong supporter of Rogers since '78. I think Rogers has always considered Blackstone a sort of father figure and key advisor. I wouldn't want to express such suspicions if I were in your shoes. You write the ads and fly the mission, my friend, and we'll watch Sky Chief's backside."

Watching the two old friends come to terms, Jeff refrained from commenting, but privately wished he could.

Chuckling at Chet's retort, Ben said, "Yeah, well, an imagination is a terrible thing to waste. Guess I'll stick to my creative guns. But I don't plan to feature Toland very heavily in my ads; he'll scare the shit out of the women and children."

"Right, but for now let's get you back to your hotel. You have a big day and some challenging weeks ahead of you, and we wouldn't want you anything but well-rested when you get back to working with the lovely Laura tomorrow," Chet said smiling, giving Ben a good-natured wink. "The car should be here in five minutes, and Jeff and his troops will whisk you back to fun city. Connie wanted Laura to spend the night, so she'll come in with me tomorrow."

Within minutes, Ben had hugged Connie goodbye with a promise to get together soon, had heartily shaken hands with Chet, reluctantly hugged Laura goodbye, and had climbed into a large limousine with Jeff and his girlfriend.. Putting his head back, Ben let his mind wander as the two chatted quietly. Jeff said nothing to him as the limo cruised through suburban streets past comfortable homes and small parks reminiscent of Currier & Ives engravings of a century earlier on its way first to Ben's hotel.

In a trailing car, two men sat silently, keeping their focus on maintaining a careful distance behind the large government vehicle. They didn't need to speak; they had been doing this sort of work for a long time.

CHAPTER THIRTY-THREE

Commutus Interruptus

June 26, 1992, 11:30 PM

Raymond Davenport walked half a block down the muggy, steamy street in an exclusive suburban neighborhood feeling smug and totally satisfied, as he always did after being with Kirin. It had been twenty years now and Kirin still transported him to places he never could have imagined without her. Married to Anita, with two college-aged children, Davenport had established a traditional lifestyle in order to fit into the typical American male stereotype. But he had never been typical, just clever and lucky, with more of the latter. As a senior CIA executive he had access to all of his annual performance reviews, background investigations (conducted every five years per standard CIA procedures), training program records and other background information. Working with a trusted data technician, he had either altered or eradicated any information that might be unfavorable to the advancement of his career, figuring this was common practice among the senior CIA cadre. The technician was rewarded with unwarranted promotions and extra vacation time, so everyone was happy, which was the way things work in Washington. "See no evil, hear no evil, but maybe do a little evil," he thought, arriving at the black town car waiting for him at the curb.

"Roland my man, right on time," he mumbled to the driver with an alcohol-induced slur as he slipped into the back seat. "Sorry to keep you up so late. Let's head on home." Settling his heavy body into the soft leather seat, he glanced out and noticed a similar black limo headed in the opposite direction. New York is not the only city that never sleeps, he thought, wondering who else was out at so late an hour. Hell, it could be anyone in this crazy city.

"No problem, Mr. Davenport," Roland responded. "Overtime is my life, and Carla loves it when I am out making money and not around to bother her and the kids. I'm hungry, so I may stop for something quick on the way back. Want something?"

"Uh, no thanks, I've just had my fill," Davenport said with a wry grin. Anita is going to wonder why I'm having so many late meetings, he thought, but this job pays well and she doesn't mind spending the money. It sure seems like my life is all about doing what other people want, so sometimes I need to do something for myself, he rationalized. Hell, no one cares anyway. Everyone I know has someone on the side. Why shouldn't I get a little comfort from a bottle and a woman, especially one as hot as Kirin? Shit, she still has it after all these years. The things she does must be illegal somewhere. That little tongue of hers never knows when to quit. Maybe other guys needed special pills to get it up, but I only need Kirin. And she only needs me, or so she says. But I believe her, especially after all these years. A perfect arrangement, he assured himself, putting his fingers to his nose to see if he could detect any lingering perfume from her.

Minutes later, his reverie was disturbed when the car phone rang. Who would be calling at this time on a Friday night, Davenport wondered as he reached for the headset and pressed the button to raise the glass partition behind the driver's seat.

"Ray. It's David. How are you and where are you?" rasped the Chief Justice, sounding as if he were close by. "I know it's late, but I wanted to tell you what your associates at the FBI discovered about the assassination attempt and the weapon used."

"Christ, David, it's late and I'm heading home from headquarters following a briefing with the President earlier today. Can't this wait till the morning? I'm really bushed," he complained, trying to conceal his irritation at Blackstone for finding him in his town car, and for knowing things about the assassination attempt that he should have been informed about first.

"No, actually Ray, it can't wait. Things are moving fast and I wouldn't want you to be left out of the loop on this stuff. You always keep me abreast of the Cuban drug operation, and I want to return the favor. Apparently, the weapon used in Vermont was a computer-guided 50mm cannon with a gun controller programmed with photos of the person or persons to be shot. That's how it can locate and shoot its target even in a crowd, just like it did with the Secret Service guys in the group of guests at the resort. It kills only its target, avoiding any collateral damage, you know, like other people, and hits only the intended victim in *both* eyes at the same time! Amazing, scary technology that was developed somewhere in Russia. Did you know about this?"

"No, never heard of anything like it, but it sounds like something the Ruskies would invent. They always want their kills to be clean but harrowing, using terror weapons that scare the shit out of people, like poison darts that spring out of shoes, and stuff like that. So, what do you want me to do about it now? I'm almost home, for Chris' sake."

"Well, you're not going to believe this, but one of the three gun units the FBI found is parked at a gas station near your house. We're not sure how it got there, or why, but I want you to join several units that soon will be converging on it. We need your immediate leadership and you're already close to the scene. This is an FBI kind of thing, ya' know? You can beat Hoover's boys to the punch, big fella, and it'll make you look good to be Johnny on the spot, my boy." Davenport flinched at the familiarity of the remark, suddenly losing his composure, his face breaking into a sweat.

"On the scene, what are you talking about? And just how did you find out about all this, David? It sounds crazy. I'm hanging up and calling my watch agent at Langley," he almost screamed into the phone. Hastily pressing the intercom, he told Roland to pull over.

As Davenport pushed the numbers for the CIA watch office on his secure line, the town car pulled to a stop near an all-night gas station. Roland turned around to speak to him, but with the glass partition closed he just pointed to the snack bar near the gas pumps to indicate he was going in for something. Davenport waved him off to focus on the phone call. Hearing the sound of the limo's front door closing, Davenport looked around the area where he sat alone, with only the sound of the engine idling.

The car phone rang again while he was waiting for his CIA connection. Seeing it was Blackstone again, Davenport disconnected his call to Langley and picked up.

"Ray, it's David again. Sorry for the confusion, but you don't have to do what I just told you. The units were called off. The report was a fake, apparently called in by whoever was behind the attack in Vermont. But the information about the terror gun was correct. They said its enclosure was constructed to look like a boat smokestack and that the gun zoomed out of it to lock onto its pre-programmed video target, just like on the yacht that blew up at Basin Harbor."

"Okay, David. Thanks for the call. I guess I'll continue on home now, once my driver gets back from the snack shop at this gas station," he muttered looking toward the store, but not seeing Roland. Must be in the can, he thought. He should have done that while he was waiting for me. With the glow of the alcohol and the sexual encounter with Kirin fading, he was feeling tired and impatient about Blackstone's call and his desire to get home. What's taking Roland so long, he wondered? Then noticing David was still on the line, he asked, "David, are you still there?"

"Yes, Ray. Say, do you happen to see a shiny white pump, to the left of the gas pumps in front of you? It looks like a smokestack, Ray. Can you see it? Roll down your window, Ray. I want you to see it clearly."

Automatically, almost hypnotically, Ray rolled down the right side window and saw the shiny pump about fifty feet away. It stood oddly alone and almost appeared to sit on a low trailer, but why would that be? I must be more tired than I thought, he yawned. Where the hell is Roland? I have to get home.

"Ray, do you see the pump? Doesn't it look real? If you had been at Basin Harbor, you would have pretty much ignored it, wouldn't you, because it looks so authentic? Ray, are you listening to me, don't you get it? Well, Ray, it gets you. Goodbye, and thanks from all of us for a job well done," Blackstone cackled. Suddenly sober and certain of what was happening, Ray reached for the opposite door handle to escape. His last mistake, as it turned out, was to look back at the oddly placed pump and the incongruous appendage rising out of it with its black snout swiveling toward him. In the next instant gun and man connected, and the rear compartment of the town car exploded.

The ensuing investigation would reveal that twenty well-grouped rounds had been expended into the four-foot-square area, with no other part of the automobile incurring any damage. Most of the rounds were concentrated on both of the victim's eyes and on his lower abdomen, obliterating his sexual organs, but not damaging other parts of his body. A review of CIA records kept for over half a century would later reveal no similar style of killing, with the exception of a few 1930s Cosa Nostra murders in and around New York City. But those had included slit throats or other similar cruelty. This murder was unique in its high-tech accuracy and gruesome simplicity.

Just a few miles away, Blackstone lay back on the same leather sofa that recently had held Davenport, enjoying the oral ministrations of a beautiful, dark-haired woman. Placing the phone down, he admired the lovely face looking up at him, eyes holding his, mouth and fingers busy.

"Turn around now and enjoy the fruits of your labor, my beautiful thing," Blackstone said, as she turned to reveal her smooth, tawny backside, sliding down his length in a slow, sensual dance. Bracing herself with her hands on the glass-top coffee table in front of the sofa, she glanced back at him with moist eyes. Eyes of ecstasy, he thought. Eyes that would see only his from now on. He couldn't see her face once she turned from him, concentrating on the act she knew so well. He also couldn't see the tears of fear, and sadness that welled up in her eyes and fell silently on the thick glass.

"Oh, that's good, so good. Just the two of us now, Kirin. Just us."

CHAPTER THIRTY-FOUR

A Day of Rest

June 27, 1992, 8:50 AM

Slightly hung over from the exotic cognac at Chet's and two more at the hotel's bar, Ben took his time in the shower. He thought briefly of Sunny. Had that encounter only been a few days ago? It feels like another era; an era of random relationships that is history now, Ben realized. As his thoughts turned to Laura, he felt pleased he had little room in his mind for anyone else.

Saturdays were like any other day in timeless Washington, D.C., so today would be just another workday. But perhaps I can find a way to build in some fun, Ben thought. He pondered calling Laura, ostensibly about their discussions of yesterday, but was interrupted by the phone ringing by the bedside.

"Coleman," he muttered, rubbing his hair with a thick white towel emblazoned with the hotel's ornate gold crest.

"Hi Flyboy," Chet hailed, "I know it's Saturday

and a workday, but Jeff and I thought we ought to show you around the Chevy Chase Golf Course where the President will be playing later. It's the best in the city, bar none. And they let women in a few years ago, so you'll have something to take your mind off your loneliness," he laughed. "We could start off with brunch. What do you say?"

"Well, I was going to ask Laura to put in some more time, but it is Saturday and I'm not that strict a taskmaster," he said, suddenly remembering telling Marie he would see her at the office.

"I sense an ulterior motive, but I won't challenge your professionalism, Ben. We'll pick you up in forty-five minutes, so grab some coffee and read *The Post*. The Vermont attack is still front page news."

Replacing the receiver, Ben approached the closet to select clothes appropriate for golf. His Porsche had arrived two days earlier with two suitcases packed by the ever-capable Helen Mayfield. She even had included a box of cigars and a cutter, cuff links, and assorted toiletries. A bottle of his favorite scotch was the icing on the cake.

As he turned to enter the bathroom, the phone rang again.

"Ben, we have a big problem," Chet said in a voice so agitated that Ben dropped his towel on the parquet floor.

"The Special Assistant to the Director at the CIA, a guy named Davenport, was found murdered in his limo in Bethesda. Not sure why it took so long for Jeff or me to hear about it. No one noticed the car all night because it just looked like a wreck abandoned in the parking area of a gas station. The rear passenger compartment was completely destroyed but the rest of the car was undamaged. Davenport took over twenty rounds in the head and groin. And just like Vermont, shot in both eyes. No sign of the CIA driver who had been with him for years.

"I have to get out there and Jeff is joining me, so we'll have to postpone chasing the little white ball around," Chet said. "This is going to be a big mess because no one has a clue what Davenport was doing there. Won't be long before this is on the wires and all hell will break loose. Shit, a high-level assassination within twenty minutes of the White House. There will be one large shit-storm, you can bet."

Before Ben could say anything, the connection was broken. A cold wave of apprehension he had not felt since launching at night with orders to bomb the bridges south of Hanoi washed over him. Trying to clear his head, he quickly shaved and dressed. Wearing Levi's Dockers, a yellow polo shirt and polished Bass Weejun loafers, he headed to the dining room for a quick breakfast before hailing a cab to his office.

As the cab pulled out into the dense Saturday morning traffic, Ben realized he should call Laura, who would likely be frantic at the news of another attack. *Hell, she's probably been at the White House for an hour while you were considering playing golf. Time to focus, Ben,* he told himself sternly. *Now, more than ever. Save the fun for after you deliver the goods.*

The driver of the dark car parked a safe distance behind the cab turned to his partner and joked, "Maybe we should give him a lift one of these times, Ori. Make a few bucks on the side!" he laughed, putting the car into gear and moving quickly into traffic.

"I like it better when he's with the redhead, what a looker! She should be easy enough to grab after this caper is over, and that shouldn't be too long. Right, pal?"

CHAPTER THIRTY-FIVE

Just a Madison Avenue Hotshot

June 27, 1992, 10:10 AM

"Ben, what are you doing here?" Laura exclaimed, standing in his office doorway, her red hair slightly askew.

"Laura, I thought you'd be here so I came right away. Chet called and told me about the Davenport killing."

"So, you heard the horrible news? Davenport's been murdered, actually assassinated from what they say, and here you are plugging away on advertising, of all things!" She looked at him incredulously.

"Laura, I just got here," he said defensively, feeling somewhat confused by her tone. Then he noticed her flushed appearance and understood she was upset, even afraid. Quietly he pulled her to him, realizing how deeply he cared that she feel safe and unafraid, the way she said her father used to make her feel.

Yielding to his embrace, Laura slumped against his

chest with her arms limp at her side, shaking slightly with release. I shouldn't do this, she thought, but it feels so good and I can't take much more of this crazy killing. Ben's arms are so strong, just like Brad's, just like Dad's. I'm glad he's here.

"Thanks, Ben. I'm sorry I broke down," she cried, clutching him and realizing she didn't want to break the moment. "Everyone is confused and upset. What is going on?" Continuing to hold her, Ben eased her to the nearby couch. Her shivering subsided and she slowly began to relax. Finally she looked at him and smiled slightly, embarrassed. "I am really sorry. It's just I've never been close to this sort of thing before, Maybe seen it in movies, but not for real."

"Listen, let's go to the cafeteria and get some coffee. I can't really concentrate knowing how upset you are," Ben consoled her. "Come on."

Walking past Marie, who was surrounded by several people looking nervous and concerned, the two made their way down the corridor. The staff they passed seemed to be rushing faster than normal and while attempting to appear calm, fear was clearly etched in their eyes. Arriving at the large cafeteria, Ben bought coffee, and at the last minute decided to get two brownies. "Perfect for national emergencies," he asserted, much to Laura's quiet amusement. Pleased to see her relaxing, Ben guided her to a remote table.

Minutes later, Chet and Jeff, fresh from a Presidential briefing on the recent situation, strode quickly through the cafeteria intent on a quick lunch. When they spied Ben and Laura, they approached them. Jeff immediately asked why they were in the West Wing.

"Where else would we be?" Laura responded. "We

all have our jobs, Jeff, and they happen to be right here."

"Hey, sorry. I didn't mean to imply anything, it just seems like the entire White House staff suddenly descended on this place and I'm not sure why. What can they do?"

"I guess in a firefight, everyone turns to what they know best," Ben replied, his eyes fixed on the CIA agent. "And that's what we're seeing here. A firefight, right here in River City."

"He's right," Chet said sitting down across from Ben. With concern clouding his face, he asked "What was that you were saying last night about Toland and Blackstone? You know, about them being odd, out of place or whatever."

"I said Toland doesn't seem like he is American and Blackstone appears other worldly, out of some foreign, earlier era. Like he studied old Hollywood black-and-white movies to develop his style. That's what my wild imagination, as you referred to it, came up with; and I'm still wondering about them. Have they been attending your briefings?"

"Matter of fact, no, come to think of it," Jeff said, looking quickly at Chet. "And the Vice President should have been there, for gosh sakes. He's always getting his nose into security issues, so where is he now when we have a big one?" Reaching for the buzzing pager on his belt, he said, "Well, back to it. We have a code yellow meeting, Chet. See you folks later."

Giving them a half salute as they departed, Ben turned to Laura, who held his eyes with hers. God, she is gorgeous, he thought, and she really felt wonderful in my arms, fit just right. Wish it wasn't only fear that made her fall into my arms. He smiled at her, hoping to keep her spirits up.

"Let's leave now, too. We can't do much in all this craziness and I need some air," Ben told her. "We can get in my car and get lost, okay?" She smiled back and nodded quickly, relieved to be breaking free from the highly-charged environment.

Inside the elevator on their way back up to the Oval Office, Jeff massaged the back of his neck and turned to Chet saying, "Other-worldly, un-American looking? Your buddy is a good guy, but he ought to focus that imagination of his on advertising and let us worry about the bad guys. We've had our share of concerns about Blackstone for sure. The calls over the years, the encryptions, his close relationship to Rogers," he continued while Chet listened thought-fully. "But I think Ben Boy is off the mark. Your Jet Jock is just a Madison Avenue hotshot who ought to stick to advertising."

As the elevator doors opened, the two men exited, moving hurriedly down the hall past the crush of rushing people. "Give it a break, Jeff. You're just pissed that he flew jets, something you wanted to do. Don't hold it against him. There's a lot more to Ben Coleman than you realize, maybe even more than I realize. But one thing you can count on: he's smart and doesn't bullshit. Maybe he's actually onto something. If I were you, I'd check it out more thoroughly."

Entering the Oval Office, Jeff did not have an op-portunity to respond, but his emotions were white hot, especially regarding Chet's dig about his never having made it into the Navy's flight program. Goddamn knee, he thought, still favoring it slightly as they took their place near the front of the expansive office, close to the President. He found it hard to believe some advertising guy might have noticed something that had eluded both the FBI and CIA. No way, he thought.

CHAPTER THIRTY-SIX

Exercising the Speedster

June 27, 1992, 12:16 PM

Ben's Porsche 356 convertible speedster zipped out of the hotel parking lot and raced towards the country-side west of downtown. The little red rocket, deftly piloted by Ben, quickly left the madness behind as they hurtled through low tree-studded hills that once were home to the Kanawha Indians. Laura closed her eyes and laid her head back, trying to recall the last time she had been whisked away in a convertible.

Ben glanced her way, smiling broadly as he down-shifted through a tight curve in the road, large colonial homes and tall trees speeding by in a blur. He wished he could read her thoughts, but concentrated instead on his driving.

Growing up in the pleasant outskirts of Chicago, Laura had enjoyed the typical existence of a suburban high school prom queen, dating the jocks, making sure she wore the right clothes and got invited to the right parties. She was carefully raised by her exceptionally beautiful mother and adored by her airline-pilot father. The oldest of four children, she realized on her eighteenth birthday that chasing boys, smoking forbidden cigarettes and sneaking beers were not for her. When the eldest child "early maturity" syndrome took hold she chose Northwestern University in Evanston, Illinois as her college objective. Graduating with the class of 1976, Laura experienced the waning of Vietnam college protests and the slow return of universities, and in fact the entire country, to a more sober and conservative era of recovery. Discovering her passion for understanding people's behavior, Laura pursued an undergraduate degree in psychology, followed by a Masters in Human Development at Manhattan's New York University.

Lured by the excitement and power of politics, she worked in Mayor Ed Koch's administration in the Department of Mental Health. When she met Congressman Bradley Rogers at a political symposium, she was struck not only by his ambitious vision for health care, but by his boyish looks and sex appeal. At the suggestion of a colleague, she applied and was accepted for a position on his staff with responsibilities that included helping draft mental health legislation. Exhilarated by the new responsibilities thrust upon her as she moved to the center of the political universe, she also discovered there was no shortage of handsome young men in Washington, D.C. who were interested in penetrating her regal beauty. Laura began burning the candle at both ends, but within a few months she officially took herself out of the running after a passionate weekend with Congressman Rogers in Bermuda. At a Department of Health conference on Early Aids Treatment, he had suggested they take a well-earned break and join a small group on a friend's yacht for an overnight cruise. Telling only her best friend of her plans, Laura had received a vigorous thumbs-up and "Go Girl" before rushing off to pack her bag. As it turned out, she needn't have gone to the trouble; she didn't wear much of anything for the rest of the weekend. Returning to Washington Monday morning on the Congressman's private plane, she dozed all the way back with visions of the bright blue Atlantic sky and Brad Rogers dancing in her head.

For the next three years, she managed to remain close to Rogers while maintaining a professional profile that seemed to fool everyone. When Rogers announced his run for the Presidency in 1987, he made two proposals to Laura. The first was he wanted her to take charge of the polling operation that would provide voter information critical to his campaign. The second was that they terminate their relationship before it was discovered, which would wreck any opportunity for either of them in this or any other city that mattered politically.

Conflicted by the opportunity to be deeply involved in the politics she had come to love and, on the other hand, losing the man she had come to love, Laura accepted the first proposal and ignored the second. She thrust herself into the Washington social scene with a cool and sophisticated persona, creating numerous valuable allegiances and relationships that cemented her role in the campaign. Several times in the next few months, Rogers lost his resolve, accosting her in her office or calling with urgent demands to meet again. With her new aloofness firmly in place, she calmly reminded him of his request and what it required of both of them. Crestfallen, Rogers actually contemplated discontinuing his campaign, going public with their earlier affair and departing politics to be with Laura. However, the lure of being the most powerful man in the world and achieving his legislative goals took precedence, and he found himself being faithful to his wife for the first time in twenty-six years of marriage. He easily won the election, which had been skillfully managed by David Blackstone. When sworn into office in January 1989, his wife held the Bible while Laura looked on from a dais thirty feet away, her blue eyes misting as the most remarkable man she had ever met was formally wedded to the leadership of the nation.

At the inauguration, a Navy officer standing near her, sharply decked out in his blue uniform with aviator wings of gold and a white bridge cap, was immediately taken by her. He wondered what would cause such a gorgeous woman to weep at a Presidential Inauguration, and he boldly promised himself to help ease her pain. Much to his surprise, when he introduced himself moments later, she grabbed his arm saying, "Let's go Commander. I'm ready to celebrate and I hope you party as good as you look in that uniform." With a quick glance of appreciation to the heavens, Commander Rick Whitehouse guided her through the crowd and toward his staff car, wondering if his first strike in this wild city would be "a hit or a miss" in fighter jet lexicon.

Two days later, Laura returned to her Chevy Chase apartment five pounds lighter and thoroughly aware of what it meant to "Fly Navy." She never looked back, but began moderating her personal activities, letting her new job dominate her waking hours.

So here I am with another jet jock, she thought to herself as she returned from remembrances of the past. He's not as tall, but certainly is a very nice specimen. Too bad he wasn't around four years ago. It's been a quiet period, too quiet, she reasoned with herself as she glanced over at Ben's clean-cut face, firm jaw, blue eyes and *hair*! What has happened to men and their hair? Even guys with nice hair have it cut too short, she grumped. What kind of trend is that? Hair should be allowed to flourish, and flourish it does on my friend Ben here.

"Where are we going?" she shouted over the wind, noticing there were fewer houses lining the road now.

"How would I know, I just wanted to get away from there," Ben said as they crested a hill, revealing a small village in the depths of deep green woods. Arriving at a crossroads, Ben instinctively turned left and pulled off the road in front of a rambling white lodge advertising rooms and an old-fashioned tavern, or Taverne as the gilded sign proclaimed. After finding a remote spot in the gravel parking lot, Ben opened Laura's door with an Edwardian flourish, mentioning a much-desired drink and perhaps lunch, "If you are of a mind, my lady." Laughing, Laura grasped his arm and walked with him up an ancient flagstone path into the quaint restaurant.

"You probably always thought a bar and grill tavern was just that, a bar with food, right?" he asked, holding an antique wooden armchair away from an oval-shaped maple table for her. "It really refers to a bar with metal grills, like that one over there," he gestured across the comfortable paneled room where a long bar was bordered by ancient metal grillwork. "In early times, barkeeps had to pull those heavy metal screens across the bar when they closed up for the night. If they didn't protect their stock of liquor, it would be gone by morning. No honesty among thieves, especially in those days. So, now you know about a bar and grill." A waitress who had arrived at their table a moment before and had listened to his description thanked him for explaining the origins of the term.

"Oh, he's just a New York know-it-all," Laura quipped, smiling at the woman. "You know, driving a woman into the countryside against her will and plying her with drinks and lunch at an out-of-the-way hotel with high hopes!" she giggled, suddenly feeling far removed from her normal life, and happily so. Ben and the waitress joined in her mirth, then the waitress took their order: one dirty martini for Ben and a vodka gimlet for Laura. "A gimlet! Well, that's unexpected. I haven't heard one ordered since my Mom used to enjoy them when I was young. But then, Laura, you are a timeless woman. I appreciate that, but it does make you very mysterious, and I like to unravel mysteries, kind of like I enjoy solving *New York Times* crossword puzzles."

"Me too," she breathed, starting to feel happy and relaxed. "This is probably the place for that. Look at the old gaming room through that doorway, with little tables for checkers and dominoes and other games. This place is truly out of another era. How did you find it?"

"I didn't. My trusty Porsche speedster did. Someday cars will be able to read your mind and take you where you want to go with just a thought. But my little jet already does that," he smiled, reflecting on how Laura and the Porsche were really quite similar— sleek, gorgeous, sinuous and sporty—yet classic and, hopefully, breathtaking at high speed.

Almost reading his mind, she said, "Your car is so much like you—sporty yet sophisticated, quick and powerful. But then, your profession would most likely cause you to be discerning when buying a car. You would want it to be more than just a vehicle. You'd want to communicate something, I imagine. Is that true?"

Usually, Ben would sidestep such a personal question, especially one that struck so close to the truth, but Laura seemed so…what? So sincerely interested in who he was instead of just impressed by his business success? Nice, he thought. "Yes, the Porsche was on purpose," he divulged. "A bonus several years ago that I had not expected was happily converted into the purchase of a classic 356 speedster in the only color worth having—red."

Having lived well, Ben generally shopped well, and when it came to cars he emulated his father in selecting large German cars like Mercedes and BMWs. Patriotic only up to a point, Ben felt his auto purchases should reward manufacturers who had earned his business. In his late teens and twenties, however, he had been thrilled by the muscle cars of the 1950s and early '60s. Their throaty exhaust rumble and exhilarating speed were just what a young pilot wanted to be driving. His first car purchase had been a new 1967

Mustang GT convertible with twin pipes and bold white racing stripes, bought in Pensacola with his first paycheck as a new Ensign and student pilot. He and his classmates celebrated their new "hotshot" status by buying brand new cars at the numerous dealerships along the "Miracle Mile" adjacent to the air station. The local auto salesmen profited nicely. They called it "The Pensacola Turkey Shoot" and veteran salesmen could predict, usually with uncanny accuracy, exactly what brand and model each new officer would want the minute he strode through the dealership's front door.

Ben had proudly driven his British racing green Mustang back to the base, his head pivoting excitedly to see if any classmates were nearby and to ensure that no other drivers threatened his "cherry ride." Parking in the far reaches of the Bachelor Officers Quarters parking lot at the training station, he draped a new car cover over the Mustang to protect it from blowing sand and the intense Florida sunshine, pulled out his personal gear, and checked into his new home away from home.

Flight training immediately consumed Ben's every waking hour, from "0 dark thirty" flights to hours of ground school punctuated with more flights and more schooling. It turned out to represent a watershed period in Ben's life. An average student in high school and college, he had been stimulated by few subjects beyond English Literature and Women 101. He liked the dual benefits that a liberal arts curriculum offered: pretty girls and gay professors, because both groups liked him a great deal and rewarded him accordingly with hot dates and good grades. Once he entered flight training, however, he grew serious and immersed himself in a rigorous regimen of engineering, aeronautics, navigation and other technical courses. Ben realized he had better master the subject matter or he would risk his ass when he finally got the opportunity to fly an airplane on his own. As a result, he consistently scored at the top of his class in academics and in actual flights, which amazed his parents, especially his father. "If I had studied in college half as hard as I do here, I would have been in pre-med," he joked with them over the phone one evening. "But, it's my butt that's on the line here."

A few months later, his father had proudly pinned the Navy "Wings of Gold" on Ben's white uniform, quietly telling him "I always wanted to fly. Now you have done it and I'm real proud of you. The world is all yours now, Ben. Good luck and be safe—for your mother's sake, of course." Then smiling and slapping Ben on the arm, he returned to his seat in the audience of other thrilled parents and friends.

"How's your drink?" Laura said, putting hers down and blotting her lips with a napkin. "Mine is strong. These country folks know how to make their customers happy."

"Oh, great, yep, just fine," he responded, returning to the present and her steady gaze. He wondered if the buzz he felt was from the drink or from Laura's stimulating presence. Probably a little of both. Looking around the tavern, he was reminded of the roadhouse movie set in the Bing Crosby film "A White Christmas." And it's just as schmaltzy, he thought, laughing out loud.

"What's so funny, Ben Boy?" Laura asked with a

coquettish smile.

Immediately conscious that she was flirting with him, Ben found himself enjoying it. "Oh, just thinking of things of long ago, but also of here and now. I guess I was comparing you to my car, a well-oiled, sleek machine capable of winning whatever race you enter." Suddenly embarrassed by his outright expression of his private thoughts, Ben hesitated.

With dancing eyes, Laura reached for his hand. "Well-oiled, sleek, capable. Hmm, I guess I should feel complimented." With her hand on his, she took another sip of her drink, enjoying every bit of the flirtation. She quietly recorded it in the secret garden of her mind that had been lying fallow for quite some time. Inadvertently, she squeezed his hand then self-consciously pulled it back to smooth her hair.

"Another drink?" he asked leaning forward, looking as though he might kiss her right then and there.

"No, not right now. This is so nice. I really feel wonderful. Maybe in a few minutes, Ben."

They sat quietly in the warmth of the moment, enjoying the serenity and peace of feeling safe and far from the harsh realities of the world.

Outside, a large car pulled into the circular drive, tires crunching on the gray gravel. As it pulled into a parking spot at the end of the lot the driver said, "Well, the little transmitter is just chirping away, Dmitri. The way he was speeding, I'm surprised it didn't fall off the Porsche."

Later that day, an informal convoy consisting of a small red Porsche and the larger, non-descript American-made car trailing behind it, wound its way over the steamy asphalt path leading back into the confines of the nation's capital. In one car, two people were quietly celebrating their afternoon escape to the country. In the other, two people were complaining about their afternoon trip into the country.

CHAPTER THIRTY-SEVEN
The VEEP Speaks Russian?

June 27, 1992, 5:30 PM

The West Wing garage reverberated with the roar of the Porsche's powerful six-cylinder engine as Ben wheeled into the second level. Carefully shutting the engine down, he looked over at Laura. "End of the tour, madam. Thanks for coming, and thanks for flashing your parking pass at the guard," he joked. "Almost as good as a trip to New England. Fun, wasn't it?"

"Yes, it was, and you are a great travel guide, even if you don't know where you're going! It must be nice to trust your instincts with such excellent results," she said, clapping her hands just like a little girl. Ben felt his heart thump, his hand moving to his chest before he could stop the subconscious reaction. Wow, this is too much, he thought. Forty-five years old and I finally feel what Lord Byron was talking about in those poems. "Heartfelt" was a word Ben had always wondered about; what was it like? Now he knew he had a

235

clue.

Opening the car door and helping Laura from the low-slung sports car, he said, "Guess we should check in to see what's transpired. Wouldn't want to appear disinterested, right?"

As they ascended the stairs leading into the West Wing offices, they heard car doors slam shut on the parking level below and voices speaking loudly in a foreign language engaged in a heated exchange. Although people of many different nationalities frequented the West Wing, Ben sensed something sinister. Placing a hand on Laura's shoulder, he eased her out of sight against the wall and leaned over the railing to peer around the corner onto the floor below. The argument continued unabated. Standing twenty feet away, two men stood in the shadows away from the overhead lighting. Even though their backs were to Ben, one was instantly identifiable. The other was taller, bulkier and more formally dressed, and was forcefully gesticulating with papers in one hand and with the other pointing toward the adjacent property. The smaller, slight man with dark hair seemed unmoved by the other man's point-of-view. He said little, except "Nyet!" and a few other indistinguishable comments." Not fully understanding the situation, but realizing they should not be seen, Ben put a finger over his lips and guided Laura toward the entry door.

"Who are they?" she asked once inside, her hand grasping his arm.

"Hush, let's just head to my office."

Moving quickly through the corridor, which was still full of frenetic activity, they avoided eye contact with the crowd of people moving quickly around them and eased their way to Ben's office. He closed the door behind them as Laura sat down in a chair across from his desk. Sinking into his large desk chair with a feeling of relief and foreboding, he glanced idly at the pile of pink phone messages stacked near the lamp. Suddenly, there was a loud knock on the door. Looking cautiously at Laura, he opened it and was relieved to see Chet and Jeff standing there, but they both looked upset.

"Where have you guys been?" Chet inquired heatedly.

"The answer is 'out.' And oh, by the way, did you know the VEEP speaks Russian?" Shutting the door, Ben proceeded to briefly tell them what had just occurred.

"Now, we have an even bigger problem," Chet said to Jeff. Easing his lanky frame onto the sofa and leaning forward toward Ben and Laura, he said, "And you two are part of the solution."

"Well, okay, I always liked 'Mission Impossible,'" Ben said sitting on the edge of his desk so Jeff could sit down.

"This, my friend, has to be 'Mission Very Possible' with no mistakes," Chet asserted. "So listen very carefully. There's not a lot of time." Then he looked over at Jeff, who immediately walked to the large whiteboard where he wrote one word in capital letters: SITUATION.

CHAPTER THIRTY-EIGHT

Un-Selling the President

June 27, 1992, 6:13 PM

"First, Ben, I owe you an apology," Jeff said, his face set in a hard grimace. "It's difficult for a Gyrene to admit to a Navy squid but what the hell, when someone has it right—even if they pulled it out of their everlovin' ass—I'm the first to say, right on. And you got it right. There is 'something rotten in Denmark' and we're in the same building with what's smellin' bad," he said, in a voice reverting to his native South Texas drawl, something that happened only when he was moving into deep battle readiness. "You two are hereby sworn to secrecy, mostly for your own safety. This 'situation' is bigger than all of us.

"First, as you know, there was the attack on the President a few days ago, then Davenport got wasted in his limo late at night with his trusted driver missing, presumed dead or kidnapped. Too many people getting shot at by some kind of wild weapon we've

never seen, which was probably dreamed up in a foreign lab. What gets really strange is the connection to a
bunch of phone intercepts we've been getting at Langley for several years, sixty-four messages over the
past six years to be exact. When we cross-referenced
the calls to President Rogers, we found they started
about two years before he decided to run for President—August 5th of 1986 to be exact. The phone calls
all emanated from scramblers we were able to isolate
to phones in several locations: at the Chief Justice's
house, beginning well before he was appointed to the
High Court; at the Vice President's house, ever since
he was elected as a Northern California Senator; and at
several other locations worldwide, involving the Assistant to the CIA Director and other people connected
to California or national politics. We only know the
calls took place, but we have no way of knowing the
content of the conversations. I've had a small team
working this angle for several years, mostly because
we wondered why the Chief Justice would have a sophisticated scrambler that was not government-issued.
In fact, the FBI is responsible for all such devices in the
U.S. and they have no record of allocating this kind of
equipment to either Blackstone or Toland. So add all
that up and you smell something spelled conspiracy.
Being overly cautious is part of my job, but whistling
an alarm this time feels justified. Just does," he summarized, looking around the room at the shocked
faces. "So our little group knows way too much, but
we may be the only ones who can do something about
it."

Clutching her stomach, Laura glanced at Ben and
Jeff, then turned to Chet. "There's nothing about the

President that would allow for his having any kind of a role in a plot like this. Who would they be plotting against? Who?" she asked, looking again at each man.

"Laura," Chet cautioned, "no one is thinking the President is part of this. What we're thinking, getting convinced of in fact, is that he's been carefully duped for years and that he is the unwitting target of some sort of conspiracy. All of the others surround him in government. They've been totally involved for years, and probably manipulated his climb to the Presidency. Remember it was Blackstone who ran Rogers' campaign. He raised the money from somewhere and pretty much determined the direction of the campaign, who Rogers saw, what Rogers said. Ben mentioned to me the other day that Blackstone had grilled him about the new campaign the minute he met him at the Yeltsin reception. And you even suspected Toland wasn't 'American.' Right, Ben?"

"Yeah, that's right, but I can't believe this is happening. It's like a runaway Hollywood movie, complete with the bad guys. Really bad guys," Ben remarked as he stood up and walked around his desk to grab the water pitcher and some glasses. "Water anyone?" Feeling slightly useful, Ben handed each person a glass before draining his in three quick gulps.

"The capper is your encounter with the Vice President just now," Chet continued. "There is no record of his studying or speaking Russian. The transcripts from his last two years of high school and Stanford show his language curriculum consisted only of Spanish, with average grades. Otherwise, he was a straight A student. The man he was talking to in the garage must have been General Sergei Petrovich Petrov. Fits your description.

"Petrov has been around for decades. He was the Russian top dog in the Cuban missile fracas with Kennedy. We think he knew Kennedy would get tough with restrictions, like the Naval embargo that finally did the trick. We also think they withdrew to feign compliance with the new American President, but meanwhile, they gained valuable intel on our military presence in that region. Russians always take the long view, like the Chinese. Petrov probably hoped the U.S. would figure we had won the war, not just the battle, which turned out to be true. It gave him years to operate quietly behind the scenes; just what we're not sure, but there is certainly a lot of Russian armor secreted away on the sandy, sunny island of Cuba that the Mob so loved in the '50s. Ever wonder why Fidel and the Mob were so pissed off at Kennedy? Instead of reopening Cuba to U.S. residents, Kennedy cut both of them off from all that U.S. gambling money, costing the Mob and Fidel millions, billions. Supposedly, Fidel kicked the Mob out of Havana, but he was actually planning to let them operate in the Guantanamo region so they could be the money machine that he planned to use in exporting his personal Socialist vision into other South American countries. Why did we assume he only wanted to dominate Cuba? He wanted the whole South American enchilada. But instead, the U.S. built a Navy base on Guantanamo and refused to allow Americans into Cuba, or Cubans into the United States. End of game. No mob money for Fidel, or no money we can find beyond what the Ruskies give him."

Ben, drawing small blocks with names linked by

dotted lines on his legal pad, said, "How does Blackstone figure into all this, and the Vice President? What do they have to gain from a plot to assassinate the President or from killing Davenport? They helped put the President where he is, and Davenport was a key person protecting them and the country. The whole group goes way back in their relationships. It doesn't make sense, suspecting them in all of this because of a bunch of phone calls. Yeah, the scrambler is weird, but not that weird, given the high-level security games that politicians play. Shit, look at 'Tricky Dick' Nixon and his squad of burglarizing wire tappers."

Jeff held up his hand, suddenly alert. "Wait, you said these relationships go 'way back.' Way back! Hang on! I have to make a call, and we have to get out of here. This is the wrong place for us to be talking about this. Chet, you and I will leave first, then Ben, you and Laura leave. There will be two cars out front. We're going to Langley." Scowling into his radiophone he said, "Gilman here. Get me the Duty Officer."

Thirty minutes later, the four were ushered from their cars and into the elevator of the expansive CIA headquarters garage. "People were so busy when we left the White House, we could have been on fire and no one would have noticed us heading out," Jeff said, trying unsuccessfully to lighten the oppressive mood. "Chet, are you covered back at the 'Big House' with backup?" he asked as they continued riding down the high-speed elevator deep into the earth. No floor numbers were displayed on the elevator panel, just lights of various colors blinking quietly, revealing nothing.

"Yeah, no problem," Chet answered, then added, "I'm really interested in what you want to show us. Not sure why we had to come to Faulty Towers to see it, but I hear the coffee here is the best," Chet kidded, smiling at Laura. For her part, Laura had lapsed into silence, struck with all that was happening. Ben also was quiet, lost in thought about what events he might have set into motion. He just hoped his instincts were accurate.

The elevator whispered to a soft stop and they were ushered down a long hallway. Numerous cameras followed their progress, swiveling silently in ceiling fixtures, recording everything. When they arrived at a steel double door, Jeff tapped a code on the glass panel, pressed his palm to it, and stared into a small aperture before the doors sprang open to reveal a large briefing room. Sitting inside were seven CIA employees of various ages, mostly young, all wearing crisp white shirts and dark slacks or skirts. As soon as they sat down the oldest of the group began to speak.

"Hi, I'm Don Garrett, Special Assistant on Domestic Government Personnel. Sorry there aren't more of us here to help you, Mr. Gilman, but everyone else is on Code Red working either on Davenport's murder or the Vermont attack. Haven't found the weapon or his driver or anything else of significance. Anyway, everything the four of you will hear today is Top Secret. Mr. Coleman, your Top Secret clearance from twenty years ago as a Navy officer has been reactivated. You are hereby sworn to secrecy along with everyone in this room, with the usual consequences for failure to do so. Is this clear, sir?" he asked.

"Yes, of course, Mr. Garrett," Ben replied respectfully.

"Okay, enough preliminaries," Chet said impatiently, turning his lanky frame sideways in his seat to get comfortable. "I'm responsible for the President, so my need to know is pretty high. These two are along because they stumbled into some weird stuff that may figure into some high-level treachery. Ms. Sinclair already is rated Top Secret, so let's get going."

"Good enough. This will be brief," Garrett replied. "Mr. Gilman called and asked us to do a quick search of records on the Chief Justice and the Vice President in their formative years. It didn't take long because we didn't get much. Both men grew up in Modesto, California. It's an agricultural town, full of conservative, church-going citizens. Friday night football is the big deal. Both men went to 'Sac State' for two years," he said, pointing to an overhead monitor in the front of the room with a large screen displaying the two men's college transcripts. "Then both went to Stanford University for their last two undergraduate years, and both went to Boalt Hall School of Law. Nothing odd there, just one hell of a coincidence. Must have known each other."

"Okay, that is a coincidence," Jeff said. "Both were probably Young Republicans from solid-citizen families. Took the classic route to politics, although Berkeley was a hotbed of liberal politics in those days."

Smiling in response, Garrett pointed to the screen, where two membership cards appeared next to one another showing the title and seal of the California Young Republicans Federation printed above their pictures and signatures. "Straight-arrow all-American boys. No red flags. No trouble from these two. The background records, which are now three decades old, revealed nothing unusual on either of them. The problem is these checks were done a few years apart and the data was never placed side by side as we are doing right now. It almost seems they were joined at the hip for years," he observed, while changing the slides to pages titled "Formative History." Both pages were almost blank.

"This is where it gets pretty tricky," Garrett admitted, running a hand through his thinning hair. "There's nothing about their grade school years or junior high activities—nothing until their last two years of high school. 'Not available' is written in several parts of the file, without any notes or explanations. Whoever did the background check was sloppy, or poorly briefed or just stupid. Basically, we have no record of anything prior to their junior and senior years of high school," he concluded. Dropping his notes on the podium, Garrett said, "In my twenty years here, I've never seen anything like this. Never. It's a real problem, but it's kind of late to start questioning them. They're powerful people now."

Ben noticed the nervous sweat on Garrett's broad forehead and felt his own stomach tighten and fists clench, realizing that something was seriously awry.

Chet was the first to speak. "Frankly, my brain is struggling here. What do you guys think is going on?" he asked, his eyes searching the faces of the CIA professionals.

"We don't know," one of them said bluntly. "I'm Specialist Hallman. I did the search. Nothing else is anywhere in the system. It's like they both just popped up in high school at the same time. No church records, birth records sure, but they could be bogus, falsified or whatever. All of this is just way outside of reasonable coincidence, and the CIA doesn't operate on coincidence, just cause and effect. The facts are simply missing—not there. So it's quite possible that neither the Chief Justice nor the Vice President were in California prior to 1955 or 1956, and may not have been living in the U.S. for that matter," she concluded with a quiet confidence that belied her youth.

"From the moon or from somewhere else, huh? Some background checks," Chet grumbled. "Toland could be President at the drop of a car bomb, and we don't know anything about him before he turned seventeen or eighteen. Same with Blackstone," he said, scribbling concentric circles on his legal pad.

"We actually don't know how old they are, just what they've told people," added Jeff. "They have been entwined in the fabric of American politics for so long, no one felt it required the typical deep background check that an overnight political-come-lately would have been subjected to. Well, this is getting thicker and thicker. Okay, thanks for the briefing. Good work. We need some time alone now."

Jeff shook the hand of each CIA staff member as they filed out of the room. Garrett remained long enough to hand a thick printout to Gilman. "Also, we have been tracking calls made to Blackstone and Toland's phones for several years; looks like they've gotten more frequent recently. Mr. Davenport is also in there. Limited content beyond a consistent "trees, please" phrase is available, but the connection is there. Good luck, folks."

The group of four moved to a table at the rear of

the room where sandwiches and coffee in a ceramic jug with cups bearing the CIA logo were waiting for them. "Probably the only place in the world where the coffee cups are safe from pilferage. Not like my favorite West Coast restaurant, Trader Vic's, where everyone steals the funky little salt shakers, thinking no one is onto them," Chet joshed while pouring coffee for everyone. "We're missing the donuts that would make this a truly authentic cops meeting, but what can you do?" he said with a slight smile before sitting down and asking Gilman to share his thoughts about the "Situation."

Gilman replied, "We're a pretty small army to be taking on what appears to be a pretty large and deep-rooted threat. I'm not even clear what it amounts to beyond some loosely aligned evidence that includes a Russian-speaking VP and a fifties-era Russian general who has been posted to the Embassy here for years; a precise, brutal special weapons attack on agents protecting the President and another precise killing of a top CIA official; a bunch of phone calls with 'the trees, please' mentioned in the conversations; a dead senior CIA officer; and a meddling Chief Justice who has been intimately involved in Roger's public life and a weird vice president. Something seems to be linking all of this in our minds, so we have to try to decide what the thread is, and what the threat amounts to."

Feeling like an alien peering in on the developments that had transpired over the last few hours, Ben stretched his arms over his head and glanced at each of the others. Laura was dazed, clearly upset, and he mistakenly assumed it was due to fear. Little did he realize that the source of her concern was the President having been compromised by the mysterious benefactor who loaned him the use of his yacht several years ago. She could only imagine the numerous videos she was sure had been shot of the two of them.

Chet looked like he used to in the ready room on the Navy aircraft carrier when they were being briefed on night missions over Hanoi. Eerily relaxed and thoughtful, he was obviously running through the checklist of threats he had just mentioned, trying to see some pattern that made sense. Jeff, still shocked at the failure of the CIA and FBI to have conducted complete background checks on Toland and Blackstone and the newly-revealed evidence of CIA wire-tapping of the primary suspects, gave Ben the impression he was mentally trying to rationalize the data void.

"Well, all I know is that I'm under the gun to get an ad campaign built," Ben said firmly. "Blackstone was insistent that we show him something soon, like next week, and I'm not close to anything I would want to present," he explained, thinking of the two or three not-so-great concepts that had emerged from the first brainstorming session. Something about "Red, White, Blue and Rogers" and "Rogers and You—Winning the Future Together" he ruefully recalled.

"Did Blackstone say that to you?" Jeff asked suddenly, his attention returning to the group. "When did he say that?"

"At the Yeltsin reception, just after I met Laura. He came over and lectured me on the urgency of getting out a good campaign to guarantee that the President would win a second term with not just a victory, but a 'total victory.' His words. He said he didn't want to take any chances; he wanted a big win," Ben recalled.

"*He* wanted to win!" Jeff exclaimed. "What the fuck does that mean? This is amazing. It sure looks like he manipulated Rogers like a puppet to get him into the Presidency, but Blackstone's continued involvement seems strange."

"Yeah, it does seem over the top," Chet agreed, drinking half his cup of coffee in one excited swallow. "Laura, what do you make of all this?"

The coffee's warmth had calmed Laura, and so had Ben's cool demeanor in the discussion. She recognized that his combat experience in Vietnam, like her father's in Korea, offers the kind of heads-up training that never leaves a person, so they're always prepared for danger. "At the time, I thought it was just Blackstone's typical bullshit," she admitted. "Always has to be top dog, even with the President, and I guess I thought this was just more of the same. Rogers seems to respect him and take his swagger in stride. Theirs is almost a father-son relationship," she divulged, tucking a strand of hair behind her ear. "But, if you look at this situation with a clear mind, you cannot help but see something is really amiss. My big concern is Toland. Why was he always on these 'the trees, please' phone intercepts with Blackstone and Davenport and sometimes other people? What were they discussing, and why the coded secrecy?

"What worries me much more," Laura continued reluctantly," is the weapon. My dad was an Air Force pilot and a student of military history. He once told me about two famous young Russian sharpshooters who helped stop Hitler's attack on Leningrad, almost by themselves. It was a strange story. The brothers, who were only nineteen, had been excellent rifle shots on their father's pig farm. They could hit anything at two hundred yards or more. The Russian Army conscripted them and gave them high-velocity rifles capable of killing a man at a distance of a mile or more. The young men were the best at their deadly sharpshooter craft and one day, on a lark, they decided to kill a man together by shooting him in both eyes rather than between the eyes. They picked a German soldier through their scopes and each targeted an eye, right or left. After killing more than fifty German troops in this bizarre fashion, they were hunted down by a special Nazi hit squad, killed and hung from the same tree. But, not before the terror they had visited upon the German invaders had resulted in mass defections. This could be the origin of the horrible weapon that killed the Secret Service agents and Davenport."

"Laura, that sounds likely and it's a piece of the puzzle we never knew," Jeff admitted, glancing at her admiringly. "Add that to the situation and it spells Commies and conspiracy.

"Okay, so if Toland, Blackstone and Davenport weren't just golfing buddies, what kind of buddies were they? What were they meeting about? And why was the last call to meet at 'the trees, please' so close to the Vermont caper?" Jeff asked the group, even though he knew no one could answer those questions. "Tell me this, Chet, what in your imagination would be the most sinister end game here? What could all this be adding up to?"

"Well, my mind always goes first to the worst-case scenario," Chet suggested, "which means the President is in danger. Then you back up from there until something makes sense. We already have an at-

tempted attack on Sky Chief; although it did not harm
him. Most agents on the scene suspected it was a dry
run. Yet there it is, a big black mark we cannot ignore.
And then the killing of Davenport in a similar treacherous fashion."

"Taking that idea further," Ben wondered aloud,
"who would benefit most from the President's murder?" His query caused the others to look at him intently. Even Jeff had to admit it was a question he
should have asked, not only of this group, but all the
members of the Special Unit staff who were working
in another part of the building.

"That's the $64,000 question," Gilman said, and we
have a means to perhaps solve it, four floors up. Let's
go." Reaching for his radiophone, he punched in some
numbers and immediately gave an urgent order. As
they rode up the elevator, Jeff said regretfully, "Should
have done this earlier, like days ago."

Ushered down a long corridor into a room almost
identical to the one they had just left, the foursome
joined several people who looked up at Gilman with
respect. "Okay, team, you all know most of the facts,
but there are a few more items to plug into your clever
computers. The Chief Justice has been close to the
President for years and has played a key role in his
success, from fundraising to helping him negotiate
treaties and agreements around the world." With each
fact, he pointed at the screen of the five-foot-high
overhead monitor in the front of the room, as if conducting an orchestra.

"Next, the Vice President speaks Russian. I know
that sounds nuts, but plug it in. General Petrov is still
manipulating things and he may be closer to the Vice

President than we knew.

"Next, the Chief Justice is close to both Davenport and Toland. They met several times at a restaurant, which we just learned from Secret Service records is Au Boir, just west of here. It's surrounded by mature maple trees, ergo 'the trees' code name.

"Next, why was a code name used on scramblers? In fact, why a code name at all?" Gilman asked, glancing toward the analysts who were busy inputting the information he was barking out. All of their input was displayed on the overhead monitor as each one manipulated the data based on previous war game and doomsday scenarios, which had become a major staple of counter intelligence operations.

"Okay, next, Davenport is murdered in a fashion similar to the Vermont attack. The same sort of unusual weapon, a highly sophisticated, heavy-gauge rifle guided by some sort of computer graphics targeting system, was used in both attacks. It's designed to shoot both victims eyes out simultaneously and may have originated with the Soviets, as Laura has pointed out.

"Next, Davenport's driver is missing. Roland is a highly trained veteran CIA officer, so plug him in as a potential accessory to the bad guys, based on my instincts.

"Another instinct call is Ben's impression that the VP isn't American, so plug in 'alien,' 'foreigner' or whatever words you bright people choose to include." Turning to Chet, he asked, "Have I missed anything?"

"Seems to cover it pretty well, at least for starters. Always wondered what you guys did over here besides write up requests for more funding," Chet laughed, releasing some tension among the group. Leaning back in his chair, and again trying to get his long legs comfortably stretched in front of him, he nodded toward Ben, "Any other Ad Guy ideas?"

"Well, just that all this, whatever it is, has been going on right in front of one of the brightest and most intuitive people I've ever met," Ben said gesturing to Laura, who glanced up in pleasant surprise. "She told me Rogers' approval ratings over the years of his Presidency have been almost perfect. That is something that should be plugged into your little board game. Not sure how you would phrase it, but Laura, have you ever noticed anything out of the ordinary among these guys?"

Laura felt Ben was reading her mind because something had occurred to her in the last few minutes that she felt she should have realized earlier. "Yes, two things come to mind. On trips with the President, especially several years ago, he sometimes spoke of Blackstone in the way a truant son would refer to a formidably strict, controlling father. The other thing is that Brad," she almost blushed at her misstep, "the President, does not like the Vice President. He had only agreed to put him on the ticket at the specific behest of Blackstone, who had insisted the President needed a West Coast politician with strong legal credentials on his team. There was no alternative to Toland, but soon after they were elected, the President spent as little time with him as possible, giving him lots of chores that always involved being out of town, on the road, out of the way."

"So next," Jeff said to his team, who were clearly moved by Laura's revelations, "plug those things in:

Blackstone dominates Sky Chief, and the President doesn't like the Vice President; in fact, keeps him at a distance. If this conspiracy includes the VP, we have a possible motive.

"You will not believe what comes out of this Cray when the team makes it dance. It can scan millions of pieces of data from thousands of data banks, examine trends within that data no matter how obscure or un-related they may be, make various assumptions and grade the probability of each one," Jeff explained. "It can even produce a prioritized series of conclusions in scant minutes, so we mere mortals can make decisions based on the facts.

"Team, we're looking for some real hot rock 'n roll from you!" he said expectantly. A couple analysts looked his way, smiling nervously, then went back to their computer keyboards, fingers flying. "Almost for-got," Jeff added. "Include Ben's comment about the nearly perfect approval ratings, and the fact that Blackstone was involved in a lot of what Sky Chief accomplished diplomatically around the world. Also, plug in the notion of the President somehow being a 'puppet.'" Anything else? Jeff wondered to himself, sitting down in a chair next to Chet.

"Sounds like enough to frame an initial scenario," Chet muttered, reaching for his coffee cup, which had been refilled earlier by one of the young team mem-bers.

"This may take a bit, gang. More coffee?" Jeff asked. "We could get some sandwiches and cookies down here." Chet nodded his agreement and Gilman picked up his small radiophone.

Five minutes later, one of the technicians exclaimed, "We're there, sir."

"Okay, put it up, Rob," Jeff answered, turning in his chair.

When Ben read the text below the single word "ASSESSMENT" that was illuminated on the screen of the overhead monitor, he gripped the arms of his chair in surprise.

"Jesus, mother of Mary," Chet barked, standing up with his hands on his hips. "Fuckin' A," Ben exclaimed. "Oh, no!" Laura gasped. Jeff Gilman simply stared at the screen looking stunned. The eyes of everyone in the room were riveted to the monitor, reading the words that blazed from the screen.

ASSESSMENT
ULTIMATE LEVEL OF US THREAT. CONFIDENCE LEVEL 98%. ATTEMPT TO ASSASSINATE PRESIDENT ROGERS IS IMMINENT, TIMING POST REELECTION. MAJOR CONSPIRACY IMPLICATES VICE PRESIDENT, CHIEF JUSTICE, DEPUTY CIA DIRECTOR (deceased), AND OTHER CO-CONSPIRATORS INCLUDING GENERAL PETROV AND PEOPLE IN OTHER COUNTRIES AND U.S. CITIES. PLOT LIKELY IN PROCESS MINIMUM OF SIX YEARS PER "THE TREES PLEASE" DATA INVOLVING NOTED CO-CONSPIRATORS. PRESIDENT ROGERS UNAWARE OF DETAILS OR BEING TARGET OF PLOT. ROGERS CAREFULLY MANAGED AND DUPED (PUPPET) BY CO-CONPIRATORS AS RECENTLY AS DAVENPORT BRIEFING OF YESTERDAY AT WHITE HOUSE. DAVENPORT ELIMINATED TO REDUCE SECURITY THREAT TO PLOT. LIKELY PLOT LEADER BLACK-

STONE. PETROV LIKELY LONGTIME SOVIET (USSR-ARMY-KGB) CONTROL AGENT. BLACK-STONE AND TOLAND LIKELY TRAINED MOLES PLACED IN U.S./SACRAMENTO/ MODESTO AREA IN LATE TEENS. BOTH HIGHLY TRAINED AND PREPARED BY KGB AND OTHER SOVIET RE-SOURCES (REF: "CIA SUSPICIONS REGARDING DEEP MOLES IN U.S. PER STALIN/KGB PLANS CIRCA 1953-59"). DAVENPORT CONVERTED TO PLOT LIKELY IN DIPLOMATIC SERVICE OR JUN-IOR CIA YEARS THROUGH UNKNOWN METH-ODS. LOOK FOR SEXUAL LIAISON AS USUAL TURNCOAT TECHNIQUE BY KGB. BLACKSTONE LIKELY DOMINATED DAVENPORT; ELIMINA-TION DECISION AT RECENT "THE TREES PLEASE" MEETING. GOAL OF PLOT: ELIMINATE ROGERS, TOLAND ASSUMES PRESIDENCY. BLACKSTONE AND TOLAND STONEWALL U.S. GOVERNMENT EFFORTS TO UNCOVER PLOT. ALSO STONEWALL U.S. REACTION TO PLOT TO RETURN RUSSIA TO COMMUNIST STATE UNDER SECRET KGB LEAD-ERSHIP AFTER BRIEF DETANTE UNDER YELTZIN. PLOT STRUCTURE AND OTHER OBJECTIVES UN-CLEAR. POSSIBLE LIAISONS WITH OTHER SENIOR U.S. GOVERNMENT OFFICIALS, FOREIGN OFFI-CIALS AND SOVIET PERSONNEL ASSUMED GIVEN LENGTH OF TIME CORE TEAM ACTIVE IN U.S. (More data is being examined from other sources) PLOT REQUIRED SUBSTANTIAL FINANCIAL AND POLITICAL RESOURCES BEYOND U.S. CELL'S CA-PABILITY. PETROV THE SENIOR MILITARY REP-RESENTATIVE DURING CUBAN MISSILE CRISIS. POSTED TO RUSSIAN EMBASSY TWO YEARS

LATER. CONSIDERED BRAIN BEHIND THE CU-
BAN PROVOCATION WITH KENNEDY. LITTLE
KNOWN ABOUT HIM INTERVENING YEARS. FI-
NANCIAL REVIEW NOTES: CONSPIRATORS LIVED
ABOVE ASSUMED INCOMES.

ALSO DAVENPORT: ACTIVE IN RETIRED CIA OR-
GANIZATION. INFLUENTIAL AMONG EX-
OPERATIVES POSSIBLY INVOLVED IN THREAT.
ALLOWS THEM TO CARRY ARMS AT ALL TIMES
ESPECIALLY WHEN PLAYING GOLF. RESULTS IN
MAXIMUM PROTECTION FOR DAVENPORT SO
CIA DIRECTOR SMITHSON NEVER NIXED PRAC-
TICE.

(All government, Interpol and friendly/cooperating
foreign government records have been scanned, summarized, interpreted, presented at this point- 6-27-92-
194602). CRAY OUT.

"Get me security!" Jeff shouted into his phone, jerk-
ing all eyes from the screen. "Don't anyone move,
please. I am establishing Code Alpha-No Foreign-No
Distribution-No Record on all of this.

"Rob, plug that in right now. Print one copy. Store
it in Code Alpha world. No Further Distribution! Got
it?"

Rob gulped and anxiously followed orders.

"I have never seen anything like this before," Jeff
exclaimed. "Talk about leaping to conclusions, but
that's what this Cray is designed to do. It took millions
of dollars and thousands of hours of programming
and file matching to get it to do that trick. This is
overwhelming, but the logic of it hangs together, at
least I think it does. The only thing the Cray didn't

predict is where all the money was coming from to run this op for several years, pay bribes to our agents, manipulate foreign governments and much more.

"Rob, ask the Cray for 'Recommendations to Thwart Threat'" Jeff ordered, and within seconds the screen was filled with two lists.

OPTIONS TO THWART THREAT

1) President must immediately resign position and Toland also.

2) President must not win re-election; plot depends on re-election to second term.

3) President must immediately expose plot and conspirators on television under highest national security level; hold all possible conspirators under armed guard and incommunicado.

4) Key conspirators must immediately be eliminated to terminate threat.

OPTION ASSESSMENT:

1) This option unlikely to be agreed by Toland. Nothing to prevent assassination at any time.

2) This option considered best option. If President convinced of plot it provides opportunity to safely fail to win re-election, Toland candidacy to replace President negated. Reduces threat of national and international hysteria, political consequence and financial fallout.

3) This option relies on agreement and response by Rogers. Requires President to acknowledge accuracy of plot/treat and punish people in error.

4) This option considered most effective. Impossible to fully implement due to lack of identity of entire co-

conspirator group.

Everyone sat glued to the monitor, minds racing. The silence was quickly interrupted by a knock at the door. Jeff answered it and gave the Security Captain orders to seal off the area from other CIA personnel. When he rejoined the group, Jeff's deep brow was knotted. As he grasped the back of his chair he said solemnly, "The safety of the country is closely linked to the safety of the President, so I think that's our foremost mission. Chet, you're the guy primarily in charge of safeguarding the President. What do you want to do?"

"Never thought I would be agreeing with a computer," Chet answered, "but I think the less made public the better—fewer people outside of this little tea party who know all this. I'm still a little stunned, but I agree with you, Jeff. The Cray's assessment and options make sense, and they're the best we have to go on. However, I disagree with our Cray friend here about advising the President. He'd never believe all this and agree to take action because his pride wouldn't let him. I also think we have the right guy here to move forward with our friendly computer's best option," he said smiling at Ben.

"Ben, buddy, this little squadron has a new mission," Chet announced. "And you're in the pilot's seat once again, only without your big fat jet. We're going on a bombing mission of sorts but this time you're going to miss the target, my friend, miss it big time. You're going to create one terrific ad campaign that's going to thrill Blackstone and Toland by making Rogers appear to be a national hero *and* neutralize this plot at the same time."

"Chet, this is one screwed-up briefing. Get real and spell out how I'm going to do that with some TV ads," Ben urged.

Catching Chet's drift, Laura interjected, "You're going to do something totally contrary to your best instincts, Ben. You're going to come up with a message about Rogers that, as they say in the world of politics, is going to un-sell the president—carefully and effectively, with no one being the wiser."

"No one will realize what's happening including Sky Chief," Chet reasoned. "He'll never believe it until it's all over on November third. By then, this treachery will eat its own tail and the bad guys will be in full retreat, suddenly powerless and country-less. They'll be losers in the U.S. and pariahs in the Soviet world. They'll be out of business with nowhere to run. Get it?" Chet asked, leaning forward and pulling out a chewing gum package that he offered the others. "Want some?"

Taking a piece, Jeff added, "We know Sky Chief won't believe people that he trusted betrayed him so he's got to be kept out of the loop. He'll lose the Presidency, but gain his life. Not a great deal, but not a bad one either."

Ben stood up and softly squeezed Laura's shoulder, which caused her to smile up at him and relax enough to give Chet and Jeff a thumbs up. "Perfect. This is just perfect," Ben said. "An ad guy is going to save the world. But you make accomplishing the mission with some TV ads sound pretty simple. Screw up and we win; lose the election and we foil the 'dastardly plot,' as they used to say in B-movies. Manipulate the election so the other guy wins and we're heroes, al-though no one will ever know. *The Un-Making of a President* will be written and become a bestseller, but the President and the bad guys won't understand how it happened.

"And, you know how we'll do it?" Ben said beaming at Laura and suddenly galvanized with an inspired idea. "All that research you showed me about how Rogers has been such a successful diplomat while holding tough on Russia and China. 'Almost by magic,' I think you said. Now I can guess where that magic came from: from Blackstone, Toland, General Petrov and others. With a lot of money, they paved the way for Rogers' success around the world. God knows where they got it, but they engineered his perfect results. Funny that the President never seemed to wonder about all that. Just did what he was told.

"So here's the gist of the logic behind an ad campaign I think will work," Ben continued. "Consider this: What do people dislike most in their lives besides being cold, hungry or horny? Change. They don't like change. In the advertising business you avoid changing your product at all costs because people have become used to it, complacent, happy with the status quo. You continue to focus on what you've always said about bleach making clothes whiter or drinking a beer with impunity because it's 'light.' Sure, you make improvements along the way, but you don't change the basic product."

Chet and Jeff, along with CIA techs seated further away, listened to Ben with growing interest. Here is a guy with a plan to deal with a threat they never could have imagined, and he's doing it off the top of his head. Not a military agent or think-tank executive, just an ad guy from New York comparing selling light beer to solving their worst nightmare.

Sensing their concern, Ben gestured to the monitor, which still displayed the information that had so galvanized the group. "We're going to treat this just like you would treat an enemy in combat," he explained. "We're going to distract the conspirators with what will look like a perfect weapon to win the election. We'll give them something new to talk about, something 'New & Improved,' that bright red stamp we have seen on so many products in stores and ads. The President is going to do what everyone always avoids: change. His public image is going to transform from a Cold War hawk into a peace-seeking dove. Now that Yeltsin has agreed to the big treaty and the Berlin Wall has come down around the Commies' ears, it's a brave new world and President Rogers is going to lead it by becoming new and improved, warmer, softer, more open. People are going to love it—at first. No more Cold War, no more worrying about the bomb, no more concerns about Cuba and Castro and other South American Commie wannabes.

"Nope, now the President will declare it's time to stop spending billions on defense, reduce our overseas commitments of military bases and troops, and reinvest all that money and manpower back in America. 'President Rogers, Peace Warrior.' Congress will love it. Everyone from Blackstone and Toland to the men and women in the street will love it. Why wouldn't they? It's peace and that's what we've always wanted, right? And the Commies are out of business, right? Well, yes to the first question, but as we've seen tonight up on that screen, NO in capital letters to the second. As the Cray just demonstrated, the Communist enemy is hardly defeated. The fear that the Wall coming down was only a minor hiccup in the grand Commie plan of world domination is embedded deep in the American subconscious. That unstated fear, augmented by the Vermont attack and Davenport's murder, is going to help this campaign do just what Laura said it has to do carefully and effectively—unsell the President."

"How do you know this will work, Ben?" Jeff asked, glancing skeptically at Laura. "What if you're wrong about all of this ad stuff, and Sky Chief keeps his job? Then the bad guys take him out despite our best efforts and disaster occurs."

"Here's why I think it will be effective," Ben answered. "Remember when the Coca-Cola Company introduced 'New Coke' a few years back?" he asked, walking over to pick up a Coke can sitting in front of one of the techs. "They made a big deal of the change, saying the new formula was going to make people love Coke even more. Well, people accepted that message of 'New & Improved' in droves and sales went crazy. But only for a while. In just a few months, sales dropped dramatically. New Coke literally fizzled out because people realized they missed the taste of the original Coke. They wanted the old, familiar, comfortable Coke back. The new product had been positioned and advertised as something 'New & Improved,' but people didn't—and don't—want things they like tampered with. So the original formula was reinstated as Classic Coke and life went on happily. It was a rude and expensive lesson for the Coca-Cola Company and for the entire marketing and advertising industry. The Company's chairman even apologized on national TV!

"So, that's why I believe this will work. People will initially like the idea of the President changing his stripes, becoming more trusting and open-minded. However, once they consider what it could mean to the country and their safety that their comfy good-old President has changed his flavor, they'll realize the President is the wrong guy to lead them forward in a world full of Commies and other enemies, such as the dangerous Muslim factions in Iraq and Libya. It's the only way I can think of to prevent his re-election and the subsequent assassination the Cray is predicting." Pointing at the screen, he remarked, "Too bad you can't program this advertising approach into that big guy and see what it says."

Rob shook his head glumly. "Yep, the big unknown for Cray boy here is the American electorate and how they react to political campaigns. Historically, there have been too many upsets to effectively program political elections into the computer. Sure would be a great idea and a real moneymaker, I imagine," he said. Smiling at the other techs, he added, "Maybe that's what we should be doing in here instead of scaring the shit out of ourselves!"

"Well, we've talked this to death, I think," Jeff said. "Time to move into action based on what we've seen, learned and discussed. Obviously, we have few options so having Ben move ahead makes sense. We'll keep tweaking the Cray model, but go ahead and get started, Ben."

Reaching to pull out Laura's chair, Ben asked her, "Want to learn how to build an advertising campaign around your big idea?"

Standing up, she smiled at Chet and Jeff as she replied, "What's a girl to do when she has a chance to help change history?" Then in a more serious tone she told Ben, "The thrust of the campaign you conceived sounds sensible in connection with all that's occurred in the Communist countries. We must make it work, and I'd love to help."

"Great!" Pulling on his blue blazer, Ben said, "We'll need a lift back to the hotel. "Chet, I assume you or someone can fetch us tomorrow morning?"

"No problem," Chet replied. "I guess it's time for this mission to get airborne. Speak to you tomorrow, Jeff, and thanks everyone," he said, smiling appreciatively at the young techs. "Welcome to the latest crazy video game called 'New & Improved,'" he chuckled, hoping to help them relax from the terror of the past hour.

Accompanied by members of the CIA security force, Ben and Laura and Chet made their way back to the garage, where Chet's car was being protected by another security detail. After releasing the three agents, Chet said to Ben, "Well, partner, guess you're back in the pilot's seat after all these years. I'll fly wing as necessary, but you'll be calling the shots!"

"Chet, this isn't going to be a walk in Hanoi Park," Ben said solemnly. "This is even scarier. If what we saw tonight is correct, and we all think it is, then our weapons and our aim are going to have to be *plus quam perfectum*—more than perfect."

CHAPTER THIRTY-NINE

Dinner Alone

June 27, 1992, 8:45 PM

Ben and Laura waved to Chet as his car eased away from the curb in front of the Mayflower. "Feels like old times, that's for sure," he reminisced, placing an arm around her shoulders. "Twenty-plus years later and Chet and I are still flying insane missions." Nodding to the doorman as they passed through the large brass entry door, Ben steered them toward the dining room. "This Navy travels on a full stomach and we need something besides CIA Cokes and cookies," he said, recalling how the Coke can on Jeremy's desk helped spark his thinking about what to do to turn the tide on the traitors.

Sliding into a large red leather booth, Laura smiled appreciatively at Ben, almost giddy with relief at being swept into the warmly-lit environment. At this hour on a Sunday night the large dining room was surprisingly full. Ben realized that all the recent activity had attracted rather than repulsed visitors to Washington, D.C., another example of the public's peculiar behavior in reaction to danger and disaster, like "moths to a flame," he thought. The new waiter who took their drink orders—a Gimlet and a Glenlivet on the rocks— walked off wondering if the handsome couple was from Hollywood. When he returned with their drinks, he asked if they would like hors d'oeuvres, and Laura selected calamari. After he left, she squeezed Ben's hand saying, "Thanks so much for getting us out of there. This whole situation is way too much to comprehend, but I feel safe with you, and also famished!" Her blue eyes glittered.

Ben found himself immersed in her beauty and was glad they were finally alone again. Their early afternoon countryside escape seemed like it had happened days ago. Once their drinks arrived they were quickly consumed, so minutes later Ben ordered a bottle of wine. "Certainly better than a Coke, New or Classic," he joked, dipping a piece of calamari into some spicy red sauce.

Ben and Laura ate their dinners ravenously. While eating, Laura suggested they play a game, inventing stories for each of the groups seated around the restaurant. Laughing at the ribald cynicism of their tales, they polished off the Sauvignon Blanc from Zina Hyde Cunningham, a boutique winery Ben recognized from a trip to the Anderson Valley in California a few years earlier. "Like all the wineries out there, this one has a great history behind it. Have you spent time in the California wine country?" he asked.

"Yes, but only briefly. It seems my travels have always revolved around work, so while I loved the area

I didn't get to explore it or run into your buddy, Zina."

"Well, maybe we could change that sometime," he ventured, thoroughly enjoying the luxury of a good dinner, a great wine and a spectacular woman. "So, what story would other people be making up about us, do you suppose?"

"Oh, let's see. They would think you were someone famous, a friend of the President's, in town on your way to Europe. You're so handsome they might wonder if they had seen you in a movie or on television. They would imagine you had met me at some fancy reception, which is true, and that we were having a torrid romance right in the middle of the Capitol. They'd say you were plying me with good food and drink in a beautiful hotel and telling me how you were going to save the world and take me away from all of this to a shiny castle. But first, you were going to lure me to your suite and take liberties with my body," she giggled, reaching for his hand.

"Wonderful story, partly true too. Now let's make it all come true!" Ben said affectionately, reaching across the corner of the table, taking her chin gently in his hand and kissing her softly, then more deeply on her parted lips. Quickly scribbling a sizable tip and his room number on the bill, Ben pulled Laura close as they departed the restaurant. As they made their way to the elevators, several couples smiled at them, secretly wishing the attractive couple an exciting evening, which they had, several times over.

"Yep, they're off to beddie-bye, Boss," the man said into the lobby payphone. "Arn will take over for me at eight in the morning, like always." Hanging up and turning from the phone, the dark-haired heavy-set man ambled across the lobby and resumed his vigil, opening the *Sporting News* to the Off-Track Betting page. Hell, maybe I'll get lucky tonight too, he thought, imagining the attractive couple in a torrid embrace. I hope, like that guy, that my bet is on the right filly.

CHAPTER FORTY

"New & Improved" Comes Together

June 28, 1992, 10:12 AM

The ringing telephone on the nightstand woke them up at 7 o'clock. Reaching a long arm over Laura, he answered, "Ben."

"Picking you up in an hour," Chet said. "I know its Sunday, but no one here rests much on Sundays. Lots going on as you can imagine, and Gaines wants to see you today. Remember, 'radio silence' on the mission as we agreed, until things begin to sort themselves out. Copy?"

"Absolutely," Ben said, replacing the phone and sitting up with his legs draped over the edge of the bed. Laura stretched her lithe body like a sleek cat, her red hair splayed across the pillow. "Come here, just for a minute, my Ben. I hope you still think I'm everything you said I was last night," she purred, causing him to crawl back next to her warm, sensuous body, half-covered by the luxurious sheets and covers. "Only an advertising man could compliment a woman in so many colorful ways, but I hope you meant it all," she teased.

"All and more, my lovely beauty," he murmured, pulling her close. As she caressed his hair and nuzzled his neck, his hand traveled down, softly stroking her smooth backside. Kissing him deeply, she suddenly sprang from the bed, revealing the fullness of her beauty. "Rise and shine, Mister Coleman. That sounded like a reveille call from your wingman, and I need time to put on a professional appearance, rather than look like a disheveled mistress. Gathering her clothes, she scampered toward the bathroom and disappeared behind the thick, paneled door.

Gazing after her, Ben got out of bed with some reluctance, realizing the strong impact she was having on him. "A new man," he chortled, wrapping a robe around himself and looking out the expansive double-paned window. The park across the street was filled with school children on their annual field trip to the nation's capitol. Their exuberance and innocence evoked tender feelings that Ben kept tucked away most of the time, but now gave full vent as he took in the pleasant scene and ruminated on the amorous experiences of the previous evening.

With breakfast requiring far less time than dinner, Laura and Ben walked out the front door of the hotel just as Chet pulled up in his Oldsmobile. Climbing into the rear seats, Chet turned to greet them from the front.

"Hello my fellow thrill seekers," he said, immediately noticing Laura's day-old attire. "Meet Agent Kevin Morse, my special assistant. He's going to be your driver and close buddy for a while, available to meet your every need. We assign agents to people working closely with the President, even if they are on 'temporary active duty,' as it were." As Ben and Laura reached over the seat to shake hands with the handsome young man, Chet continued the introduction. "Kevin's been with the Service for five years and knows the ropes, so feel free to ask for anything...within reason," he said grinning.

"Not sure how much help I'm going to need," Ben stated, "but you're going to be getting a fast course in advertising if you're interested, Kevin."

"Sure, Mr. Coleman. My sister works in an ad agency here in town and loves it. I especially like watching beer commercials; they look like whoever made them was having too much fun."

"That's because beer is supposed to be fun," he said, "and call me Ben, Kevin. Okay?"

"Sure thing. It's a pleasure to meet you and Ms. Sinclair."

"Laura, Kevin," she urged, and they all laughed.

Arriving within minutes at the West Wing, they disembarked and made their way up the same parking-garage staircase where Ben had seen the Vice President quarreling with Petrov. Glancing at Laura with concern, he put his hand protectively on her shoulder as they moved through the door held open by Agent Morse. Arriving at his office, Ben moved to the desk and sank into his black leather chair. Meanwhile, Kevin got each of them a cup of coffee, then stood in the doorway as if awaiting orders.

"Grab a chair, Kevin. You might as well join in the fun if you're going to be my back-up wingman for a while. Even though I appreciate Chet's concern, I think this place is pretty tight security-wise," he said, probing Morse for a response.

"Never been tighter, Mr. Coleman, er, Ben. Not only because of the two attacks, but because Yeltsin's visit brought more Russians around here than a vodka-fueled bear-baiting contest in the Ukraine. Frankly, I'm curious why Mr. Greenwood assigned me to you. You seem pretty capable, from the reports of what you did up in Vermont. Seems to me we should hire you, not protect you," he laughed. Then glancing at Laura he added, "And it seems you have your own protective detail, right Ms. Sinclair, er, Laura?"

"I certainly do, and he's going to stay close to me until I feel safe again," Laura stated with conviction, eyes flashing. "And I intend to do everything I have to in order to make his stay in Washington as pleasant and stress-free as possible," she asserted, with a wink to Ben that the vigilant agent appeared to miss, probably due to good manners and training.

With Kevin looking on curiously, Ben and Laura began discussing the framework of the "Peace Warrior" campaign Ben had proposed. Periodically, they were interrupted by phone calls. One from Charlie Gaines, who registered his and Blackstone's escalating interest in seeing some results soon. Others were from Ben's staff in New York, including Helen Mayfield and Dan Roth, who were suddenly working Washington, D.C. hours to coordinate numerous aspects of campaign development with Ben's creative and media staff. "Just like home," he said. "Always 'get it to me yesterday', and when yesterday comes something always needs more work that takes you into tomorrow.

That's the drill, Kevin. Not as cut-and-dried as riding shotgun for politicians." Realizing he had unintentionally denigrated Kevin's profession, Ben was about to apologize when Kevin smiled and said, "No problem, no offense taken. It's why I'm in this business. We have our procedures and they rarely change. We're either on or off duty and always wired for incoming threats that we've studied ad nauseam. Black and white, meat and potatoes, the simple way is best for me," he said candidly. "I find my creativity on weekend afternoons yelling plays at the college and pro football teams on TV. They never listen to me, though."

Nodding his head in sympathy, Ben returned to working on a large sketchpad where he was literally laying out the campaign. It was his habit to create a visual roadmap of an ad campaign on a large pad with black marker headlines, examples of initial text or scripts, notations of the media to be employed, mass mailings and other elements of a complete marketing and communications plan all sketched out. Writing "Peace Warrior" across the top of the page, he wrote down headlines for several TV and radio spots and for ads to run in *The New York Times*, *The Wall Street Journal* and other major U.S. newspapers. It was rare for a Creative Director to select the media. Generally, the ad agency's media department would determine the best outlets to be used to target a creative message to its intended audiences. Ben instinctively approached his craft with a more holistic view. He knew the message was only half the battle; the medium was also the message, as communications theorist Marshall McLuhan so eloquently stated years ago. Ben's approach ensured that the main message, the key selling idea as he called it, would be consistently expressed on TV, radio, in print and wherever else it appeared. In most cases, he worked closely with an art director to define an especially powerful image that would reinforce the message across multiple media platforms, after the viewer or reader had seen or heard it in its original TV, video and audio formats. To explain this technique of consistent image management to Laura and Kevin, he used the example of The Marlboro Man, which was first portrayed in tobacco commercials on television and finally only appeared in print ads and on billboards.

Suddenly, Charlie Gaines burst into the office, interrupting their work and conversation. "Morning folks, how is everything going?" he asked abruptly, signaling Kevin to leave the office with a brusque gesture. As Ben stood up to shake Gaines's hand, he told Kevin to return to his seat, explaining to Gaines that Kevin was proving useful and he'd like him to stay. With a brief "Whatever" response, Gaines took a chair and accepted the cup of coffee handed to him by Marie, who was used to his bluster. "So, where are we?" Gaines pressed.

"Charlie, 'where we are' is that we have identified a theme we like and we're laying out the various pieces of how the campaign will work. I'd like to withhold the punch line until I have it pulled together. Would this same time tomorrow work for you?" Ben asked, feeling as though he had been put in this position way too many times in the past. "I think you're going to find it pretty powerful, especially after the last few days of fireworks," Ben promised. Feeling

Laura's compassionate regard, he continued. "Basically, we're going to position the President as an even stronger and more thoughtful world leader than before, someone who reads the mood of the public and historical events and responds to them with a new vision, a new message of achievement and success for America."

Visibly impressed, Gaines sat back in his chair. "Well, that sounds pretty good. It would certainly fit with what President Rogers has accomplished, especially with Yeltsin being here." Gaines, who managed all things concerning Brad Rogers—under Blackstone's constant oversight—had worked with numerous advertising and marketing people while running his family's bank in Philadelphia. He had participated in several Board of Directors meetings and watched many account executives make pitches on behalf of well-known advertising agencies located in his hometown, as well as in New York and Chicago. Ben's quiet confidence reconfirmed his decision to hire him. He was willing to wait another day because there was something exciting in the wind. He could smell it. His nose never failed him, especially in politics and dining. Smoothing his expensive Hermes tie over his sizable stomach, he stood, grinned at Ben and Laura and turned to go, waving easily at Kevin.

"Son, don't let 'em out of here, except for meals," he joked. "See you tomorrow, Ben and Laura. I may have one or two interested parties with me. Hope you folks can get things done with all this other stuff going on. Horrible about Davenport. Salt of the earth, that man. Brad really liked him; he played a lot of golf with us. Lousy golfer but he told the best jokes, short of

Rodney Dangerfield. Well, I'll get out of your way, lots to do."

As Gaines left the office, he reprimanded himself for not having arranged better accommodations for his new friend, Ben Coleman. Better take care of that, he realized. This guy is key to another four fat years for me and the Missus—and my other ladies. Ahh, yes, the ladies, he mused, chuckling out loud, which caused several young people in the hallway to look his way. Hang in there, kids, he thought, politics is fun!

Ben and Laura continued to work until Marie walked in with a white-clad older man carrying a large tray. Placing the tray on a table, he took their drink orders and left to get them another pot of coffee and some cookies. The latter was requested by Ben, who doted on chocolate chip cookies in the afternoon.

"What's Gaines like, Kevin?" Ben asked the young man quietly observing their activities.

"He's a pretty good guy, kind of like a brother to the President, like Bobby Kennedy was. From what I can see, President Rogers is pretty even-keeled, but no one is as cool as Charlie. He grew up on the Philly Main Line with Sky Chief and other rich kids. Was an All-American halfback at Penn when the President was playing quarterback. Party boys, which they still can be when they have time. Like the President, he's powerful in his own right, but he's always an easy person for us to protect. No vanity, no grandstanding. If Mr. Greenwood wants him to take certain precautions, he does it, no argument. He'll even wear a bullet-proof vest on occasion if requested," Kevin finished, then said he was going to take a walk and check in with Greenwood.

"Nice kid," Ben said as the door closed to the outer office. "Strange world when we have to expose Secret Service staff to protect people like us. Crazy pecking order. Not much of that needed in New York, unless you venture into the wrong parts of the Bronx."

Kevin soon returned to find Ben and Laura speaking on the intercom to New York. Ben was giving directions to several art directors and media department staff on the other end, while Laura watched with deep interest as he described what had to be completed and delivered via Fedex so he'd have it by 10 a.m. tomorrow. Kevin was slightly confused by Laura's obvious interest in Ben, especially because her current Secret Service moniker, which had changed from "Madonna" to "Ice Princess," was based on the broadly held assumption that she was impervious to men's advances. There was still some talk among the team about her old affair with the President, but his popularity with his protectors squelched much of that commentary. Now it was clear that whatever Ben brought out in her, he was bringing it out in truckloads.

Well, why not, Kevin thought. People deserve happiness, even in this crazy city. Me, too, for that matter, he mused, thinking of his girlfriend, a pretty and buxom airline stewardess named Sunny. "I'll be back in two days," she had said. Not soon enough, he contended, fussing with his earpiece to ensure it was properly functioning. Yep, come on home, Sunny. Come on home to your one and only, he thought, feeling the heat rising in his groin at the thought of her. Only four weeks into our relationship and she makes me feel like I'm the only guy in the world.

CHAPTER FORTY-ONE
Blackstone Loves It!

June 29, 1992, 3:02 PM

"Blackstone will be here momentarily," Gaines told Ben as he, Laura, and Kevin entered the well-appointed conference room in the West Wing. "You could launch a war from this room, y' know. It's got everything, so hopefully what you have to show us, Ben, will be as effective as a war strike, but safer."

Ben wondered whether Gaines would ever know how close he had come to describing what he was about to present, a formidable defense to save the President and the country from a terrible threat. Laura gave Ben a knowing look then glanced toward the door as it opened to reveal the Chief Justice, followed by Chet.

"Afternoon, lady and gentlemen," rasped the Chief Jurist as he entered the room with a domineering presence. "I feel like a youngster going to a Saturday afternoon matinee to see his favorite action film. Only thing

missing is popcorn. Oh, I see we even have that," he
chortled, moving to the array of food and beverages
on a nearby table. Grabbing a small bowl of popcorn
and a Coke, he gestured toward Chet. "Ran into your
buddy on the way over and thought he would enjoy
sitting in since he's the head babysitter for our action
hero, Brad Rogers," Blackstone bellowed, taking the
prime seat at the head of the table.

Winking at Ben, Chet grabbed some snacks and a
soda and took a seat a few feet down the table. "Wow,
Classic Coke! Where have I heard about that before?"
he asked with a sly grin, glancing out of the side of his
eye toward Ben and Laura. Ben squirmed a little at
Chet's playfulness, but then realized Chet was probably as nervous as he was, maybe more so.

"I was hoping the Vice President would join us,"
Blackstone said, "but it's probably better to keep him
in the dark until we present to Sky Chief. Vice President Toland tends to forget that loose lips sink ships,
even advertising ships. Don't you agree, Chet?"

"Yes sir, Your Honor. The fewer folks in the know
the better, I imagine," Chet replied, placing his Coke
can on the broad mahogany table littered with speak-
erphones, legal pads and pens. Looking up, he noticed
a mysterious half-smile on Ben's face. It was a look
Chet had seen many years ago in Vietnam, in the
ready room of the aircraft carrier shortly before a dangerous nighttime launch.

Walking to the front of the room and turning to
face his audience, Ben said, "I'll try to keep this brief,
but also give you a complete sense of a campaign I
believe will re-elect the President in a landslide, as you
have suggested, Mr. Chief Justice. I want you to know

exactly what words we'll use in our message and exactly how that message will be communicated to the American people. Working with Laura, who has been terrific in making sure our approach reflected voter research, and with my staff in New York, I think we have a knockout kick-off to the campaign. But let's start at the beginning."

Blackstone's eyes were fixed on Ben. Reptile-like in their intensity and focus, a penetrating laser-bright energy seemed to emerge from his cobalt blue eyes. Taking a deep breath, Ben momentarily flashed on a night carrier launch, realizing he had never been in the gun sights of a more dangerous threat.

"A great deal has changed in the world in recent years. President Reagan bankrupted the Soviet's military program, which began a major thaw between the world's two superpowers. That culminated in the tearing down of the Berlin Wall; major concessions by the Soviets in arms negotiations; positive trade agreements reached with heretofore difficult adversaries, including China; mutually-manned space exploration; the creation of the multinational Space Station and other heartening achievements. To your credit, four years ago you positioned presidential candidate Brad Rogers as an extension of Reagan's unyielding anti-Communism—a Hawk, yet a moderate Hawk. The overriding theme was 'Keep America strong; don't let down our guard until they capitulate.'" Ben watched Blackstone's and Gaines's reactions, the former nodding slowly, the latter alertly gauging the other man's response to this pronouncement.

"That's exactly right, Mr. Coleman," Blackstone remarked. "President Reagan held the line with Russia, forcing them to overspend their treasuries on defense. We kept that faith and triumphed four years ago, and with great results as we all have seen. I am proud to have been part of the Republican Party's thinking behind the President's approach to world affairs. Brad Rogers inherited the mantle from a terrific predecessor and has done a good job of carrying the torch of freedom forward, with some help from his friends," he chuckled, seeming unusually relaxed. "Hell, Laura, you've tracked it all. He's carried the ball after some great previous quarterbacks, right?" he said, staring at her with a broad smile.

"Your Honor, that is very true," she said awkwardly, feeling the fear she always did in his presence. Remembering Ben's recent advice to avoid letting Blackstone unnerve her, she took a deep breath. "President Rogers has the popularity and poise of President Reagan, but he also has a 'boyish quality' that added an additional measure of trust in the minds of the voters. He has been close to the electorate in ways that few presidents have ever been."

"Sort of an intimate 'hands-on' style?" Blackstone asked, appearing to be amusing himself at her expense. "Would you put it that way, Ms. Sinclair?" he inquired, taking a deep swallow of a second Coke, which Kevin had placed in front of him. Blackstone couldn't help comparing Laura to Kirin. Two beautiful women desired by every man who saw or met them. One trapped by her background of servitude, the other a product of upper-middle-class America. One who thought she had to allow men to dominate her in order to survive; the other who knew her survival in this city required her to avoid subjugation by a man at any cost, even for love.

"Yes, hands-on, Your Honor," Laura responded firmly. "That, I believe, is his most outstanding virtue, his strength with voters. They trust him because they feel he knows them. Must be those baby-blue eyes," she joked, flashing a smile at Ben to try to warm his icy blue eyes, which had turned cold at Blackstone's denigrating tone. Gaining confidence, Laura continued more boldly, "Perhaps he is too trusting of people, of the people around him and of people in the general public. But, the electorate can smell his fundamental interest in them and they love him for that. They want it, and they vote for it."

"Ms. Sinclair, beautifully stated. You represent exactly what you have just expostulated about the American voters—a believer in a good man. Mr. Coleman, would you please continue?" Blackstone said, helping himself to a handful of popcorn.

Ben had been mesmerized by Laura's courage, standing up to an intimidating, powerful man. She knew the extent of his power, yet she had spoken her mind simply and eloquently. He would never forget this moment of witnessing a remarkable exchange between the old world of fear and menace, and a new world of hope and courage. He wondered if the influence of his creative talent would be enough to empower the latter to prevail in order to protect President Rogers and the Free World. I guess we'll find out, "Madison Avenue Hotshot." So here goes.

"Gentlemen, I present for your consideration the theme for President Rogers' re-election campaign, a headline that embodies everything we will communicate to the American people as we build toward the

Republican Convention in August and expand expo-
nentially in the months leading to Election Day."
Reaching for a remote control, he pressed a button that
caused a simple headline and graphic image to appear
on the large screen in the front of the room.

A warm, full-color photo of the President in shirt-
sleeves, hair slightly askew, hands spread apart as if
preaching to the camera, surrounded by a circle of
children, young men and women, and their elders all
smiling up at him happily and confidently. In deep
blue letters the headline stated, "President Rogers,
Peace Warrior." The text below was the ultimate in
simplicity: "Now is the time to put down our arms
and turn our guns into ploughshares, our enemies into
friends, and our fears into our children's faith in the
future."

"We intend to recognize the sea change in international relations that has occurred since the fall of the
Berlin Wall," Ben announced. "The dramatic easing of
East-West tensions has culminated in recent nuclear
treaties, improvements in trade with China as well as
coordinated efforts among key world powers to dilute
and eradicate the threat of emerging terrorism in Iraq,
Iran and other countries. The time for guns and threats
is over. The time for peace is upon us. President
Rogers knows this, so he's changing his stripes in favor of peace without surrender. Peace through world
cooperation. The Peace Warrior. Now and into the Future. For All of Us."

Ben turned to the group, his face devoid of any
emotion or expression. It was an unbiased technique
he had used for years to prevent his clients from being
distracted by anything but the creative idea he had

presented. So often, other creative executives went to great lengths to act out their ideas, to exhibit Broadway emotions, or even add Vaudeville high jinks to their presentations, hoping that a large measure of theatrics would convince clients that the ideas they had presented were really exciting. Ben relied on the power of the main selling idea, one simple concept on which he would gamble everything. In some cases it failed to elicit a strong positive response, and that was fine with Ben. So be it. He'd be back tomorrow or next week with a different approach. But in most cases, the powerful quality of a single solid concept presented in a simple format made the value of what the viewers had seen breathtakingly obvious, and they would erupt in appreciation and approval.

"Peace Warrior! What the hell...Peace Warrior!" exclaimed Blackstone, standing up and spilling his drink in the process. The Chief Justice could hardly believe what he had just seen and heard. Here in front of him was the final gift, he thought, a gift that Stalin and his mission planners could never have imagined. Here was America giving up, just when she had the Soviets where she wanted them, flat out of business. Kaput, as they say in Germany. Blackstone was amazed that this guy from Madison Avenue had just handed him and his fellow conspirators the capping prize to their decades-long effort to dilute any American response to the apparent demise of the Soviet Union. Rogers was going soft. Americans would love it, he speculated, and it would reduce the pressure on his native Russia. The campaign looked like it could really work to re-elect the President. And then all hell can break loose as we activate the "end game" with no one

here willing to do much about it. We'll be "home free,"
he speculated, as ironic as that seems.

Blackstone's supercharged mind was having difficulty fathoming that he and his far-flung team were so
close to finalizing their covert plan, their long-held
dream of bludgeoning America in its finest hour. They
would just have to let America do what it does best, to
its own detriment—give up just when it has victory
tightly held in its freedom-loving, capitalist-driven fist.
What fucking fools, Blackstone thought darkly. And
this ad guy is making it all look so irresistibly attractive!

"My God, I heard you were good, but this is outstanding," he exclaimed, to the surprise of the group.
"Peace Warrior. Those two words are exactly right for
these changing times, for this President and this country, given everything that has occurred on the international political scene. America is where it has wanted
to be for many years: back in the business of bringing
peace to the world. After World War II, in fact after the
First World War, America's been given the ugly job of
being the world's policeman and has been totally un-
appreciated for her efforts; but those days are gone.
This is the future: peace on earth. This is exactly what
Rogers and this administration are all about. In a few
days, Mr. Coleman, you got us right, captured our essence in a few crisp words. Gaines, great stuff. This is
perfect, don't you think?"

Ben could not believe his ears. Blackstone is one
smart guy and for him to jump onboard so quickly
and with such enthusiasm was simply unbelievable.
What am I missing, he asked himself. I figured he'd at
least want to see more or discuss it; but he gets it and

seems to like it. Maybe he's not what we think he is, maybe he's just shining me on because he thinks it doesn't matter what I come up with, because Rogers will win anyway. Looking over at Laura, he could see his thoughts reflected in her wide-eyed expression of surprise. Chet's poker face betrayed nothing, but Ben thought he glimpsed a quiet 'thumbs-up' in his eyes.

"Mr. Chief Justice, thanks for your enthusiasm but would you like to see how the campaign works over time?" Ben queried, noting that Gaines was clearly elated, but seemed unsure why.

"Ben, I imagine this idea can be put on TV and in newspapers, or bounced off the fucking moon or whatever you have in mind, but the main idea is powerful," Blackstone replied. "It says we succeeded because President Rogers led the way. It says 'here's where we're going because President Rogers knows the right direction to take now, the direction of peace.' I doubt we need more than that to cause every 21-plus-year-old registered American voter to flock to the polls in four months. I say, get this thing going full-bore," he demanded, enjoying using an American expression that rolled so readily from his lips. "Get it on the air, on radio ASAP, in all the places where America can see and hear and react to it. Nice job, good going!"

"Come on Charlie, we have some other things to attend to," Blackstone commanded.

Gaines, who had said nothing to this point, simply stood up and placed his hands on the tabletop. Looking approvingly at Laura and Ben, he said, "It looks great to me. Let's plan to present it to the President when you are ready with whatever other elements you want to include. Perhaps in two days, Ben? Thanks Laura. Great work!"

Moving toward Blackstone, Gaines smiled widely saying, "Mr. Chief Justice, I'm pleased that you like it."

"Like it? I love it!" Blackstone replied with delight, looking like a child with an ice cream cone instead of the man who had so artfully designed and overseen the implementation of every behind the scenes detail of the last four years of an American President's term of office.

The two men left the room ushered out by Kevin, who did not return, perhaps on silent orders from Chet.

"What do you think?" Ben said, collapsing into a chair. Chet scribbled a note on his yellow pad and inconspicuously turned it to show Ben and Laura: Your hotel restaurant 8 PM, as he replied, "What I think is that you guys did great, you're underway and you have a big meeting with the boss in two days. See you soon," he said, and rose to leave.

Ben reached over and took Laura's hand, kissing it in old-world courtly fashion. "My lady, shall we celebrate our success with dinner at the famous Mayflower Hotel?" he winked, playing along for whatever cameras were busy recording them in this suddenly very public room.

"Why, of course, kind sir. I agree with the Chief Justice, excellent work. And how might we reward you for your brilliance?" she teased, enjoying Chet's chuckle as he walked out the door.

Gathering up their material, Ben reflected on what had been the fastest and most likely, the most important creative presentation in his life. Another happy client, he thought, but a dangerous one. He couldn't help but have lingering doubts. Why was it so easy to impress Blackstone? What does he know that we don't?

What Do We Do Now?

June 29, 1992, 8:15 PM

"Mind if I join you?" Chet asked as he reached the table in the Mayflower's dining room where Ben and Laura were sitting. After ordering a Manhattan made "with Maker's Mark, extra bitters, no cherries, on the rocks," he observed, "You two look like a hard-working couple taking some time off from the fast-moving business of making commercials."

"What's up with you, old buddy?" Ben asked, reluctantly releasing Laura's warm hand. "You seem particularly ebullient, like a cat that just swallowed a canary."

"It's the canary your new clients, Blackstone and Gaines, have eaten that's the good news here," Chet said. "You obviously won them over, Ben. Those guys swallowed the 'hook,' and the advertising 'line and sinker,' and that's going to turn out to be fortunate for a lot of people, especially the President!" he pronounced happily, taking a swig of the cocktail that had been quickly delivered to the table. "Gosh, that's good! Why are these always better in a restaurant? I make 'em the same way at home, but somehow, they just don't taste as rich. Maybe it's the ice," he said shrugging.

"Anyway, Gaines wants you to show your stuff to Sky Chief the day after tomorrow, so be on your toes. The heat's really on to make your miracle advertising scheme work the way we need it to, but you've got a little space. They have other problems to handle, like what to do about Davenport and the continued threats from the Vermont attack. The spin doctors in the media are working overtime, but it doesn't look like any of it is getting in the way of the President's agenda. I recommended that we back off his public appearances for a little while, but Gaines has got the President on the road as of Thursday, the day after your presentation. That's what I was doing before I got here, getting the travel plans from Gaines."

Chet recollected the meeting an hour ago at the White House, during which all of the plans had been discussed at length with various Presidential advisors and a few Congressmen. During the meeting Vice President Toland had finally spoken up, advocating the need for Rogers to continue to present a strong and confident public persona. Toland had seemed passionate, almost frenzied, in his advocacy of continuing with a "business as usual" posture. Just as the assembled men and women were becoming aware of Toland's uncharacteristic outspoken behavior, the Chief Justice, who had been sitting quietly in a chair to the side of the room, put his dark pipe down on an ash-

tray and said chidingly, "Mr. Vice President, you reflect the appropriate thinking regarding our next steps,
although with perhaps a bit too much fervor, my good
man." Being a highly-trained observer of people as a
central part of his job, Chet recalled the look of shock
and sudden hostility on the Vice President's face. "Yes,
business as usual is the best course to contain any
nervous reactions on the part of the public, but I suspect that Mr. Greenwood's expression of caution is
worthy of consideration, too," the Vice President had
said sullenly, almost like a chastised schoolboy.

Picking up Toland's cue, Chet remembered saying
to the group. "Of course we have to maintain appearances, as it were, but I would like to ensure that the
President's schedule for at least the next week or so is
designed with maximum attention to locales that we
know to be low-risk security sites."

"That's fine with me," Gaines had broken in, gazing curiously at Blackstone. "Appreciate the help,
Your Honor, but I think we have things in hand now,
thanks to the Service, along with the FBI and CIA folks
who are still working overtime to unravel the mystery
behind the recent tragic events. But we have to keep
pushing forward. The convention is only six weeks
away. Fortunately it's in Philadelphia, where it all
started for our little team four years ago. Most of our
stops along the path to the President's nomination on
August 24th are in key cities that voted heavily for
Brad Rogers four years ago. So we should be okay,
especially with stepped-up security, which most folks
won't notice, right Chet?"

"Yes sir, Mr. Gaines. That's the plan, as you and I
discussed earlier today," Chet recalled saying. "My

guess is that the Vermont attack was some sort of anomaly. Not so much an assassination attempt as some kind of test. Yes, the President was exposed, but had he been a clear target we still would have prevented that with our immediate escape procedures, which worked perfectly." Thanks in part to Ben, Chet had thought, remembering how after he and his backup agent had thrown themselves on the President and his wife, Ben had protectively covered Laura.

At that point, Brad Rogers had stood, back in command after allowing his staff and the others to have their say. "Okay, I've heard enough. Thanks to all of you. I mean it," the President had said, glancing with a faint smile at the Vice President, who sat glaring at Blackstone. "I think we're in good shape," Rogers continued, "so let's start focusing on the primary goal for all of us, a knock-out convention. Let's enter that Philadelphia stadium looking like leaders, but with the eagerness and excitement of a contender. We want to achieve a clear and unmistakable victory at the convention and in November. No overconfidence, no assumptions of success. Let's start with the same energy and conviction we all had in 1988 at that great restaurant in Philadelphia, Le Bec Fin. Besides the beef, what I remember most about that night was the enthusiastic energy. I want that now, from all of you. You're either 'inna or outta the boat,' my friends," he had concluded, smiling at allowing himself a rare dip into his forbearers' working-class dialect.

Immediate outbursts of "bravo, Mr. President" and "we're here for you" had erupted as the group broke into clusters. Slapping backs and shaking hands,

President Rogers had signaled Chet that he was departing and within seconds he was through the door, away from the clamoring mob of advisors.

"Chet," Rogers had said as they headed for his living quarters, "hopefully your buddy's advertising is going to not only get the electorate excited, but it had better get those guys back in the saddle. Four years of fat living has made them complacent. Well, maybe they have a right to be a little confident. We've all earned it with everything that's happened, Vermont and Davenport aside. When it happens, shit happens big time around here, it seems. But we all have to keep our eye on the ball.

"Okay, guys, this is a far as you need to go. Mrs. Rogers will take it from here, I'm sure," the President had remarked with a wink to his security detail, which immediately broke up and manned pre-determined security positions at various doors and windows, and rechecked the weapons and electronic communications in the closets.

"See you tomorrow, Chet. Drive safely," Rogers had said.

"Yes sir, Mr. President. Thank you. I'm stopping by the Mayflower to see Ben. I'll give him your best wishes for a breakthrough campaign," then he had added, "I'll probably have to give him some ideas, like I did in the good old days."

"Good old days are nice to drink over, but it's the great new days that I'm thinking about. Tell Mr. Coleman that for me, Chet," the President had said with a meaningfully glance. Then, opening the large paneled door leading into his living quarters, he added, "Tell him we need something really exciting.

We need to drive hard to November. Hard, Chet, hard.
We're all in this together, on the same damn team. No
let up, not now."

Snapping out of his reverie, Chet glanced over at
Ben and Laura, then surveyed the large dining room
for the fifth time, noting only a couple of heavy-set
men eating at a table in the far corner as being possibly
out of place. After quickly putting a mental tag on the
two, he said, "Well, Ben, the President has high hopes
for you, my good friend. It was 'fat cat city' in the Oval
Office tonight. Everyone seemed to feel sure Rogers is
on a clear ride back into office in six months. I think
some of them were even comparing notes on what
they were going to wear to the inaugural ball! Politicians. What a bunch of wild-assed jerks, but whatever.
Guess we all have a role in this giant pageant."

"Well, my secret air wing, we start some of our
own story-spinning tomorrow. 'Peace Warrior' has to
get on the air ASAP according to Blackstone, and I
have to start earning my paycheck, with the help of
my friends, of course," Ben smiled. "We'll take the VP
and President through the campaign on Tuesday, but
now, let's order."

On their way out of the restaurant an hour later,
Ben and Laura were oblivious to the many people who
looked their way, but Greenwood made a point of noting the incongruous duo still sitting among the well-
dressed diners. In the half-light of the restaurant one
of them looked his way. He almost seems to know me,
Chet thought. Memorizing their features in an instant,
he also observed they were drinking a clear liquid
from regular beverage glasses, rather than tumblers or
wine glasses. No ice, just clear liquid. Well, they're not

drinking water, Chet figured, because they have full water glasses with ice sitting unused on the table. Vodka, neat. Well, fellows, you're either still here with Yeltsin and company or you work full-time here like me, possibly doing the same sort of thing, except doing it for someone else.

Planning to include this observation in his daily report before he went to bed, Chet gave Ben and Laura each a hug before leaving them to each other and the night, and to what lay ahead in the heat of the summer.

CHAPTER FORTY-THREE

The Republican Convention

August 18, 1992, 11:10 AM

Philadelphia's 18,000-seat indoor stadium, The Spectrum, had not seen such excitement since December 9, 1980, when Bruce Springsteen and his E-Street Band opened a fan-packed show with a statement regarding the recent murder of John Lennon. He said, "It's a hard thing to come out and play, but there's nothing else we can do." In a sweaty, four-hour musical marathon, Springsteen performed thirty-four songs, culminating with a rousing version of the sixties rock and roll standard, "Twist and Shout."

Now, twelve years later, it was the Republican Party's big chance to twist and shout, and re-nominate their incumbent President for four more years.

Beginning at noon the day before, over five thousand Republican National Committee delegates from all fifty states had convened at the stadium and loudly proclaimed their support for the re-nomination of their favorite President for another four years of diplomatic, economic and social achievements. Young, middle-aged and senior members from all walks of life had responded enthusiastically to the first night's speeches, beginning with the Democratic Governor of Pennsylvania, Robert Casey, Sr., who graciously welcomed the Republicans to The City of Brotherly Love. "Even love for Republicans when you bring ten million dollars to Ben Franklin's hometown," he had said to waves of good-natured laughter and catcalls. Casey was followed by Tom Ridge, the highly popular Republican member of the U.S. House of Representatives, who would eventually succeed him as Governor.

"This is the only city I know of that can be hotter than Washington, D.C.," President Rogers commented to the twenty or so people gathered the following afternoon in the Presidential Suite of the historic five-star St. James Hotel in Center City. "I traded one hothouse for another it would seem, but it's my hometown for better or worse. Too bad our forefathers didn't designate San Francisco as our capital, right Alan?" turning to the Vice President, who was busy checking his appearance in a large gold-leaf mirror. "That city's not far away from your hometown, Alan, so you deserve battle pay for having left that beautiful part of our fair country. But that was a long time ago, wasn't it?" President Rogers teased the V.P. good-naturedly, but with latent enmity. Still stuck with this odd duck, he privately bemoaned his fate. But no matter; Charlie will send him on a plastic-chicken-and-handshaking tour in the boondocks the week after the election.

Nodding pleasantly to the President, Toland glanced at the Chief Justice with a sense of impending success and impatience to have it all happen now, not two-and-a-half months from now after the formality of an election. Patience, he thought, patience. Not my strong suit by any means, but so far so good. Rogers is such a typical American jerk, all puffed up over his anticipated acceptance speech tonight. Charlie is boldly counting on a positive first-ballot win for him via a voice vote and quick acceptance by the standing convention. Little does he or Rogers know how carefully and skillfully a small, dedicated cadre of my comrades has brought this administration to this moment of impending victory. It's too bad Rogers will have scant months to enjoy it all, but as my hero Joe Stalin used to say, "people are subordinate to the State, and therefore, expendable. All of us, all of you, and myself included!" he would roar, obviously unconcerned about any harm that might befall him. Rogers, too, is expendable, thought Toland, and when the long arm of Stalin reaches forward through time to the fall of 1992, the secret mission that was so well conceived half a century earlier will draw to a decisive conclusion. Yes, this President and his presidency have only a few months of life left thanks to Uncle Joe Stalin. Yes, Uncle Joe, your plan to keep America on the sidelines while loyal comrades reclaim Russia for the Communist Party was well-planned and will succeed, he assured himself smugly.

"Charlie, thanks for a terrific convention. You and your people here and all over the country have done it again!" Rogers said smiling broadly at Gaines, who was standing across the room with Ben and Laura.

Spying them, Rogers added, "And hats off to Ben Coleman and his brilliant team, including our own Laura Sinclair, for fashioning a winning ad campaign. When I first saw it I admit it was not quite what I had expected. But as we have seen, it's blown the doors off the electorate. They love the new 'kinder' me, and so do I. And so do Mrs. Rogers and my mother. But that's why we have pros helping us out in all types of professions: in law, education, agriculture, defense and more," he asserted, making eye contact appreciatively with the Congressional, military and administration leaders standing around the room. All were happily holding glasses of champagne, which they raised as Rogers hoisted his glass and bellowed, "To my family, to all of you, to the United States of America, and to four more years, Cheers! To four more years!"

"Too successful," Ben whispered to Laura, who glanced back at him with a flushed face. Continuing to speak softly he told her, "I have to start thinking of ways to get this thing turning on itself like we planned. The advertising is simply too effective. I never thought I would be anything but pleased with such results."

Catching a glimpse of Chet's rueful grin, Ben felt his buddy had read his mind. *Maybe my old 'wingman' will have a bright idea like he used to when he'd suggest that we dive to avoid a SAM missile launch, or leave the crowded bar at the Marine Corp Recruiting Depot's Friday night bacchanalia in San Diego before drunken members of the Navy's "sister service" took serious offense at our success with the local ladies.*

Chet's mind was moving along the same lines. *Ben has got to start putting the brakes on this runaway ad* campaign and get it to begin to show the signs of weakness he intended, or we'll end-up re-electing Rogers and facing the dire consequences. We still haven't identified any of the members of the Commie team other than the V.P. and Blackstone. The Secret Service knows how to do its job, but the Vermont and Davenport events clearly show the limitations to our ability to defend Sky Chief against unknown assailants with such sophisticated weapons. Better to have the President defeated than to lose his life days later.

Standing apart from the "American fat cats," as he often referred to them in his private ruminations, Chief Justice Blackstone noted the nonverbal exchange between Ben and Chet. Having made a point of staying abreast of the ad campaign results—while manipulating various Supreme Court decisions to his satisfaction, and simultaneously influencing the handling of various details of Rogers' public appearances through his unsuspecting friend Charlie—he had to admit Coleman was clever. He's proven that, Blackstone thought, so why do I trust the guy as far as I can throw him? Because he's the only person in here who has never really given me the time of day. Too independent; knows he can return to his comfortable life unscathed by anything that happens here or in Washington. He has an entire other world to return to in New York when he's done. Beyond politics, the prick, Blackstone steamed. Big time ad guy, a real American icon, but he's just an oddity to me. I don't have much experience influencing smart-ass Americans, just gullible ones. My success has been using weak men to do my bidding, like Davenport. Even Brad Rogers fits that mold, especially in the beginning when he was hungry for political fame. Coleman couldn't care less. He was brought here to do a job, get paid and get out. That's pretty clear, pondered the Chief Justice. But why do I think there is something more going on?

I had better pay more attention to Ben and his buddy from their old days of flying jets and bombing the shit out of our Vietnamese allies. Better not underrate the brotherhood of the military, as proven by our Army, which held Moscow with terrible casualties and kicked Hitler back into his rotten bunker and oblivion. War forges strong bonds. I've got to stay alert to everything and everyone so we can put America where we put those cocky Nazis years ago. Out of our way. Well, we're almost there, just a few more months and we're home free.

As he watched Chet turn to speak quietly with Ben, Blackstone thought, yeah those two are real chummy aren't they? Got to keep an eye on them, or rather more eyes than I already have following them. Cocky bastards. I hate people who ignore me. Greenwood and Coleman and that brassy bitch Rogers was banging for years, thanks to the invitation to my yacht years ago. Maybe we need a little more excitement around here. Instead of six more Secret Service agents getting drilled by our fancy super-gun, perhaps Greenwood and his ad buddy need to be in our cross hairs. I'll have to think about that—sure would make me feel good, and I like to feel good.

Blackstone looked out the large, multi-paned hotel window. God, what an old, crummy city Philadelphia is. Charlie sure picked a cauldron for a political event. With temperatures as high as 95 degrees and 90 percent humidity, what was he thinking? Well, I'm staying in here with the booze and the air-conditioning, and a woman or two. If only Kirin could be here, but forget that. I'll just have to settle for second best, which is always pretty good around Republican events like this, he anticipated with a smile.

"How about a trip over to the cradle of our country, Independence Hall," Chet suggested quietly to Ben, in earshot of Laura. "My team is in charge here and I'd like to get some fresh air, if you get my drift. You'll find the historic site fascinating, particularly when you learn that our bold forefathers were evenly split on the issue of secession from the King and his tax agents. They finally got an absent representative, from Delaware I think, to show up on his big white horse and cast the deciding vote in favor of independence. The rest is history."

The rest will be history, too, if we allow Sky Chief to win, Ben thought as they quietly left the celebration. After six weeks of living with their secret plan to diffuse the threat they had discovered, Ben still was finding the whole situation unbelievable. During that time, the Cray had noted an increasing amount of traffic emanating from personal phones belonging to Blackstone, Toland and several other suspects, including General Petrov, all of which seemed to confirm their earlier suspicions. Petrov had not figured in any intercepts until a week after the Vermont attack, but they had yet to break the code used to scramble the transmissions.

Also, Gilman had reported numerous arrests of retired CIA and FBI agents in connection with suspected drug smuggling from several South American countries, including Cuba. Chet and Jeff told Ben this was the missing chess piece, because it explained Davenport's role in the illicit plot as well as the source of its massive funding. Apparently, Davenport had used his extensive friendships and influence to convince ex-agents that they deserved a better lifestyle following years of dangerous but unrewarded service. In his high-level position at the CIA, he had made it easy for the retired agents to get their fair share of the good life. When Gilman and his team confronted the suspects with insurmountable evidence of their culpability, most of them spilled their guts in return for leniency and were sworn to secrecy in order to prevent the conspirators from suspecting that their grim plans were at risk.

Little did Gilman realize, however, that Blackstone had fully expected this portion of the overall conspiracy to fail after Davenport was eliminated. In fact, the Chief Justice had taken pleasure in knowing that U.S. agents who he had helped, via Davenport, to turn against their own country would be revealed as traitors and would likely be put to death or forced to live out their days in prison. In his mind, Davenport and these weak sisters had served their purpose of bankrolling his mission and they, like the President, were now expendable. Best of all, it seemed to Blackstone, there was no way they could incriminate him because Davenport unwittingly had done all the dirty work himself.

Ordering another vodka at the bar in the Presidential suite, Blackstone could almost visualize the satisfied smiles on the faces of a few well-placed officials in the Kremlin as they contemplated the successful completion of his lengthy deep-cover mission on foreign soil. They had waited forty years to take control of the U.S. Presidency so they could blunt any American re-action to the KGB's efforts to rebuild the Communist state. Too bad he would receive no public recognition, Blackstone thought, but his reward was in knowing no one could play political chess as ruthlessly as he. Now he had the lovely and sensual Kirin all to himself and after the November elections and Rogers' assassina-tion, he knew he would be even more politically influ-ential with Toland in place. The only shortcoming, of course, will be having to deal with Toland, whose ego is bound to bloat enormously after he ascends to the Presidency. Well, we'll face that when we come to it, Blackstone consoled himself.

Maybe that will be the right time for me to finally retire from all this subterfuge and take that round-the-world cruise on my eighty-foot Hatteras yacht "Czar," the Chief Justice contemplated, chuckling to himself that the only public reference to his true origins, the name of his beloved pleasure craft, was an indiscretion that had never raised questions, even from his ever vigilant wife. With a sinister smile he thought once again of the voyage on Czar several years ago in the Caribbean, when a popular Congressman and one of his attractive staff members had been videotaped in the throes of passion by the well-hidden cameras imbedded in the rich mahogany ceiling trim. "Ice Princess" hell, he mused. "Red hot tamale," as his Mexican deckhands would say, was more like it. Too bad I had to influence my friend Rogers into terminat-ing that little romance once we got underway getting him into the White House. The films are great.

Glancing again around the room, Blackstone noticed Greenwood and company had departed. Got to keep a closer eye on those folks. Too fucking smart for their own good. Gotta admit though, Coleman's ads are working better than I ever suspected. The polls are tracking north each week and victory seems assured. Well, it's time to join these party hacks and have another vodka, Blackstone decided.

CHAPTER FORTY-FOUR

The Liberty Bell

August 18, 1992, 12:20PM

Entering a Secret Service car parked outside the St. James Hotel, Chet gave the driver their destination and soon they were passing through the narrow streets of Philadelphia on the five-block trip to Independence Hall. Exiting minutes later, the three were impressed with the size of the large crowd surrounding the historic site where the Declaration of Independence had been signed many years before. Chet presented his credentials at a side door guarded by local police and was given a nod to proceed. Standing only fifty feet from the impressive Liberty Bell, the trio took advantage of the din of the crowd to converse.

"So, hotshot, now that we have everyone at a fever pitch, when's the campaign going to turn on itself?"

"Cool your jets, Chet," Ben urged. "It's only been a few weeks and this kind of advertising generally peaks after a two-month period, so we have a ways to go—probably mid-October, which would be perfect. Then the campaign's Achilles' heel will hopefully take hold and begin to erode people's faith in the new and improved President Rogers we're promoting."

Laura, who had been quietly troubled by the unprecedented strength of the campaign in generating positive impressions among nearly every element of the electorate, took advantage of Chet's discomfort to speak up. "Ben, I think Chet's concerns are valid, especially when you examine the poll data. The early results from your campaign are decidedly stronger than we experienced from the campaign four years ago when Brad won with 55% of the vote. Our current projections are that he could take almost 61% of the vote if the election were held today, and there are two more months to go! That's perhaps too much momentum for your plan to turn around in time. The ads are too good!"

"Nothings 'too good' just like 'nothing's perfect,' Laura," Ben reminded her, although he appreciated her insights, a feeling he might not have been as comfortable with had anyone other than Laura caused it. "But if your data is accurate, we have to think of a convincer, a fool-proof idea that will guarantee that the President's popularity will drop when the electorate begins to distrust and dislike the notion of a Peace Warrior. Any ideas, my clever crew?"

"Well, Ben, the Democrats have a charismatic candidate in Senator Lucas Lee Hightower," Laura advised. He's only forty, but he's a strong visionary with a rugged, western profile that plays well, not only in his home state of Arizona but in the southwestern and southeastern states. As a moderate Democrat, he has taken firm supportive stands on a few key conserva-tive issues, such as the budget and immigration, and his strength is that he's also well-known in the north-eastern states for being the "level-headed liberal" that Walter Cronkite called him two weeks ago on the eve-ning news. However, Hightower is not nearly as well-known as Rogers is throughout the country."

"I've met him several times," Chet said, "and I agree he's solid. A handsome dude too: college All-American from the University of Arizona, military service with Naval Intelligence prior to returning home to run his family's investment management business years ago. Was Mayor of Phoenix, then ran successfully for senator. He's a bright guy; a lot like Sky Chief, if you ask me; just less well-known, as Laura said."

Ben thought about Senator Hightower. He had studied the competition, just as he would in any mar-keting program. "Rock solid" was the impression he had of him from reading the news stories in recent years, and the research data Laura provided sup-ported his intuition. Ben had seen several of High-tower's commercials and TV interviews and found him to be a concise, thoughtful and credible proponent of old-fashioned American values, unlike other De-mocrats who favored "big government" and its associ-ated runaway costs. His one-sixteenth Cherokee Indian heritage, coupled with good looks and western charm, was an attractive complement to his political acumen. Chet and Laura are right, Ben concluded. He's a "sleeping gun" that hasn't been effectively promoted by his own staff. The Democratic campaign, while visible virtually everywhere one could find advertising, was predictable and almost sophomoric in its theme: "Hightower, A Fresh Choice from the West." Hightower's people did, of course, leverage his handsome profile. The headline and ad copy were reasonably well-written, but lacked focus and energy. In Ben's estimation, it was not the kind of hard-hitting, persuasive advertising campaign that Hightower deserved and needed in order to overtake and defeat a very popular sitting President.

"Hell, maybe Hightower needs some help," he declared, reaching for a notebook from his jacket pocket. "Laura, what could Hightower say in his ads that would convince a voter to support him over Rogers?"

Laura pursed her sensuous lips in thought, causing Ben to momentarily forget his question. "He would have to say something to cause voters to worry about Roger's leadership, his ability to truly change his stripes and be more liberal while remaining an effective President. As you said back in June, people don't like change. If Hightower could raise serious doubts about Roger's new direction he could possibly succeed."

"Sounds right. Thanks. Chet, any thoughts?"

"I think it's a question of who captures the heart and the intellect of the voter first. It seems to me that political advertising is mostly emotional. But this time, your campaign for the President is more intellectual. It relies on people agreeing with the premise that it is time for the U.S. to act nice because we have won the 'good fight' in the world. If Hightower could launch a message that exposed Roger's move from a Hawk to a Dove as premature and misguided, even dangerous, it could cause the President's ratings to begin to decline.

But you'd have to use facts, in addition to an emotional tack, to prove it was wrong and misguided."

"What a team, I'm taking you guys back to New York and paying you big salaries so I can sit back and just watch things happen," he grinned. "Let's see what we could say. Hmmm...yes, here it is. Scribbling a few ideas down quickly, he read from his notes to Laura and Chet. "Something like this: 'I'm Lucas Lee Hightower, U.S. Senator from Phoenix. Out here, we believe that a safe home is a well-protected home. And a safe United States of America is a vigilant USA. Yes, the Berlin Wall's come down, the Cold War may be won, some treaties have been signed, but the Communists haven't gone away. Bad guys don't just ride off into the sunset. Keep our vigilance, maintain our strength. Vote for a safe and powerful USA. Vote for me, Lucas Hightower.'

"Every ad would feature photos of Russian submarine pens, and airport tarmacs still covered with bombers, evidence of the strength of the Soviet states, even with the USSR supposedly out of business," Ben proposed. "People will believe this because in their hearts, they know it's true; bad guys don't just go away quietly. The Communists and their KGB buddies will not go away, they'll just change their organization's name and job titles. It's the perfect foil to our Peace Warrior message. And when it airs about three weeks before Election Day, our good friend Brad Rogers will lose his job, but will win his life."

Laura and Chet were riveted by Ben's concepts and choice of words, which he had so hastily conceived and scribbled down. Chet was the first to speak. "Straight talk from a straight-shooter. Perfect!" he

said. Ben wrote the clever line at the top of the page
before giving him a thumbs-up.

"Ben, it's really good! Where do these ideas come
from?" Laura asked, beaming at him.

"From a great team, that's where. And that's how it
always works in real life, or at least in my life in advertising. My job primarily is to polish and finalize great
ideas, ideas that come from any number of sources, as
you two just demonstrated."

Ben had that thrilling feeling of sinking a hole in
one. This was exactly the kind of message that would
stop the "Peace Warrior" in his tracks, the Sidewinder
missile strike that would drop the Republican campaign bridge into the rapidly flowing river of political
history.

"Well, this may seem crazy, but I guess our next
steps will be going to see Hightower himself and
'pitch' his account. How do we get to him?" Ben
asked, closing his small notebook and putting it back
in his pocket.

"I have some friends who can get us a meeting
with Hightower," Chet acknowledged, "and I bet Jeff
can get us the kinds of photos you would need. Yes,
I'm sure of it. Let's get back to the convention. The
person we need to speak to first is one of the convention delegates from Arizona. He's a Republican, but
politicians work in mysterious ways. They all know
each other, even the guys on the other side. Let's go
pay him a confidential visit," Chet said grinning ear-
to-ear, feeling like they had just lifted off an aircraft
carrier on the most exciting and critical mission of
their lives.

As the trio walked out the side door they had entered, two overweight visitors disengaged themselves from looking at the crack in the Liberty Bell and followed them out of the building. Appearing to be just two more history buffs, the men discussed the brochures they carried as though they actually cared about the history of America. What they were really interested in were the people getting into the government vehicle thirty feet away. "Those three sure spend a lot of time together. In Moscow, we would have broken them up weeks ago and sent them to places nastier than Philadelphia," he laughed, relishing a vision of the redhead in one of Russia's treacherous Gulag prison camps. "A little something special for the guards to enjoy," he quipped.

Ignoring his accomplice, the other man spoke briefly into a small radiophone as they walked to their car, which was parked in front of a fire hydrant across the street. Removing the ticket on the windshield and flinging it into the gutter, they got in the car and followed the government car.

"Your dirty mind is going to screw you sometime, my fat friend. Just keep your mind on the mission and tell me when you see them turn. According to the boss, we have to stay on these guys tighter than before. We may be getting some wet action soon, and they may be the targets. Then you can have your fun."

CHAPTER FORTY-FIVE

Ben's New Client

August 22, 1992, 10:45 AM

"Ms. Sinclair, Mr. Coleman, Mr. Greenwood and Mr. Gilman, it is a pleasure to meet the enemy, as it were," Senator Hightower said with an outstretched hand of welcome as he moved across the spacious living room in the hotel suite of New York's famous Waldorf Astoria. "Fred Siegel, my Chief of Staff, told me that my favorite Arizona Republican and trusted friend, Judge Perry Booth, had called to request this curious meeting.

"I must say, I find your request to meet most incredible, quite bold, and frankly, more than suspect," the towering Democratic Senator from Arizona admitted candidly, motioning them toward an arranged grouping of sofas and chairs, "Please make yourselves comfortable, but since I have to be on the road in an hour, let's get to it."

"Senator Hightower, first, thanks very much for

agreeing to meet with us," Chet said, speaking cautiously yet firmly. "As you are aware, I head up the Presidential detail of the Secret Service; Mr. Gilman is a senior CIA operative with whom you are familiar; Ms. Sinclair has been on the President's staff for over six years as a Senior Research Specialist; and Mr. Coleman is the New York City advertising executive that Charlie Gaines, the President's senior advisor, hired to write President Rogers' re-election campaign. Ben also happens to be a fellow Navy pilot and squadron mate of mine. We were stationed on the U.S.S. Saratoga aircraft carrier off Vietnam in the late '60s and ran into each other again when he came to Washington in late June. Since that time there have been several high-level assignation attacks. Sir, I don't have to tell you that we live in perilous times, but these times require unusual actions." Chet picked up his coffee cup, drained it, and continued. "I am going to brief you on a major threat to our country. This information has been shared with no one outside this group, save several of Mr. Gilman's CIA technicians who have been sworn to secrecy, and has been corroborated by the CIA's primary strategic computer system, the Cray 5500. As Chairman of the Congressional Committee on Security and Espionage for the last several years, you are no doubt familiar with it?"

Nodding his head, Hightower, eased back into his chair. "Yes, it's an amazing machine, one of the few government investments in information technology that has proven its worth. What has the Cray learned, Mr. Greenwood?" he asked, glancing at Fred Siegel, who was taking notes.

Chet switched on a small computer projector,

aimed it on a blank wall, and described to the Senator, Siegel and his three top staff members, the most elaborate and potentially successful threat to the safety of the United States in its more than two-hundred-year history. As he reviewed the events of the last two months, including the Presidential attack in Vermont, the Davenport assassination, and other details of the plot including the Cray's data, the members of Hightower's team who had been standing sat down in response to the gravity of the situation.

"Senator, that's how we see it, and that's why we're here," Chet concluded.

"Alright," Hightower stated, running his hands through his full head of dark hair. "All of that is quite disturbing but it seems to make sense. Assuming it's the truth, we normally would arrest these people and limit their ability to proceed with their plans to assassinate the President. But, as you said, beyond the machinations of a myriad of little computer chips, there is scant evidence. Blackstone, Toland and whoever else is involved, are big players, very big players. It goes without saying that this whole thing had better be airtight.

"Well, I can't imagine you would have come here without some sort of proposal that involves me," Hightower continued. "So have at it, I'm all ears."

Chet signaled Ben that it was his turn in the barrel. Standing up and walking to the fireplace, Ben began. "Senator Hightower, I'm an advertising man from New York City. I've worked with big companies on big marketing projects that really mattered to them. But, frankly, I haven't been involved in the sort of threat that we just described since Mr. Greenwood and

I dropped bombs on the Viet Cong. At least then we knew who our enemy was, and most of the time, we knew where to find them. But the problem we have here is a puzzle to which the only solution lies in saying the right words, in the right way and at the right time to the American public. Normally, I write ad campaigns for one player in a marketplace; one brand, one product. Yes, I study the competition, just like we researched you in depth with the help of people like Ms. Sinclair. But instead of creating a campaign to beat you, we were faced with the unusual challenge of creating one to defeat President Rogers.

"We designed a campaign that would look good to him and to the bad guys: Blackstone, Toland and whoever else is part of their crew. So far we've succeeded. They all love it. We hoped that the strategy of changing the President's spots would cause voters to like the idea at first, to rally around an exciting new American vision of real peace. But, we intended that the initial euphoria would evaporate as the electorate and the media began to realize the full import of the "Peace Warrior" message and started to question a sitting President with ideas so in opposition to his long-established conservative, Hawkish values of protecting our country against an old foe. Frankly, we have done too good a job promoting the call for peace, helped by the media's sensationalism of the two assassination attacks. President Rogers' popularity ratings keep moving up, as you well know, although polling results indicate some weakening of certain aspects, including "foreign relations leadership" and "military leadership." It's becoming urgent to do something that will accelerate concerns among the U.S. electorate regarding the risk of going soft on the old Communist regime and other potential enemies around the world.

"The plot that Chet described makes it clear the Communists have not gone away; they've just gone underground until they can reorganize and re-establish the Union of Soviet Socialist Republics, or whatever their ultimate goal may be. We have to make the true aims of the Soviets and their allies clear to the electorate and avert the re-election of President Rogers, his resultant assassination, and the lethal usurpation of power planned by this devious group. We have to clearly explain this threat to the American public without tipping our hand to the plotters, and it needs to be done on a careful timetable with a specific advertising campaign. We need your help to accomplish this."

Pausing to take a drink of water, Ben realized that now was the time to lay his plan squarely in front of Hightower, so he sat down across from him. "As crazy as this sounds, and it certainly does seem surreal," Ben admitted, "in order to prevent the scenario that Chet outlined we need you to allow us to write your advertising campaign. The team that created your competitor's election campaign finds itself with no choice but to work to get you elected as the next President of the United States. If we fail, the presidency will be 'rent asunder' as they used to say, and America will become something none of us want to imagine."

"Fred," Hightower said firmly, "cancel my schedule for the rest of the day. Team, do the same with whatever you have on your plates, but be cool about it. You've all worked with me for years in delicate situations. This is the most delicate one of your careers, so treat all of this most carefully. This is one meeting and one project that will never make it into your memoirs." Nodding with sober faces, they all headed toward the phones placed around the room to make the necessary changes to their itineraries.

"Ben, let's say that you're right and all of this is true. What can you do with words that someone else could not do better by directly confronting this bunch of coyotes?" Hightower asked in his easy western drawl.

"We can position you as the experienced diplomat that you are and the moderate Hawk this country desperately needs, whether they know it or not. We can do it with something like this," Ben said, pulling his large art portfolio close. Reaching inside, he pulled out a presentation board and rested it on the back of an armchair in the front of the room. Turning the poster-sized board around, he revealed a photo of Hightower astride his handsome horse Sunriser with a headline that read, "Straight Talk from a Straight Shooter."

Below the photo was the essence of the campaign's message:

Bad guys don't just ride off into the sunset.
Stay the watch, maintain our strength and vigilance.
Vote for a powerful USA. Vote for Lucas Hightower.

"It's single-minded and speaks to voters' concerns about what is going on in the world beyond their hometowns. It gives voters a clear solution, a clear choice to remain safe and secure, which is the most important thing to any human being, especially when they are made to think about it," Ben said, placing his hand on the top of the poster. "We can have it produced in the next two weeks and air it later in September, just when we expect Roger's ratings will plateau and begin to decline in some parts of the country. This campaign will hit the TV, radio, magazines and billboards throughout the country within the same week. It can either be produced by your agency or by a small, independent team of my old advertising friends who would be pleased to help, although they will never know the true reason for this plan. Your message of maintaining vigilance and our military strength will be in sharp contrast to our campaign for President Rogers and it will do exactly what we need it to do. It will establish the ongoing Communist threat and clearly portray you as a rugged independent Congressman whose governmental experience and defense leadership support your assertion that 'Bad guys don't just ride off into the sunset.' It presents you as the clear-cut, favorable choice for President."

"Good God, you just came up with that in the last few days?" Hightower asked Ben. "Fred, what's our advertising say now, something about 'Hightower —A Fresh Wind from the West'? I liked that when you showed it to me, but obviously these guys not only are onto something rotten in our fair capitol, but have what looks like a bulls-eye campaign concept that might just solve both problems: my election and the undoing of Blackstone and Company. I never did like that guy, or Toland, for that matter. Good instincts, right?" he laughed. "Ladies and Gents, it looks like we have something worth working on. What do we do now? Are you sure the President isn't hip to this?"

"Senator Hightower," Gilman said, "there is no

way we would be here if Sky Chief suspected anything. Much to our dismay, Blackstone has gained a very strong influence over the President, so Rogers would not be able to look at the evidence with an open mind. We also cannot risk the President going into action on his own, angry and embarrassed as he would likely be. And there is nothing to keep the plotters from going ahead with the assassination earlier if they are tipped off in any way. Toland would be in the Oval Office the next day, and with all the post-assassination confusion, he probably would be elected. Nope, this is the only way to go. Clean, precise, and likely to work."

Nodding in agreement, Hightower turned to his staff. "I guess this is all legal. Everything's fair in love and politics, and in this case it's also pretty strange. Okay, let's start working out the details. I want to sit in with these folks on the planning. It's too wild to miss out on anything, and frankly I like looking like the Marlboro Man, even if I don't smoke. Well, maybe a little in college," he joked, winking at Laura, who smiled back, suddenly feeling like she was in the middle of a surreal movie.

For the next couple of hours, the small group formulated a plan. They did not have military forces, guns or even bows and arrows to help them accomplish their objectives. They simply had their wits and Ben's well-chosen words with which to forge a counterattack on Joseph Stalin's vindictive and brutal plot to upend and destroy his oldest enemy, the United States of America.

CHAPTER FORTY-SIX

Public Opinion Shifts

September 24, 1992, 3:45 PM

Ben sat in his new, larger West Wing office—recently assigned by Gaines—surrounded by Laura, Chet and Dan Roth. Displayed around the room were blowups of the President's ad campaign posters and TV story-boards, illustrating key scenes and dialogue from the commercials that had been created over the last twelve weeks. On the largest wall, stretching twenty feet and illuminated by overhead spotlights, were three framed full-page ads that had appeared in major U.S. news-papers the previous week, the scripts of six nationally broadcast radio ads, and a muted projection of ten one-minute television commercials running back-to-back in a video loop.

"Great job all around, Dan...and really great work with your special team over at J. Walter Thompson. Where did you find them, anyway?" Ben asked his old associate, impressed with the quality of work produced by the carefully chosen team of writers, art directors and producers who had secretly pulled together Senator Hightower's new campaign in three weeks. Ben felt comfortable talking openly about the competition's advertising knowing that Chet had made sure the office was scrubbed clean of electronic bugs on a daily basis.

"My old friend at J. Walter Thompson, Bob Weekes, knows everyone on the planet and came out of retirement to build a strong veteran team, which could make it happen quickly," Roth replied. "Guys and gals like Jim Fox, Tony Foster and Jill Gabbert—all veterans. All they knew was that Bob was hired directly by Senator Hightower, had a big budget and needed to get on the air quickly with a new message. They worked with the ad theme Hightower's team gave them, which was established by you, Ben, but the concept had to be fully fleshed out, photographed, produced and distributed to all the various media venues. Ad folks like to have a Presidential campaign on their reel, no matter where the source of the central idea came from. It's always a team effort anyway. But the real source of Hightower's new advertising pitch will always remain a state secret," he said gesturing to Chet, who nodded, crossed his long legs and put his arms behind his head. "So, we're off and running. When are you coming back to the big city, Ben, now that you've launched not one but two Presidential ad campaigns in short order?"

"Not until Election Day according to my erstwhile client. Between my beating him at tennis regularly, and Laura and I being in great demand at various DC functions, I have become indispensable to Rogers, something I never thought would happen," Ben joked, smiling broadly at Laura. "And speaking of my client, how're his numbers doing lately, Ms. Sinclair?"

Laura enjoyed watching Ben finally relax after weeks of feverish work as he conferred with Dan, who obviously revered him. She shifted in her chair reaching for a folder labeled Polls-September-1992, and pulled a few sheets from the file. Glancing at them, she turned to Ben.

"Just as you hoped, or expected," she reported. "Of the twenty-two attributes, monitored by Yankelovich Research on a daily basis in forty-five major markets, the President's ratings plateaued days after the Hightower campaign first aired, which was last Wednesday. Half of those attributes are now down five to ten percent, especially in urban and some suburban markets. He is still doing well in rural markets. I suspect things should really begin to shake after about two weeks. As we agreed, I have given the President this study, but with the explanation that we experienced the same profile in the last election. Fortunately, he and Charlie didn't press to see the comparison data, which would have been uncomfortable at the very least. But they're too busy jumping on Air Force One every other day."

Just then, Marie knocked on the door and leaned in to tell Ben that Justice Blackstone had called to say he was on the way over to meet with them and wanted to make sure they were in the office.

Glancing at Ben and Laura, Chet stood up quickly. "Not sure it would make a lot of sense my being here in the middle of the day. He knows we're friends, but you never know. See ya." Waving goodbye, he walked past Marie who lingered in the doorway, her well-honed instincts alive and working overtime.

"Do you want me to get anything for you folks and the Chief Justice," she asked, causing Ben to realize she was alert to something that he had missed. "I should mention, Mr. Coleman, that as Ms. Sinclair can attest, the Chief Justice rarely comes into this part of the building. He only goes to the Oval Office or the White House proper. I'll get some fresh coffee and snacks. Be right back," she said, ducking out the door.

"Well, now comes the 'Grim Reaper.' Not sure what we have done to deserve such an unexpected visit, but it doesn't feel like something we're going to enjoy. I know the nervous client syndrome and can smell it a mile off, like Marie just did. Do what you do best, Dan, and play dumb when he arrives. The Chief Justice can be pretty overbearing, but then, you've had a lot of practice with that, haven't you?"

Minutes later, the outer door opened and like a cold wind Blackstone whooshed his way through the inner door. "All right folks, you've had six, no seven weeks to get our numbers way above four years ago, and while they were higher three weeks ago versus the last election, they're not going up lately, right Ms. Sinclair?" he spun on Laura, who was still holding the poll reports. "Why haven't I been kept abreast of things the last few days, just when the Democrats have splashed their 'man rides horse' ads on everything that moves, including the sides of Greyhound buses? We're going flat, and I want to know why, Mr. Coleman. Who's this?" he frowned, pointing his arm at Dan. "You look like an agency account man; I can smell 'em a mile away, and with good reason," he blustered. Taking a seat across from Ben, Blackstone insisted on knowing "What's being done to goose things up?"

While Ben had experienced this kind of grand-standing in New York, he had never been accosted by a client he knew to be an enemy agent—a very power-ful one. The unlucky boys in the "Hanoi Hilton" had experienced direct confrontation with the twisted minds of Communists, but this was a first for Ben. Feeling slightly warm, he reached for straws, several of which were immediately proffered by his fertile imagination.

"Well, Mr. Chief Justice, we just met with the President and Mr. Gaines who seemed quite pleased with our progress. Sure, there are some weaknesses with some measures, but overall we're just hitting a period typical in ad campaigns. It's called 'message plateau.' We max our exposure to the extent of our media budget, then wait and see how it all plays out. When we see the numbers begin to flatten out, we fig-ure out where the weaknesses are and shore them up on a targeted basis. In this case, it looks like two areas, "military leadership" and "foreign relations leader-ship," are a little soft. I would imagine the President's staff, who have this same data, would be planning some clear and decisive responses in these areas that could be translated into the campaign; photo ops and that sort of thing. We can't run policy here; we just reflect it. And we've done a good job of that so far, don't you think?" he asked innocently, enjoying the grim look on Blackstone's face as the shrewd man real-ized Ben was playing him like a rainbow trout on a long fly-fishing line.

"Don't patronize me, young man," Blackstone bellowed, causing Ben to involuntarily sit back in his chair. "You're the idea man, but maybe you're right. Charlie should be giving you fodder for the fire. That's his job. First thing tomorrow you'll have your fucking fodder and you'd better be on the air with some new, fast-moving stuff by the end of the week!" he demanded, tossing Roth a steely look.

Turning to Laura, he roared, "And you need to put more energy into your reports to the President. He seems to be too relaxed, and we have only five weeks to D-Day. It had better be a fucking D-Day or your careers will look very different after November third! Everyone on board with me?" he demanded, once again employing an inane American expression. Soon, he thought, I won't have to be "on board" with virtually anyone I know in this or any other place in Washington. Soon I'll have the run of the world with Kirin, rather than be stuck in this sophomoric, money-worshipping fifty-state part of it. Blackstone stomped out of the office, ignoring Marie who attempted to hand him a phone message.

"Wow. That guy must have been handpicked by Stalin because he is one bad motherfucker," Ben scowled, clutching his chin. Glancing at Dan, Ben smiled weakly, saying, "He's a major asshole, isn't he? But he's our asshole, so let's meet here tomorrow to figure out some way to develop some pullouts from the current campaign ads. Maybe this will just help our cause, if we're smart about it. Hell, the agency's making a fortune from all this, so we'll act like it's our job while we make sure the competition's campaign is absolutely perfect, right?"

As Dan and Laura got up to leave, Ben asked Laura to stay behind. Dan picked up his briefcase, tucked several file folders under his arm and was walking toward the door when Marie leaned in to hand Ben the phone message Blackstone had ignored. "I'm sure he's going to wish we hadn't seen this," she smiled knowingly.

On the slip was a simple message: "Call K. Urgent." Placing it in his pocket, Ben had the feeling he possessed something that would somehow become important in the days ahead.

"That's enough for one day, Laura," he said. "Let's go see what our bartender friend at the Mayflower can invent for us tonight. We need our own signature drink, don't you think?

"You look like you've just been through the wringer, my love." Reaching for her hand, Ben pulled her close to him and ran his hand across her shoulders. Then they gathered their things and left the office, stopping briefly to thank Marie for the early warning.

"No problem. It comes with the territory, I'm afraid. See you both tomorrow. I'll bring a new brand of coffee, Starbucks. Their coffee shops seem to be popping up everywhere. One is right near my condo, and I think the coffee is better than most places serve. Good night."

Taking a White House car back to his hotel, Ben overlooked the large dark car that pulled into the busy street behind them. Although he was constantly alert to client threats, it had been years since he had to watch out for threats to his rear, or "six o'clock position" of a more lethal type. Now that threat was four cars behind him.

"He's heading back to the hotel with the redhead, and has got a Service guy with him. The young one, Morse. Do we still go ahead with it? And do I get to go to Dulles right afterward for that flight home? Because if not, I'll spill the beans, dammit. You guys have safely sailed above all this, but my team has been doing the wet work and we need our reward now, not in Heaven," the solidly-built man in the rear seat of the car said into his radiophone.

After listening briefly, he responded. "Okay, got it. Greenwood and the Secret Service kid. With surprise on my side, it should be easy. Just a lot of witnesses, but so what? I look like a hundred guys, at least a hundred tough guys," he chortled, turning the phone off with a satisfied look on his face.

"Full steam ahead, Alexis. It's High Noon time for our friends, just a little later in the day than originally planned." Then I'll be on my way to my new dacha by a lake with my old KGB buddies as neighbors, he mused. About time for all I've done. It's about time."

CHAPTER FORTY-SEVEN

Ben Takes a Round

October 18, 1992, 4:39 PM

Ben and Laura climbed out of the Secret Service sedan and stood on the sidewalk in front of the Mayflower while Kevin parked the car a few feet away. Enjoying the cool late-afternoon breeze, they idly observed the comings and goings of hotel guests.

"Oh, you shouldn't have waited," Kevin said, looking around quickly to ascertain their safety.

"No sweat, Kevin. We're going to have a little celebratory cocktail inside and would love to have you join us," said Ben. "I think Chet is going to show up too.

"Thanks very much. Let me make a phone call, then I'd enjoy that drink, sir."

The three entered the hotel lobby's rich Old World opulence. Kevin headed to the public phone bank, causing Ben to wonder why he didn't use his state-of-the-art radiophone like the other agents. Guiding

Laura into the bar, they found a booth and sat down. A cocktail waitress took their order for "two Maker's Mark Manhattans, a splash of cranberry juice, bitters, chilled, up." It was Ben's idea for their new signature drink. "Let's call it the "New & Improved 'Hatten" to celebrate the first time I've done ad campaigns for two competing brands simultaneously!"

Laura laughed, finally able to relax with the man who had made such a large difference in her life in such a short period of time.

Meanwhile, Kevin was on the phone listening to his girlfriend Sunny divulge—to his stunned amazement—her brief encounter a few weeks ago with a famous ad guy from New York. Kevin had never told her who he'd been assigned to protect, but in explaining why he would be late for their dinner date tonight, he had mentioned it.

"Oh, Kevin, I shouldn't have told you. I don't know why I acted so impulsively. It's just that he's famous and handsome, and you were always so busy. It was only that once at the Mayflower. Kevin, let me get a cab and meet you so we can talk. Where are you? I can make it right for you, sweetie, really right, you know?" she teased him, knowing she could always entice him into a rendezvous.

"Sunny, this is bullshit," he yelled into the phone, causing people passing by to look with alarm in his direction, and an overweight man seated on a couch nearby to look up from his newspaper. "You bitch," he ranted. "I love you and thought you were mine. I'm at the fucking Mayflower right now, the very place you...oh, shit, Sunny, how did you let this happen?" he cried, slamming the receiver on the hook.

Wiping his face with his right hand, Kevin stalked off to the men's room to pull himself together. Hastily splashing cold water on his face, he stared into the mirror, wild-eyed. What the fuck, man, he told himself. Are you not the dumbest jerk on the planet? Midwest rube comes to Washington, D.C. and gets jobbed by the first cute blonde he meets. "Oh, Kevin, you're the most, I love you so much," he mimicked her lines into the mirror. "Major chump, Mr. Secret Service Man."

Halfway through the cocktail, Laura nudged Ben, "I wonder where our young protector has gone. Isn't he supposed to be stuck like glue to you and me?" Glancing toward the entrance just then, she saw Kevin slump into the room. She waved and caught his eye. "He doesn't look well, Ben. Wonder what is bothering him."

Ben also was surprised at Kevin's long departure and sudden reappearance. But, he attributed his evident distress to the pressure of the young man's job. "Well, maybe he's like our young account guys; they just seem to have too much on their plate, inside and outside of work," he suggested.

Just as Kevin reached their table, Chet arrived slapping Kevin on the back, much to the young man's surprise. "Well, here we all are, doing what we do best," Chet joked. "Have a seat, Kevin," he said, sitting on the outside of the booth and gesturing for him to sit on the other outside position. "We're off duty now, Agent Morse, but we still can place our burly bodies outboard to protect our happy charges here from any radicals plotting to harm them," he smiled, noting Kevin's distress, but deciding not to comment.

"So, what can we get you gentlemen?" Ben asked, hoping to relieve the tension so evident in the young officer's demeanor.

"What are you guys having, Ben? Looks somehow familiar and very dangerous. One of those for me and one of those for my associate," Chet quipped to the waiter, but Kevin sat there frowning. What's eating him? he wondered. It's hard for me in my forties to have any idea what goes on in the mind of a twenty-four-year old, although it doesn't seem like such a long time ago.

Their drinks arrived in a few moments, just as a smashing young woman with thick blond hair framing her pretty face strode into the bar. Stopping near the entrance, her blue eyes scanned the room for her date. As Chet took a deep swallow of his drink, he noticed her look intently in their direction. Realizing she recognized one of them and was fast approaching their table, Chet stood up as proscribed by his training, alerting Kevin with a terse comment, "Action, now, to your right."

Kevin, his mind still reeling, instinctively stood, his right hand going to his belt holster. As the young woman drew closer, he cried out in surprise, "Sunny, what are you doing here?" She rushed up to him and wrapped her arms tight around him, pinning his gun arm to his side.

"You crazy baby, I had to come. You are so wrong about things...I..." she sobbed, clutching Kevin even tighter and wondering why his arm was moving up to separate them. Chet watched closely, still suspicious of the stranger.

Ben, shocked at the unexplained appearance of

Sunny and her apparent involvement with Kevin, watched their brief struggle with amazement. Just then, he caught sight of a husky man rushing through the entrance toward them with rabid emotions on his face. Seeing him pull out a pistol, Ben's mouth filled with the foul taste of fear as he yelled "GUN" to warn the others.

"GUN!" Chet echoed, instantly pulling his revolver from his belt holster and raising it. "Everyone down on the floor!" he shouted, as shots rang out. The next instant, Ben pressed Laura under the table, then turned in Chet's dirction. Seeing blood streaming from his ear, Ben realized his friend had been clipped by one of the bullets. Leaping intently through the air, scattering drinks, flowers and utensils, Ben pushed Chet away from the incoming fire.

"Chet, he's aiming at YOU! Jesus, Kevin, get off a shot! What are you doing? Shoot the fucker! The big guy with the gun, you fool." Another two shots. "Hell, I'm hit!" Ben exclaimed as he landed on Chet, both men falling to the ground.

"Try to take him alive, Morse. Alive, dammit!" Chet screamed, as more gunshots shattered the air. Christ, I hope those rounds are from Kevin's gun, Ben thought, his mind crazed with sudden pain.

Rolling away from Chet, who was now back on his feet with his weapon aimed carefully at the prone figure several tables away, his eyes quickly scanning the room for accomplices, Ben felt a blazing fire in his shoulder. He instinctively reached with his left hand to check the cause of the pain and his hand came away wet with blood. Looking over to see Laura still huddled under the table three feet away, he rolled toward her and covered her with his body, oddly recalling taking the same action several months earlier.

"Morse, he's down. We got him. Take him now!" Greenwood ordered, as Kevin dashed at the fallen as-sassin. The large man groaned at the rough handcuff-ing and having his head pushed solidly against the hardwood floor. "He's clear; handcuffed; weapon's clear; bleeding from his legs; no other weapons," Kevin yelled, following Secret Service procedure. Glancing back toward the table, he saw Sunny slowly get to her feet. She looked at him with terror then fainted onto the seat of an adjacent booth.

Suddenly the bar was crowded with District of Co-lumbia police, and immediately thereafter dozens of well-dressed young men who flashed plastic creden-tials to the police before taking over the task of clear-ing the bar and hotel lobby.

"Mr. Greenwood, your orders please," one of them said to Chet, who had just noticed Ben was down and injured.

"Operation Bravo, check for other perps ASAP; alert home base; get ambulances; get a medic to my friend there; do a perimeter check; and check the other people for injuries, Officer. Keep me posted every two minutes. Get video going now," he ordered, driven by rote memory and years of training.

Turning back to Ben, who was lying on the floor with his head in Laura's lap, Chet realized his friend was bleeding profusely from his right shoulder. One of the agents was rapidly pulling medical equipment from a black bag and cutting Ben's jacket and shirt from his body.

"Hey, it's nothing, buddy," Ben said, his ashen face

belying his effort at humor. "Just a little round in the arm, no problem."

Laura continued to hold Ben, ignorant of the blood on her arms and crumpled dress. "Chet, help him. Oh, Ben, did you get shot somewhere else?" she cried, pulling his jacket more completely away from his body.

"No, Laura, just the shoulder, but that's enough. Wow, I've never been shot before—a horrible way to be treated in a nice place," he said, trying to mask his discomfort. "Who is that guy, Chet?" he asked, as they all looked across the room at the agents encircling the shooter.

"Don't know, but don't expect the answer will be anything but a Russian-sounding name. How do you feel, my friend? How's he doing, Scott?" Chet asked the attending officer.

"Just one hit, Sir. One round through the fleshy mass above his right shoulder. He was bleeding badly, but I have it slowed down. The medics are in the lobby right now," he said, adjusting his earpiece. "This guy will be fine, especially with the great nursing he's getting from this young lady," smiling at Laura who was holding a large compress tightly to Ben's shoulder, tears flowing down her face.

"Ben, you son of a bitch, it's *my* job to 'take the round,' not yours, for Chris' sakes," Chet said with deep concern.

"Hey, it was time for me to fly wing on you, buddy. Once we find out what it was all about, then I'll turn in my resignation papers. Ow, this really hurts!" Ben grimaced, looking up at Laura with appreciation. "My own private Nurse Nightingale," he laughed softly.

"Who is that woman who accosted you, Morse?" Chet demanded, now beginning to reconstruct the unexpected events. "What's she got to do with you?

"Nothing, boss. Nothing at all," Kevin replied coldly, glancing at Ben before watching Sunny being attended by two policewomen. "Let her go, Mr. Greenwood. It was all a big misunderstanding, but she may have saved our lives by getting in the gunman's sights at just the right moment, sir."

Chet looked hard at Kevin for a moment, seemed to make up his mind about something, then gestured to him to go off duty for the night. "Good work, Morse. Get some sleep and report in the morning. I have a new assignment I think you're going to like. You've earned it with that well-targeted shooting. We got him alive, thank God."

Sirens added to the din in the bar as several ambulances arrived at the front of the hotel, medics racing in to bring more medical supplies and gurneys. Lifting Ben onto one of them, the medics rushed him into one of the ambulances, helping Laura climb into the rear to accompany him on the way to the hospital.

Chet walked across to where the gunman lay handcuffed and bleeding from leg wounds. "What's your name?" Chet asked, expecting nothing.

"Your ass, that's my name," the man uttered, obviously in pain.

"Great name, fits your face, friend," Chet countered, looking at the Secret Service agents around him. "Get him up and out of here and book him for attempted murder of a government official. No visitors, no lawyers. As far as we're concerned, he's an assassin and they get special treatment. Which is not very special," Chet threatened the man before turning and walking out of the bar toward the street.

Unwinding his car from the knot of emergency vehicles, Chet headed to the White House to debrief his boss and senior Secret Service staff. This job certainly has gotten old all of a sudden, he thought, touching the top of his ear where a small bit of flesh had been patched with gauze and a wrap. Or maybe I'm what's getting old. When my civilian friends have to protect me, it's time to hang up the holster and put it behind me. Time to get to know my wife and kids, and work on my golf game.

CHAPTER FORTY-EIGHT

Getting Killed at the Polls

October 30, 1992, 5:45 PM

Days before the November 3 election, the White House was a scene of chaos and confusion. Normally serene and composed, Chief of Staff Charlie Gaines was a vision of distress and consternation as he made his way from the East Wing to the Oval Office. Shocked at the recent unraveling of President Rogers' re-election bid, Charlie's twenty-five-year career as a successful political consultant was going up in smoke. "What happened?" he worried aloud as he entered the White House proper and noticed dejectedly that a Marine guard seemed oblivious to his passing. That guy's right, he thought, I'm fucking invisible, or will be soon. Nowhere to go after this debacle, he despaired. Nowhere except to the cottage at Green Lake, back to my family's place in Northern Wisconsin where no one cares who you are or what you do, just that they know you and your family. Maybe that is the right thing for me now, he consoled himself. Haven't seen the old Chris-Craft runabout, "Knotty Lady", in fifteen years, probably half rotted but still worthy of some TLC.

Well here goes, into the lion's den, Charlie thought. My old school chum Brad "the brat" Rogers is probably crazed over the poll results. Shit, what happened? Talk about a fast thaw! As an immaculate Marine corporal opened the large white-paneled door of the Oval Office, he took a deep breath and walked in.

"Charlie Gaines, my main man!" Rogers shouted, standing up from leaning against his desk. "Here he is folks, and none too soon. Charlie, these folks have a tale to tell that you couldn't have conceived in your wildest imagination. Hollywood would kill for this story. And they might just get it. Looks like I'm going to need some income from somewhere and I think this is my story to sell. Just kidding, guys," he said smiling, gesturing to Chet and Jeff, who were seated on the two long parallel couches in front of his oversized desk. "Charlie, get some coffee and have a seat. You don't want to miss any part of this."

Gaines waved languidly at Chet, a White House fixture these days, and Jeff, whom he had met at various CIA briefings over the years. He was always glad these two professionals were on "our side" as he found them to be formidable in conducting their roles as protectors of the state. After helping himself to coffee with plenty of sweetener and cream, Charlie sat down in a leather armchair. The President walked over and sat in the matching chair beside him. Then Chet began.

"Mr. Gaines, several months ago you hired Ben

Coleman to create the President's re-election campaign. Mr. Coleman arrived in Washington in June and was with the President during the Vermont attack in which he distinguished himself under fire. I served with Mr. Coleman in the Navy. He was a flight leader in Vietnam and I was often assigned as his wingman. Ben was one of the toughest and most fearless pilots I knew. To run into him here years later was a great pleasure and, as it turns out, a very timely event for our country.

To cut to the chase, it was Mr. Coleman's informal observations regarding certain senior members of this administration—observations that frankly my professional associate and I initially disbelieved—that provided an early alert into one of the most treacherous plots against this country in its history. Had this conspiracy been successful, President Rogers would have been at immediate risk of his life and our country would have suffered an unprecedented and devastating upheaval.

Gaines looked with disbelief at the President, who simply nodded. "Right under our noses, Charlie, and for years. As incredible as it seems it all makes sense, especially with what Officer Gilman will explain in a moment."

Jeff turned on a small computer projector, focused it on the wall near President Lincoln's portrait, and began to speak.

"Gentleman, as we all know, on June 24th a coordinated attack on the President and his party at the Basin Harbor Club in Vermont was carried out by unknown assailants. The President escaped unharmed, but six Secret Service officers were killed, shot in both eyes by a highly sophisticated weapon fired from a yacht that was subsequently destroyed. While the perpetrators were never identified, we believe they were eliminated with a firebomb thrown inside their escape vehicle soon after the attack by assailants still unknown. Within days, senior CIA executive Raymond Davenport was murdered in his limousine in a manner similar to the Vermont operation. His long-term CIA Officer driver was missing at the scene and is presumed dead, perhaps another accomplice in the overall plot.

"At that time, following a conversation with Mr. Coleman, it became clear to me and Mr. Greenwood that these events might be linked to what Ben felt were the odd and 'un-American' personas of the Chief Justice and the Vice President. As implausible as these conjectures were, we nevertheless processed the entire scenario and associated details into the CIA's Cray supercomputer with the following results."

For the next few minutes, Gilman explained the Cray's projection that the Chief Justice and the Vice President were in league with unknown conspirators within and outside the U.S. government to thwart any American response to the collapse of Communist Russia. During the past five years, events such as the tearing down of the Berlin Wall and the recent attempted Russian coup all indicated the demise of Communism. Yet that same time period has provided enough time for a cadre of former KGB agents, emerging Russian business oligarchs and other members of the Communist regime to recover from these political setbacks, reestablish a new Communist presence in the old capital and reassume their earlier dangerous presence in the world order. While highly complex, the computer projection made it clear that the success of that plot hinged upon the re-election of President Rogers, his subsequent assassination and assumption of the presidency by Toland. Anything short of this would mean failure for their mission."

Rogers handed Charlie the Cray printout, stamped "Top Secret. No Forn. No Elint. No Copies" in red, with signatures of just six people. The import of the text made it seem to Charlie that the document weighed much more than it actually did. Blinking a few times, he silently gestured for Gilman continue.

"In response to the Cray's assessment, Mr. Coleman, Ms. Sinclair, Mr. Greenwood and I arranged a clandestine meeting and decided to take a direct and expeditious approach—for which we all are prepared to accept whatever punishment you and other authorities may deem appropriate. In an attempt to save the President and the nation from the dire consequences of this plot, we decided to try to neutralize the threat by using your advertising campaign to frankly un-sell the President to the public. It sounds crazy, it certainly did then, but we could not bring this to your attention for obvious reasons. Should the plot have been exposed, the threat to you and the country was too great and, therefore, unacceptable.

"So," Gilman concluded. "Mr. Coleman used the power of advertising to entice the public into believing that now was the right time to for you to celebrate our apparent victory over the Commies, to extend the olive branch to them and turn the other cheek.

"Jeesh, I remember that meeting and thinking, shit, maybe they're right," the President admitted, taking a gulp of Now Cola. "I thought it would be nice to relax and enjoy the sunshine of the supposed end of the Cold War. Who wouldn't have liked that idea? Coleman is a sweeter talker than Charlie here, and that in itself is pretty amazing."

Gaines chuckled, starting to feel relieved and somehow more relaxed than he had in years.

"Yes, you guys sold the idea of 'Peace Warrior' to some smart old guys who gobbled it up like chocolate cake," said the President, taking another deep swallow.

With a conciliatory smile, Chet told Rogers, "Mr. President, given the events of the day the idea had merit. But Mr. Coleman knew it would falter because of its inconsistency with your long-term Conservative record and the deep distrust the U.S. people continued to have about cozying up to the Ruskies. You did the right thing by agreeing to the campaign strategy, even if it wasn't totally clear to you why Coleman had recommended such a provocative position."

President Rogers walked over toward the antique grandfather clock and stood by the large window, peering out at the end of the day. His thoughts ran back to the early years of his career when he first met David Blackstone. It had been at a political event in New York when he was a prosecuting attorney for the City of Philadelphia. He had been surprised, but pleased, by Blackstone's unexpected interest in a young attorney, and over the ensuing five years was flattered to have the older sage help him advance in the Pennsylvania legislature. Soon he became his constant coach, calling him several times a week and inviting him to California to see how things were done in Sacramento.

Rogers remembered Blackstone urging him to run for Governor and recalled how he had driven his campaign, financed by people he had never met. In return, Rogers had installed his mentor in several powerful positions in the Pennsylvania administration and later in Washington. All his subsequent political successes both at home and abroad had flowed like a spring-fed river, but now, here he was staring at the abrupt end of his career. And he had only himself to blame for not having minded his store more carefully.

"Charlie, it looks like we're going to take it in the shorts next Tuesday," the President said resolutely. "We're getting killed in the polls. Well, everyone did a great job. I loved the campaign and the folks all over the country did their level best, but it looks like our friend from Phoenix is going to be moving in here soon, and most likely he deserves it. He certainly knew the mindset of the populace. A 'straight-shooter, hold the line, don't trust the bastards.' His team must have figured out something we didn't, right Charlie?

Chet and Jeff exchanged brief glances, but said nothing.

"Well, Chet and Jeff, I don't care that you guys shifted my positioning or whatever. Sometimes you have to do something you know is right. I was that kind of guy early on, but looking back at more recent years it all seemed too easy, and it turns out it was. Good old Blackstone paved my way without me ever guessing. The presidential patsy. Then he put Toland inside the tent. I should have said no to that. Never liked the guy."

"Boss, take it easy on yourself," Charlie said, walking over to the President and putting his hand on his shoulder. "We all did what we thought was best at the time. Blackstone was good at what he did and you were smart to take him up on his interest in you. Yes, Toland was a disaster, but he never screwed up too badly. He just liked cruising around handling the fun stuff, which was perfect for us. The bad deal was his complicity in this conspiracy and his intention to replace you prematurely. That we can't abide. I apologize for not recognizing what was happening. I was too preoccupied to take the time to read between the lines. I feel like I failed you."

Chet watched the conversation with growing discomfort. In his fifteen years in the Secret Service serving Presidents in close proximity, he had never witnessed such a sad display of mea culpa on the part of a Head of State or his chief advisor and friend. He turned to look at Jeff, who was also observing the interaction with some embarrassment.

"Mr. President, do you have any questions we can answer or information we can provide?" he asked, hoping for an early exit.

"No Chet, thanks. I think things have run their course, and at least now I have a better understanding of why. Please tell Mr. Coleman that I admire his insights and creative talents. And make sure Ms. Sinclair knows I understand. You folks had no choice but to do what you did, and while it puts me out of a job, it saved my life and the welfare of the country.

"Mr. Gilman, we'll need to meet first thing tomorrow to decide how we will deal with these people. As of Tuesday, they will be technically out of work, too. Charlie, please get it on my calendar. And Mr. Gilman, be sure to put some agents on Blackstone and Toland with total surveillance. Do all you can to identify the other members of this plot. My last official act will be to ensure they have no opportunity to advance their cause beyond today."

With a formal acknowledgement of the Presidential order, Jeff and Chet exited the Oval Office. As they closed the paneled door they could hear Charlie Gaines break into tears, with the President obviously consoling him. Glancing at one another, they strode past the numerous secretaries, functionaries and other White House staff aware of how soon their faces would be replaced by shiny new sun-tanned faces from the West.

CHAPTER FORTY-NINE

Hightower in a Landslide

November 4, 1992, 12:15 AM

Walter Cronkite turned his famous, silver-framed face back towards the camera having taken another glance at the big board behind him which kept an electronic tally of the national vote late on this election night, 1992. His normally jovial face, which had shepherded three generations of Americans through news of war, peace, national elections, space exploration, assassinations, the advent of the Beatles, riots and every other aspects of the American life experience, was composed as he read a news flash just handed to him.

"Tonight, at midnight eastern standard time with the closing of the polls out west, President Bradley George Rogers, the Republican candidate for a second term in office, officially conceded the race to Senator Lucas Lee Hightower of Arizona. As we all know now, Senator Hightower won a record fifty-four percent of the electorate on his campaign of a strong defensive posture towards other world powers and vigilance in protecting the interests of the U.S. This campaign reflected President Roger's campaign from four years ago which positioned him as moderate hawk and conservative politician. However, Rogers chose to change his tune in this campaign and assumed the role of 'Peace Warrior,' extending a liberal olive branch in a controversial political turnabout. The people have clearly spoken today and have registered a historical approval of Senator Hightower's conservative stance with a 54-45 percent vote imbalance, the one percent going to Ralph Nader. Well, history has definitely been made here tonight. We congratulate President-Elect Hightower, and wish President Rogers Godspeed and safe journeys in his future endeavors. I want to note that President Rogers has asked the major networks for a half hour at eleven o'clock tomorrow morning, Eastern Standard Time, to address the nation. While this is unprecedented, we at CBS and the other major networks have agreed to make the airtime available. We, of course, will be watching with great interest and will provide perspective and commentary immediately following his speech."

Walter Cronkite announced a commercial break and returned sixty seconds later.

"My friends, with our broadcast tomorrow, I will take my second retirement from joining you in your homes each evening to review the day's events. I am looking forward to returning to Martha's Vineyard and sailing my beloved sloop, writing books with my good friend Ray Ellis, and gardening with my wife Betsy. I also want to wish you all the best of everything in this wonderful and cherished American life, and hope that certain horrible events of recent months are never repeated and that America will continue to thrive under the new and, I truly believe, dynamic leadership of President-Elect Hightower. That's the way I hope it will be. Good night, and good luck."

CHAPTER FIFTY
Back to Madison Avenue

November 4, 1992, 9:36 AM

Ben and Laura hurried along the hall from the Oval Office, ignoring the crowds of White House staffers rushing to prepare for the momentous press conference scheduled within the hour.

Reaching Ben's gleaming red Porsche parked in the underground garage, they pitched their bags into the front trunk and settled into the tight cockpit, shoulders touching intimately. Smiling at Laura who was in the driver's seat, Ben reached over to hug her with his left arm, his right arm still supported by a black cloth sling to aid the healing of his shoulder wound. Instead of responding, she quickly grasped his jaw and looked him in the eye.

"I love you and I also understand you, my precious. I want you to have something, and I don't want you to question it," she insisted, her voice almost breaking with emotion. Her hand reached into her

357

purse and retrieved a small silk box. "Here, open it, read the inscription, and put it on."

"What is it?" he asked as he opened the small parcel, revealing a beautiful gold and black onyx ring. It was a handsome ring, sparkling even in the reduced light. "It's gorgeous, well, what does it say, it's too dark to see."

"To a Man and His Words, love Laura 11/3/1992" she recited, her voice warm and soft in his ears, her eyes moist, yet confident as they held his firmly, yet lovingly.

"My gosh, it's beautiful, and heavy, too!" he murmured glancing away to gather his thoughts, which were racing in circles in his mind.

"Only the best for you. Put it on," she urged. "How does it feel?"

"Like home, Laura. It feels like home."

Glancing once again at the ring, which did look right at home on his right-hand ring finger, Ben finished the kiss he had started moments ago, enjoying her lush mouth and rich fragrance.

"Let's go before they catch us down here. The press is going to want to know what happened and they are likely to guess we had something to do with it all," Laura inserted the key into the ignition to the left of the wheel, racing style, felt the powerful air-cooled engine fire to life, ready for a new road adventure, but with her driving instead of Ben. She maneuvered expertly through the underground maze, emerging with a roar into the daylight and crowds of tourists pressing against the metal police barriers to hopefully catch a glimpse of activities inside the White House. A DC cop signaled her to turn right on Massachusetts Avenue with a firm thumbs-up and large grin to Ben. She followed the cordoned-off roads until she saw signs for the Beltway and the turnpike north.

As the small car rocketed onto the highway leading out of town, Ben turned to Laura, a new smile of excitement and optimism on his face.

"Laura, the ring is phenomenal, you are wonderful, and a great driver, to boot! And I have never wanted so much to be back in New York City writing ads for stuff no one needs. And I have never felt so lucky and happy as I feel with you. Let's get back to Madison Avenue—it's saner there."

Laura hugged his arm and laughed, "Saner is right—they can have their political games. I'm calling it 'finis.'"

Ben, grinning, reached to turn on the radio. A newscaster was just announcing the defeated President's arrival at the podium in the Presidential newsroom. President Rogers began speaking immediately.

"My fellow Americans, I want to thank you first for your confidence in me and my administration over the last four years. It has been a wonderful experience for me and my family and my terrific staff. But, more importantly, I want to thank the men and women who, unbeknownst to me, thwarted a dangerous plot to bring this country to its knees. I cannot, and will not for security reasons, reveal the details of the plot nor can I publicly name those whose keen intelligence, courage and patriotism stood between this nation's safety and certain disaster. Let me assure you that we are in full control of the situation that began so horribly in Vermont last summer, and President-Elect Hightower has been thoroughly briefed by our security agencies as well as my staff.

"Again, let me thank all of those in the government including members of the FBI, CIA and the armed forces and especially some private citizens, for their resolute response to this threat. Suffice it to say that words cannot express my appreciation.

"Now, let me turn my comments to my successful competitor in our recent National election and wish him good luck in this new era for our country. Senator Hightower is an excellent man with unique and powerful talents who will...."

Ben abruptly turned the radio off as Laura expertly changed lanes to the far left, her right hand dropping the gearshift into fifth gear, the Porsche settling into a 75 MPH cruise.

"Enough. The only appreciation I, for one, need is dinner at the Four Seasons, theater tickets to a good show and you on my arm, my love."

The small red car continued its speedy trip north, winding its way between cars, trucks and motorcycles whose drivers might have noticed and remarked on the eye-catching automobile driven by a raven-haired beauty with a middle-aged man slouched in the right seat wearing an outsized grin. They would never know much about the two occupants. Particularly, the special reasons behind their tight grip on each other's hand.

Epilogue

The Washington Post broke the macabre story the following day regarding a police report that the Chief Justice of the Supreme Court had been found dead in the commodious main cabin of his large yacht, "Czar," moored at a yacht harbor in nearby Bethesda, Maryland. David Blackstone was found, to the dismay of government officials, in the company of a veteran Russian General, Sergei Petrovich Petrov. Both men had apparently ingested poison, most likely cyanide capsules, within the last eight hours. There was no sign of foul play and officials were at a loss to explain why the senior-most jurist of the United States was with a senior Russian agent who had been linked over the years to numerous Soviet incursions in the western hemisphere, including the Cuban missile crisis during John F. Kennedy's presidency. The only odd detail noted by a Bethesda County detective was a Japanese character ruthlessly scratched into Mr. Blackstone's right palm with what appeared to be a ballpoint pen. Experts determined that the mark was the Japanese sign for "devil." No evidence suggesting others had been on board was found despite a thorough search of the elegant vessel.

Several days later, Vice President Alan Toland was found shot to death in Northern California, near his hometown of Modesto. Witnesses stated that they had seen him having coffee earlier in the day, and then getting into his prized customized yellow Ford pickup truck and driving towards the town cemetery. Eluding his Secret Service detail, he was found lying next to the grave of his daughter, with a single gunshot wound to the neck. His wallet and jewelry including a gold Rolex watch had not been disturbed. He clutched a small pistol.

In a small mall twenty miles to the west of Washington, D.C., two men walking their dogs discovered the remains of a middle-aged woman, apparently of Oriental descent and once very beautiful, lying at the bottom of a deep concrete culvert. Her death was deemed a suicide although no note was found. Her identity has not been ascertained, although the investigation continues according to the authorities.

Two weeks later, a small gathering took place at a Chevy Chase restaurant favored by Chet Greenwood. Numerous public safety officers, government employees, and fifty-five veteran and retired Secret Service officers took special pleasure in helping roast the retiring agent who had served five Presidents and Vice Presidents. His remarks were brief, but poignant.

"My friends, I have flown with the best, served with the best, lived and loved with the best, and been blessed every day I have been alive, thank God. Very simply, I appreciate very much the opportunity to have lived the professional life that I did. Now, it's time to live my personal life. Thanks for coming, eat up and drink up. Cheers!" He turned on the small stage and hugged his wife and daughters so tightly they lost their breath and giggled in delight. Chet smiled at their reaction, realizing with relief that he was finally out of the business of "taking a bullet" for someone else.

Sitting in the bar of the restaurant, two large men raised their glasses of clear liquid to each other, murmured a quiet toast, and drained the vodka.

"Well, Vlad, another fish has gotten away, eh?" the first said quietly, signaling the waitress for another round. "This Greenwood was a good one, I think. Smart, alert, always knew we were around. Kind of got to be like a friend in an unfriendly land, you know? Wonder if he knows how close he came to losing his boss and maybe his own life. The whole thing just came apart around us."

"Sergey, you are getting soft like these Americans. I should rat you out to our control, but I feel much like you. I still wonder how they knew what was going on, but it's all too late now. We just continue to do our job and wait for orders. And meanwhile, we drink this very good Swedish vodka," he chortled, causing several people nearby to glance his way. Waving to them pleasantly, Vladimir Vladimirovich Putin drained his glass in anticipation of yet another, feeling strangely mixed emotions regarding recent events in this foreign land. He could only wonder where the dark world of political intrigue would take him next.

Advertising executive and Vietnam-era Navy pilot, Peter Engler worked at major New York City and San Francisco advertising agencies for over thirty years. He worked closely with creative luminaries at Saatchi & Saatchi, Foote, Cone & Belding, and J. Walter Thompson to create award-winning ad campaigns for Sony, Clorox, Lipton and other successful brands.

Engler experienced their superior powers of observation, creativity and professional courage in action many times. Ben Coleman is a composite of these brilliant advertising craftsmen and this story could have happened.

Visit Peter Engler at www.granthampress.com.

grantham press

Dear Reader,

Thanks very much for reading my first novel, *New &*
Improved! A Political Thriller.
I appreciate your interest in the story and hope you
found it as exciting and fun to read as it was to write.
Like many novels, *New & Improved* took several years of
writing, editing, re-writing and layout work. Publishing it in
September, 2013, was clearly a glorious moment that
fulfilled a teen-aged dream to publish a book with my name
on it.
I am already underway on my second novel that follows
the exciting exploits of four young Navy Ensigns as they
become enveloped in the thrills, dangers and challenges of
becoming Naval aviators during the Vietnam War. The
novel, *The Four Options*, should be available in the summer
of 2014. You can follow my progress as well as read my
blogs and short stories at www.granthampress.com.
I would so appreciate your taking a moment to search for
Peter Engler on Amazon in Books, then click on the *New &*
Improved book page, scroll down to find "Write a Customer
Review" and provide me and the world with your comments.
You can also write to me at granthampress@gmail.com.
Thank you very much for reading *New & Improved*, and
my best wishes for hours of enjoyable reading ahead.

Gratefully,

Peter Engler
Author
Grantham Press
www.granthampress.com